Orch

*'Oh, my Orchidea – my irresistible, incomparable Orchidea, love of
my life and bride of my bereavement...'*

Ah, Orchidea – the legend of the lady with the lion: an enigmatic
embodiment of elegance crisscrossing the centuries and navigating
broken hearts with an incongruous travelling companion in the
shape of the big cat snapping at her heels. It could merely be a
magic-realism myth – the wandering orphan of unknown origins
appearing from nowhere in the life of a Victorian literary sensation
before eventually vanishing into the atomic mists of Hiroshima; or
perhaps it all really happened?

A series of fantastically dramatic events shaped and moulded the
woman whose devotion to the written word engineered an encounter
with an author wounded by a tragic back-story of his own. They
were primed for falling for each other via years of isolation from the
very energy that exploded when they got together. As time sped by
beyond the bedchamber, Jeremiah Meadowbrook and Orchidea
lived their love in a blissful bubble they imagined to be for life. And
then life intervened.

In their world, a buxom Georgian patron could host glittering salons
attended by foppish aesthetes whose hedonistic appetites would span
the metamorphosis of escapism from laudanum and absinthe all the
way to cocaine; an egg discovered in the ashes of a burned house
could hatch a parasitical raven that would feast on the negative
energy of its 'father'; and an heiress could be ravished by a demon
in human form before giving birth to a lion whose violent mood
swings its mother would be in thrall to thereafter. This was the
world in which two lost souls who had known no love for so long
that they'd forgotten what it felt like found each other – at last.

Johnny Monroe's latest yarn is a love story, but not as we know it...

1

Orchidea

A fairytale
By
Johnny Monroe

'I found a picture of you...those were the happiest days of my life'

Chrissie Hynde,
'Back on the Chain Gang'

A Man Spurned

Cue background sax and flashing neon light illuminating venetian blinds.

No lie – I was willing to go straight to the furniture department at San Quentin for this dame. I'd set my broken heart on a special chair, the kind of chair that won't work unless you plug it in and flick the switch. See, I'd reached the stage where I didn't care what became of me anymore because my head was on fire and there was no other remedy for the pain; all I could see whenever I opened or closed my eyes were two laughing figures dancing in the flames – she was one of them and he was the other; only, he didn't have a face, just a hideous blank canvas where his features should have been. It was as though those features had been sanded down and rubbed away, like his face was a wooden sculpture gone wrong and the sculptor was beginning again from scratch.

Every night I parked in the shadows of the disused Catholic Mission on the corner of 67th and 71st Street. It was the perfect spot because nobody ever took a second look at the old place, let alone noticed a reject from some corny romantic B-picture driven half-crazy by a cold-hearted broad who'd pushed him over the state-line of sanity; they couldn't have been less interested in me if I was a sidewalk bum begging for a dime. People just walked on by.

Perfect.

From those shadows I had a clear, uninterrupted view of her front door and I could see all the comings and goings. If anyone called, I clocked them, and I had a pistol in my pocket primed for a doorstep delivery if I saw the sucker she ditched me for. The only problem was I didn't know what he looked like. I had to keep watching day-after-day to try and work out which caller was him. If I was going to do this, I had to make sure I got the right guy.

She lived next-door to a liquor-store and I noted she made a pilgrimage there around the same time every evening. It only ever took a couple of shots to knock her out, so I knew she wouldn't be drinking alone. Besides, she always called in at the store an hour or so before the same guy showed up.

He parked in front of the house and I only ever saw the back of his head, never got a good look at his face. Even when the time came for him to leave, his hat was pulled down so low that I could only ever really make out the tip of his nose and the outline of his jaw-line. He was built like he could take care of himself in a fight, which told me it was a smart move to say hi with a revolver and not a fist. There were no Queensberry Rules in this kind of fight. He'd stolen my girl, and that was lower than a Lonsdale Belt to me.

It had to be him. He had to be the one. He never missed a night and he never left till sunrise.

The day I became history, she confessed she'd just been on a date with some guy, but denied seeing anyone else behind my back. I didn't believe her then and I didn't believe her now. It was too soon, too close, too convenient that she'd found another bozo so quick after making me yesterday's news. I had a feeling this had begun long before then. Even though I'd never looked my replacement in the eye, I knew he was more to her taste than I was. He was everything I wasn't – and more besides. She'd had her fun with me, something a little bit different; and now she was back in the arms of a straight. And where did that leave me?

Thanks to her, I could never believe the word of a woman again, but it was so Goddamn easy for her. She was the kind of dame who could toss guys away like a ripped stocking and never lose a wink of sleep. She knew she just had to stand by the conveyor belt and pick off whichever dummy took her fancy – as long as he was loaded, of course. She didn't need to do much more than give the guy a glimpse of those sparkling sapphires peering through that yellow veil and he'd take the bait. Give her a year or maybe two and she'd have got what she wanted from him. Another one would have come along by then and she'd dispose of the poor sap without giving him a second thought.

We were all just steps on life's staircase to her.

After a week of keeping watch, my trigger-finger was itchy. I felt like kicking that front door in and laying waste to both of them without saying a word. I could just see the headlines. They'd call it a crime of passion. I'd probably be labelled a hero by all the guys in the world who'd been cruelly used by her kind of broad. On the seventh night, he'd been there a good hour and I'd had enough. It was now or never.

I got out of the car around ten-thirty and crossed the street. It was a quiet night – a hot, sticky night, one of those where the heat was so thick and dense you'd need a chainsaw to cut through it. My first instinct was to break down the front door, but I decided to check round the back. There was a narrow passage that led round to it, so I walked alongside the side of the house. The windows were open with it being so hot and I could hear them even before I reached the backdoor.

He was getting her to make the same sounds she used to make for me – *exactly* the same sounds. My eyes couldn't see them, but my mind could. I pictured her with those great legs in the air and that burglar riding her like he was the star attraction at his local rodeo. A jabbing pain poked me in the heart and the stomach at the same time. I didn't know whether to cry or throw-up. It must have been ninety degrees in the dark, yet I'd never felt so cold. The sweat cascaded down my face and back like liquid icicles and the hand clutching the gun was shaking so much I may as well have been holding a pneumatic drill. I somehow steadied myself as the sound of her running through what I now knew to be her reliable manual of ecstatic noises seemed to grow louder and more unbearable to my ears.

The backdoor was pretty flimsy. Two kicks and I was in. They were making such a racket they never heard me above the bedsprings. The heat had dispensed with sheets and I now saw with my eyes what my mind had already showed me – only twice as ugly in the flesh. I stood over the bed for the best part of half-a-minute before she realised I was there and screamed.

I guess I could've spared him if I'd been feeling more generous. But nobody else deserved to suffer what I'd suffered, and I knew if I just walked away, she'd only go on and do to him what she'd done to me. And he'd touched her, he'd held her, he'd taken her from me – even if the invitation *had* come from her, he'd still accepted it before I was out of the way. And he was such a disappointment, not the Greek God with the equine dimensions I'd expected at all. I figured he'd have to be something really special to steal her from me, to bring out the bitch in her that she showed to me, a man no woman could resist. But he wasn't. He was just an ordinary-looking Joe. And somehow, that made it even worse.

'No, Jerry – don't do it! This isn't you!'
'I am what you made me, doll.'

I emptied the barrel and soaked the sheets. They were still soaked when I shot upright in daylight; but not with their blood. I was sick of this Goddamn dream.

Part I
Falling in...

The Lady with the Lion

There is a legend of a lady who shared her home with a lion. You may or may not be familiar with it. The lady was named Orchidea and the lion was her constant companion. Like many legends, the fiction and the fact are so tightly intertwined that the join cannot be discerned and concrete evidence of the pair's existence is closer to cardboard. Not that this ultimately matters.

All that is past is fictionalised, anyway, reconstructed from fact and reshaped on each occasion the tale is told. Oral history is never set in stone and the legend of Orchidea ebbs and flows with the ease of improvisation that is dependent on the storyteller's imagination. It can be both fluid fantasy and recorded reality, for any gaps in the story of Orchidea that are generally regarded as true are filled with whichever invention fits the narrative. As with the similarly mythical challenges of King Arthur or Robin Hood, as long as any additions to the myth of Orchidea sound relatively convincing, they convince.

One version of the legend is that Orchidea began her journey as an orphan of unknown origin, discovered as an emaciated beggar wandering the rural wilderness of the kingdom's middle by a sculptor whose greatest achievement was carving the face of the King into the mountain overlooking his home, a feat that had made the region something of a tourist spot for travellers and the aesthetically curious.

According to this interpretation of the myth, Orchidea was brought into the family bosom of the adoptive father who had taken pity on her as though she were a wild animal he was determined to tame, a pet received with distrust and disgust by the sculptor's wife and son, whose antipathy towards the new arrival never blossomed into either love or acceptance. Undeterred, the sculptor adopted this stray as his daughter and tamed her less sociable habits as best he could. Little Orchidea was smart enough to realise she was on to a good thing and responded well, reserving her less feral attributes for the one generous soul who had shown her any form of compassion.

As chance would have it, fate intervened in her father's talent a year or two later when the King was returning from a visit to a distant mistress early one morning and sighted the famed sculpture of himself from his carriage as the sun illuminated his noble granite brow. Flattered and impressed, His Majesty demanded to know the artist responsible for this magnificent tribute; he dispatched a messenger to the nearest village and summoned Orchidea's father and family to his palace several days after he returned home.

As reward for such an astonishing work of art, the King commissioned Orchidea's father to produce similar sculptures across the land and promised him a lifetime's annuity in service to the royal household. Intrigued by the somewhat uncouth member of the family that Orchidea's adoptive mother had failed to dress adequately for the occasion, His Majesty at least pleased the old hag by offering to take Orchidea into service as an apprentice lady-in-waiting to the Queen.

Despite her absence of social graces, *L'Enfant sauvage* captured the Queen's heart and served Her Majesty devotedly until the Queen's death a decade later, by which time Orchidea had learnt a great deal as to what was required of her to get ahead in society. Unfortunately, as she slowly bloomed into a beautiful young woman, she began to draw a few unwelcome and aroused individuals into her orbit, chief amongst them being the debauched heir to the throne; and once the Queen was safely out of the way, an Orchidea deprived of Her Majesty's benevolent protection was then banished from the palace when she invoked the ire of the amorous Crown Prince by rejecting his salacious advances.

The scandal painted her as the guilty party and her father (largely influenced by his wife's self-interested entreaties) disowned her, fearful of losing his invaluable income as sculptor to the royal household.

Distraught by the death of the Queen as well as heartbreaking rejection from the only other person who had ever looked kindly upon her, Orchidea was forced back into roaming alone again until eventually settling in a town a considerable distance from both the royal household and her own. Eager to put down fresh roots and bury unhappy memories, she foolishly rushed into marriage with a man who turned out to be an ill-tempered rogue inclined towards regularly beating her, a cruel brute who finally battered her so badly that he ran away when he imagined this especially severe beating had killed her.

So desperate was Orchidea to escape her ill-treatment that she went into hiding and the townsfolk believed she was indeed dead, with her body buried by her missing husband; his swift capture was followed by her failing to reappear. After several months in which there were no sightings of Orchidea, the authorities declared her to be dead and found her husband guilty of her murder, an offence for which he was hanged. It was also an event she witnessed in disguise without exposing her true identity before fleeing the scene.

Once again reduced to a penniless wanderer, Orchidea drifted anonymously from town to town until a kindly peer of the realm took pity on her when he caught her stealing apples from his orchard. This aged unmarried aristocrat extended a similarly benign hand towards her as her adoptive father had, and invited her to become his housekeeper; drawing upon her experience as a lady-in-waiting to the late Queen, this was a role she performed so successfully that her master controversially bequeathed his entire estate to her upon his death five years later. Orchidea was grieved by the passing of another protector, but was nevertheless now the mistress of a considerable fortune and naturally revelled in her elevated status.

Financially secure and independent for the first time in her troubled life, Orchidea finally had the luxury of indulging in her neglected taste for finery and soon attracted the attention of eligible suitors who began knocking on her door with monotonous regularity. Few appealed to Orchidea, but she enjoyed the novelty of being wooed by gentry bachelors, none of whom would have tossed so much as a farthing in her direction not so long before.

However, the circus that swiftly formed around her blunted the instincts formed in the brutality of matrimony, and when one uncharacteristically exotic suitor stoked her increasing acquisitiveness by masquerading as a wealthy eastern prince, she took the bait. This sinister charlatan, so much more impressive than the competition, was actually a malevolent demon in disguise, a visitor from the underworld who had taken human form in order to have some sadistic fun messing with the affections of those he regarded as being in possession of more money than sense. The woman Orchidea had now become was ideal prey for such a confidence trickster. She succumbed to his charms and was mercilessly ravished by a villain who also intended to steal her fortune.

Orchidea's survival skills had been corrupted by the prospect of never having to worry about money ever again, and she had placed her survival in jeopardy when confronted by the demon's promises of a partner to share her new life with. Although she was belatedly alerted to the demon's intentions at the eleventh hour and managed to prevent the intended theft before he fled, unbeknownst to Orchidea the demon had placed a curse upon her via her surrender. She soon fell into a deep sickness and bed-ridden gestation that resulted in the eventual arrival of the product of her seduction by this demon, which took the form of a lion cub she gave birth to. The cub was called Biba by a simpleton servant who couldn't pronounce the word 'baby'; and it stuck.

Distressed and distraught at this development, Orchidea purchased and then retreated to a remote rural mansion she turned into a veritable fortress in order to raise the wild beast free from the public gaze. But the lingering legend of the lady with the lion originated from the moment she withdrew, slowly spreading throughout the land as the cub grew and expressed its natural instincts, savaging strangers straying into its territory and lashing out at its mother as she struggled to control its tantrums. She established ways and means of appeasing Biba's temper, though these would only ever have a limited lifespan, for the beast had an extremely low boredom threshold; the constant need to invent new distractions to prevent the lion from wreaking havoc took its toll on Orchidea, numbing her intellect and damaging her ability to function in any other environment.

Over time, Orchidea recruited several handmaidens she trained to help with the exhausting burden of Biba, delegating duties when she herself was in desperate need of rest and recuperation. As the lion became physically stronger, the job of looking after it became more of a challenge, reducing Orchidea to a shadow of her former self.

Believing she was now doomed to pay for the consequences of her vanity, Orchidea convinced herself the folly of one error had condemned her to an eternity of isolation and virtual imprisonment. This conviction mirrored her deeply-held opinion that, for all the riches she had inherited, she had never really outgrown that uncouth orphan, the one discovered as the archetypal alienated loner without a past – and she never would. Yes, she may have subsequently acquired the superficial trappings of material wealth, but that didn't alter the fact that she was now as detached from her fellow man as she had been in her days as the invisible infant vagabond of the rural highway.

However, there was a crumb of comfort. In those rare moments when Biba slept or was calm, Orchidea's sole respite from the madness was to lose herself in the written word, dispatching her trusted servants to towns around the land to purchase as many books as they could carry in order that her insatiable appetite for factual knowledge and fictional escapism could be satisfied. Orchidea slowly built up an extensive library in her home, housed in a wing of the residence that Biba was barred from ever entering for fear that the lion would rip the collection to shreds. The library became Orchidea's intellectual oasis, providing her with a welcome refuge of stimulation and relaxation.

After a while, Orchidea established a line of communication with many of the living writers whose works she devoured, penning letters expressing how important a form of salvation these works had been to her. She longed to invite one of them to her home, but the presence of Biba precluded such an invitation.

Nobody ever visited Orchidea because of Biba. Only Orchidea and her handmaidens knew how to handle the lion; the safety of a stranger could not be guaranteed, and a stranger would no doubt find the scenario so bizarre that they would probably take flight the moment they were made aware of the unconventional situation. Orchidea had become so accustomed to it that she often forgot how it must be perceived by outsiders, yet she was acutely aware of how the presence of Biba restricted her ability to forge friendships and find solace in the society of others. There was no hope things would ever change.

With reading being the sole escape from life with the lion, the time Orchidea devoted to it increased and the ever expanding library began to be graced with the works of newer authors, one of whose *oeuvre* Orchidea made an instant connection with.

He went by the delightfully melodious name of Jeremiah Meadowbrook, a moniker that rolled off Orchidea's tongue with such poetic delicacy that she felt it to be fate that their paths should cross, even if the odds of a meeting appeared heavily stacked against her. How on earth could she possibly engineer an encounter when she shared her home with a lion, a lion so demanding that it could only ever be left in the care of a handmaiden for a few hours at a time?

There is also another, alternate version of the legend in which it turns out Orchidea's husband hadn't been hanged after all, but managed to escape the noose. For Orchidea, the greatest fear was that he'd track her down one day and torment her anew. This interpretation sees him do just that, stalking the grounds of her home and then breaking into it to wreak his revenge on her following her disappearance years before. Even though eventually chased off by Biba, his presence meant Orchidea was no longer a widow and therefore couldn't remarry should she meet a suitable new suitor.

Of course, the likelihood of that was already highly unlikely courtesy of a certain big cat; but the knowledge that her husband was alive somewhere out there and could darken her door at any time without warning was a further blow limiting her prospects of happiness.

Which version bears the closest resemblance to the truth is open to debate, for the story of Orchidea is built on shifting sands and its individual chapters often seem to inhabit different worlds. But then, the lady herself was something of an enigma, so in this context, her story makes perfect sense.

End of a Century

The unexpected event had excited as many who missed out as it had those who were actually witness to it – if not more so. Those who were delighted to observe the gay Montgolfier vessel sail across the skyline before coming in to the most graceful of landings could report the spectacle with accuracy and authority to those who weren't there, whereas the latter were left to exaggerate and speculate. Accustomed to receiving advance warning of such incidents in the shape of highly-publicised races amongst the aristocracy, the public were caught unawares by the element of surprise, something that added to the buzz that had swelled into several stories by the time it reached a particular man-about-town as he prepared for a special occasion.

Good chum Conan had arrived at his home early and excitedly informed him that a hot air balloon had touched down on the common that afternoon.

'Attracted quite a crowd,' said Conan with a chuckle. 'Not a sight the good people see on a daily basis.'

'Quite,' replied Jeremiah Meadowbrook – for the home was his – 'nor any of us. Sounds something of a capital wheeze, though. Only wish I'd been there to witness it.'

'So do I; I don't even have the remotest notion as to who the passenger was.'

'Ah, probably a young member of the idle rich; most seem to engage in such stunts in the absence of anything else to do until they inherit their titles, after all. They need something to keep them active while waiting for their fathers to die, I suppose. And there are plenty of them around.'

'Plenty of them at the theatre this evening, I should imagine.'

'Quite! And I think this an opportune moment to change for the occasion. Help yourself to a dram, and I shall rejoin you shortly.'

'Right-ho!'

If Jeremiah Meadowbrook and Conan Blackcastle acted and sounded like caricatures, it was because they were victims of their own success. They spoke the slang of literary comic characters because that's essentially what they were; they had manufactured the men that the circles they mixed in lauded and applauded, for both knew this was precisely what those circles demanded.

The more successful they became, therefore, the more Dickensian the eccentricities of their personalities grew, and as Meadowbrook was rapidly overtaking Blackcastle in the public consciousness, he exhibited the most outré characteristics of the two. He was a bona-fide dandy whose every new ensemble was more colourful and extravagant than its predecessor as he pranced and minced his way through society, playing the vaguely ridiculous aesthete with his flowing tresses knitted into ringlets and a green carnation permanently pinned to his buttonhole.

Of course, the deliberate frivolity of his public persona would have quickly become tiresome had he not been in possession of the talent to support it; but he was. Both he and Conan Blackcastle delivered what was expected, for they were literary sensations, and this was indeed the age of them.

The spread of literacy way beyond the time when many signed their name with a cross because they had never been taught to read or write had spawned an audience with an appetite for the written word – and not exclusively that penned by Biblical scribes recounting ancient fairytales and reporting them as historical fact. A generation of giants had blazed a bombastic trail and the likes of Jeremiah Meadowbrook and Conan Blackcastle were hitching a ride on their coattails.

Jane Austen, Dickens, Thackeray, the Brontës, Eliot, Gaskell, Trollope, Hardy, Wilde – storytellers of page and stage with a worldwide following, all of whom had stolen the spotlight from verse in the name of prose so that the novel was the vehicle of expression for both the literate masses and chattering classes, united in opinion and adoration. With the honourable exception of the odd American, Russian and Frenchman, the English owned it, for England was the epicentre of this cultural revolution.

Man-of-the moment Jeremiah Meadowbrook was the latest in an increasingly long line of successful English wordsmiths to capture the public's attention, but anyone who could tell a good story with a degree of distinctive flair and imagination would be snapped-up by one publishing house or another in this fertile climate; publishers had multiplied and flourished along with the readership eager to devour the novel. Publishers wanted writers and the public wanted books. Meadowbrook was fortunate to find himself in the right place at the right time. Yes, he had talent, but perhaps talent that may not have been received so rapturously were he not an artist from an art so in demand – and had he not been adopted by an influential patron, which was always a handy leg-up the ladder.

Wealthy widow Lady Sarah Stabinbach was one of the last old-style society hostesses, famed for her lively salons and political soirees. Like many ladies of her era, the right to represent a constituency or even vote was one denied her, so she had engineered a behind-the-scenes role in affairs of state. At one time, she had even been known as 'the *real* Home Secretary' – or so she liked to tell the young, impressionable men she gathered around her; they weren't old enough to discern whether or not her entertaining anecdotes about past Prime Ministers she had known and loved were true; but most didn't care.

Half the time they couldn't even remember if it was Napoleon or Wellington that Lady Sarah claimed she had once been the mistress of – or was it Melbourne? They were too in awe of the charismatic aura that her talent for talk (and the elaborate stage she spoke from) radiated. She was a living link to a past they found infinitely more interesting than the present, so whatever yarn she spun, they swallowed.

Yes, she knew these naive devotees saw in her a means of furthering their careers, yet at the same time she was safe in the knowledge that it was wholly in her power to further those careers or kill them; she relished this power – and the power was permanent because so few of her followers had much in the way of talent anyway.

The harem of fawning, foppish dilettantes paying homage at the feet of Lady Sarah – and occasionally warming her bed – may have kept her entertained and stroked her ego, but being surrounded by superficiality meant she recognised substance when she saw it – and she saw it in the early works of Jeremiah Meadowbrook.

Still too obscure at that stage for word of his storytelling skills to have spread beyond his own limited corner of literature, Lady Sarah said nothing of him to her peers until she made contact with the author and expressed both her admiration and her willingness to help; if he accepted her offer of setting him up in a handsome residence and introducing him into society, his talents would then be regarded as further evidence she still had her finger on the cultural pulse. His inevitable success would reflect well on her and she could take considerable credit for it when it happened.

Jeremiah Meadowbrook naturally accepted Lady Sarah's offer and found her to be a sharp-witted and generous mentor of the kind he had always yearned for. A buxom woman wearing the shape of a Georgian, Lady Sarah's intelligence was stamped on her countenance, though her thin eyes prevented casual sightseers from peering into her soul's windows. Nevertheless, she had the ability to convince her favourites of their untapped greatness, and once belief facilitated that greatness to show itself they understandably credited Lady Sarah with a pivotal part in their rise to prominence.

Lady Sarah kept her promise to Meadowbrook, and within a month of meeting her he was indeed residing in an elegant townhouse situated in a highly fashionable neighbourhood populated by other artists who had benefitted from Lady Sarah Stabinbach's patronage. However, the only one he formed a bond with was fellow novelist Conan Blackcastle, who had been Lady Sarah's favourite until she discovered Meadowbrook. To Conan's credit, he bore no grudge against Jeremiah Meadowbrook when he was usurped in Lady Sarah's affections by the newcomer, for he himself fell in love with Meadowbrook's work and was eager to help notify others of that work as well as becoming a close friend of the author.

Meadowbrook and Blackcastle shared the same background – both products of provincial industrialists whose industry financed their education yet was rejected by them in favour of more aesthetic pursuits. Spurning their unenviable inheritances, had their ambitions not been boosted by the intervention of Lady Sarah, a life of Grub Street penury or a season-ticket for the debtor's gaol could well have been their dual destiny.

Both Meadowbrook and Blackcastle saw no reason to doubt Lady Sarah's intentions and their praise maintained her imagined occupancy of the plateau she portrayed herself as occupying; if enough people believed in her importance, she was important. That was the way she sold herself to those whose inexperience made them see the good in anybody who professed to see the good in them. Even if Lady Sarah was merely telling her chosen ones what they wanted to hear, however, when it came to Jeremiah Meadowbrook the inherent talent had simply required coaxing out, and Lady Sarah was the final piece of a jigsaw Meadowbrook had been trying to complete long before she appeared. This accounted for the rapid change in his fortunes so soon after Lady Sarah installed him as the Next Big Thing.

It took only six months as one of Lady Sarah Stabinbach's 'kept men' before Jeremiah Meadowbrook found himself to be the author of the best-selling book in the country. This was a novel rooted in truth, recounting as it did the tragic romance that culminated in the death of his young bride five years earlier. It touched the largely female readership with such sentimental expertise, appealing to the fashion in fiction for morbid melodrama, that the author felt any attempt to repeat its gloomy Gothic narrative would only disappoint; instead, he began to inject a more comic tone into its successors, and this masterstroke considerably broadened his appeal as a writer, providing him with a string of further best-sellers over the next couple of years.

His reputation firmly established as a novelist, Meadowbrook then decided to spread his storytelling wings into a more theatrical arena. Lady Sarah encouraged him when he expressed interest in penning a play. She was convinced he could transplant his success on the page to the stage and she part-financed the production scheduled to open in a high-profile theatre, attended by numerous other luminaries who had been made aware of her protégé's talent by her ceaseless promotion of it – prominent among these being Benjamin Disraeli, Dante Gabriel Rossetti, Aubrey Beardsley, and the established playwright Jasper Hampshire, whose opinion of the production especially mattered to Meadowbrook.

This windy, chilly evening was the opening night, though Lady Sarah herself couldn't be in attendance on account of a recurring illness that had a habit of striking at the most inconvenient of moments. Nevertheless, Lady Sarah was present in spirit and Jeremiah Meadowbrook dedicated the play to her as recognition of her role in his rise.

As all involved largely expected, the audience loved it; the critics' reaction was something he'd have to wait for, but Meadowbrook himself was relatively satisfied with the end result of his endeavours and departed the theatre with Blackcastle en route to the gentleman's club they were both members of. There would be a private reception there in which the author was expecting to reunite with some of his fellow writers as well as be introduced to a few he'd corresponded with but had never met in person. One of these was the aforementioned Jasper Hampshire; Meadowbrook wasn't certain how favourably a professional playwright would react to the debut effort of a theatrical novice, but his uncertainty was misplaced. When they were introduced, Hampshire was as effusive in his enthusiasm for the production as the audience had been.

Jasper Hampshire was an amiable individual with a scatterbrained persona that suggested he had just been woken from a deep sleep by a fire in his bedchamber – and a writer who was not as indebted to Lady Sarah Stabinbach for his success as Meadowbrook had been; he was not one of her discoveries, but was still an acquaintance of hers and lamented her absence from the festivities.

Her absence ironically made Lady Sarah the name on the lips of all present, with the sole competition for conversation being the novel spectacle of the hot air balloon landing on the common earlier in the day. By now, the rumours were suggesting that the passenger who had disembarked from the exotic flying machine had been a woman, and this was something Jasper Hampshire confirmed when he turned Meadowbrook's attention to his companion.

'Actually,' said Hampshire as a female figure materialised in Meadowbrook's eye-line, 'I happen to be in the...er...fortunate position of being able to enlighten you as to the identity of the...er...balloonist. She happens to be dedicated to the penmanship of us all, though I know she reserves the greatest of...er...fondness for yours, Mr Meadowbrook; allow me to introduce a devotee of your writings – Miss Orchidea.'

Society ladies who travelled by balloon were usually of an ilk, as it were – and they were generally only hitching a ride in the wicker basket in order that some randy rascal could have his wicked way with them several miles high and therefore win a bet. This one didn't seem the type, though. Reserved, diffident, elegant, well-spoken and snow-white tan – not cut from that cloth at all.

There was none of the gaudy vulgarity about her that Jeremiah Meadowbrook had become so accustomed to when encountering fans of the fairer sex; yes, they may have been overcompensating in the presence of nervousness by being a tad too forward, but most were chaperoned by men whose tastes tended to favour the jezebel and the jade. Even at this relatively early stage of his literary success, Jeremiah Meadowbrook was already well schooled when being introduced to female strangers who professed to be avid disciples and had developed stock answers to their stock questions, rendering the whole experience a tedious exercise he preferred to avoid. This one was different, however. He recognised the difference straight away.

There was always the possibility she was maybe overawed or dumbstruck by being introduced to somebody she had admired from afar, somebody her imagined unworthiness perhaps expected to be waved away with arrogant and dismissive disdain, what with her emanating from outside of his elated circle; in that case, she would have prepared herself for the anticipated brusque brush-off and received it with resigned disappointment. That would explain her gentle, graceful stillness, for meeting an artist whose work has touched us can be a tricky proposition.

Beforehand, we somehow imagine we will meet them in a state of unlikely preservation so that they are precisely as they were at the very moment of creation, as though the art that spoke to us with such profound meaning will be embodied in their person months or maybe years after the event. But when we shake their hand, we realise in an instant that of course the alchemist who concocted that particularly potent potion is not at home. We have no idea what kind of manic antisocial animal they may have been when engaged in the act of creation – probably one entirely unsuited for meeting and greeting their public; we are merely the beneficiaries of that act; we don't have to live with whatever consequences it might wreak on their character.

It's an impossibly high standard for the author of our most cherished and personal artwork to live up to, anyway, and realising this can be a crushing gate-crashing of reality into the intense intimacy that constitutes the private relationship between artist and individual audience member. Our way of coping with this likelihood is to tell ourselves that our favoured genius could be a frivolous fopdoodle in person. After all, we are not worthy of sharing their space, for we are not geniuses, are we? We must cut them some slack.

Jeremiah Meadowbrook knew not which approach Orchidea had taken upon encountering him in the flesh; she might simply be shy or she might think him a tremendous letdown; all he saw was a woman quite unlike the woman whose presumed persona he had constructed in a matter of seconds between Jasper Hampshire introducing her and Meadowbrook's lips making contact with the back of her hand, a woman he'd pieced together from all the fragments of all the other women who had been pushed forward as fans. This time, for the first time, he was intrigued and puzzled because he immediately found he cared what she thought of him; and that wasn't what usually happened.

Jeremiah Meadowbrook had reserved one of the club's exclusive dining rooms used for private parties and had not originally made provisions for a guest to join him, Blackcastle and Hampshire for their meal after the post-play reception; in many respects, from Meadowbrook's initial perspective, Hampshire had been viewed as the guest, with the two men never having met in person before. However, Hampshire had taken it upon himself to invite Orchidea – with whom it appeared he'd conducted a prior correspondence – and it would have seemed ungallant to have barred her from taking a seat at the table.

She accepted, though the fact she was seated beside Blackcastle while Meadowbrook had Hampshire next to him meant Jeremiah was forced into observing Orchidea from an inconvenient distance throughout the meal as he engaged in conversation with Hampshire, something that frustrated him and ultimately soured the food from his perspective. He didn't really know why, but there was an increasingly impulsive need in him to talk to her at the expense of the other two. And once the wine flowed, the pulsating magnetic messages she aimed in his direction intensified in their constancy so that he wanted to edge even closer to her. Perhaps the fact they weren't sat beside one another actually presented him with a unique opportunity to study her that ultimately made her even more intriguing.

There was also the now-annoying need to hold court at a reception at which he was supposed to be host, a need which felt as though it was getting in the way. Surrounded as he was by those who could recite his lines with greater accuracy than he himself ever could, Meadowbrook was being bombarded by sentences and dialogue he had composed in moments that felt so distanced from the present that they were utterly irrelevant to him; and he was expected to respond in kind by completing the recited lines as though he were a tiresome thespian who could reel off a Shakespeare soliloquy in his sleep.

Then he had to remember how important these passages were to his companions for the evening, and how it was the ability to compose quotes people actually remembered that was responsible for him being where he was and who he was with. Therefore, once his little audience had quoted numerous lines verbatim, he acquiesced with their requests to do likewise – or did his best to. He also overcame his reluctance because he felt the strong compulsion to impress the special guest.

Still, however, Jeremiah Meadowbrook preferred to observe rather than participate; the trio sharing the table with him were too animated by both the occasion and each other's company to notice he had slipped into the vigilant observation of human interaction that is second nature for a writer – filing away these observations for future reference, when they would emerge on the page after being reshaped and reconfigured through the creative funnel so comprehensively that their original inspirations may well struggle to recognise themselves reborn as fictional characters once they hit the first sentence.

Engaged in this almost subconscious process, Meadowbrook automatically absorbed the behaviour of Conan Blackcastle, who he knew well enough – and the seeping of Jasper Hampshire's core personality into his artistic engine was a similarly effortless endeavour too. The lady was something else altogether, though. He struggled to get an instant fix on her, but he should have realised time had to slow down in order for him to immerse himself fully.

Gradually, the sensory distractions of Meadowbrook's surroundings and his other two companions melted away as though nothing mattered but the mesmerising figure drawing his whole field of vision towards her. He could see nothing else in that room now. Something had happened, and it had happened so stealthily, creeping up on him with such sublime surprise that he couldn't pinpoint a precise moment when he became aware it was happening; but once he was in the thick of it there was no going back.

He had been caught unawares, yet he let himself go with that fabulous flow because the stream he'd slipped into was carrying him closer to a prize that suddenly seemed preordained and destined to belong to him. The leaves of a priceless volume began to open at a serenely sedate pace, a volume glowing with the promise of something new.

The stretching of the evening imbued Orchidea with an even deeper, resonant range of seductive shades than she had initially suggested, shades wrapping themselves around Jeremiah's receptive frame and plunging into his depressed, dark heart with such luminous vitality that he could feel it beating for the first time in years. The sensation had been so lost to him for so long that its unannounced reappearance felt more akin to a debut than a resurrection. He wasn't even aware he was hungry till the feast was laid before him.

Each passing second of blissful study revealed greater, more intoxicating colours than the previous beguiling layer had displayed. Like flicking through the feathers of a rare bird, every depth he delved into exposed elements of the rainbow he had never seen before. The pleasing and sweetly simplistic surface that shimmered so softly across his consciousness like a fresh breeze on an August afternoon had caught his attention; but he certainly hadn't been prepared for the astonishing spectrum of this fascinating woman as her subliminal invitation to explore unveiled a precious jewel that he felt only *his* entranced eyes could discern or could ultimately own.

Courteous Conan had the decency to leave the room with the chamber-pot when nature called – as opposed to the usual masculine custom of strolling over to the cupboard it was kept in and pissing along with the conversation; Hampshire, meanwhile, had succumbed to upright slumber as the claret sang a song of sedation. Meadowbrook suddenly had the opportunity to speak alone with the exquisite creature his arms were craving to pull towards him – and he took it.

Her voice was as soft to the ear as he imagined her hair was to the touch; it had the enchanting whisper of a little girl imparting a secret to her governess during an elocution lesson. She giggled nervously, as though overawed by the company; he tried to transmit the unprecedented ease she generated in him back at her. He didn't cross-examine, but probed with a delicacy coaxing replies which slowly increased in their word-count the longer the time they enjoyed without interruption.

The concise economy of her first reply – 'It's complicated' – was expanded upon as the chat progressed. She confessed there had once been a husband, but didn't go into detail; Meadowbrook was told nothing of the hanging or even the alternate version in which her husband returned to torment her. She also admitted she had a 'child', but the truth was understandably skirted around.

She said she'd used the balloon as a vehicle on account of the favourable wind that day and how it could cover the lengthy distance from her country home to town far quicker than a coach; she would spend the night in a nearby hotel and would return by the same means early in the morning; her manservant would be keeping guard on the moored balloon in her overnight absence.

Meadowbrook gathered-up snippets from their conversation as if he were an archaeologist searching for the remains of a Saxon warrior but who'd had to settle for a few unearthed trinkets at the end of the first day's dig. There would always be tomorrow's dig, after all. Yet, there was an undeniable urgency to the way in which Jeremiah Meadowbrook tried to get to know Orchidea in the brief window without company, almost as though the world was scheduled to come to an end the following day and he only had this night to act on his intuition.

Perhaps the death of his wife, the tragedy he had described with such moving eloquence in the book that made his name, had instilled within him the need to move fast should he ever encounter these feelings again. He knew only too well how they could be cruelly snatched away and how every moment in the presence of a woman who provoked them had to be cherished. He wanted more of those moments, and he was determined to grab them.

All too soon, Conan returned to the room and then Hampshire stirred from his winks as all forty appeared to be up; the assembled quartet recognised that time was being called on the evening, and Orchidea's early start played its part. The three gentlemen escorted Orchidea to the hotel, which was conveniently no more than two-hundred yards from the club, and she embraced all her chaperones in the doorway.

She planted a kiss on the respective cheeks of Conan Blackcastle and Jasper Hampshire, yet didn't grant Meadowbrook the same affectionate farewell gesture, as if to do so would have exposed a greater depth of affection to the other two when she wanted to privately assess what Jeremiah had stirred in her before making it public. She knew something of immense significance had happened between them, even if neither had acknowledged it to one another in words. Maybe she also knew – as he did – there was no need to kiss him goodbye when they would shortly reunite. The Gods had already embellished the stars with the script.

Jasper Hampshire hailed a cab a couple of minutes after Orchidea disappeared into her hotel, while Conan strolled with Meadowbrook to their shared neighbourhood; it was only a ten-minute walk away, for their whole world revolved around an area encompassing little more than a square mile. The two friends parted outside the Meadowbrook residence, having had quite a memorable evening in each other's company. Jeremiah had claimed tiredness as a reason for spurning Conan's eagerness to prolong the day with some laudanum, but he was far from tired. He was more awake now than he had been in years.

The energy levels in him were flying so high that he knew he couldn't simply wait a few days before writing a reflective letter to Orchidea; he wanted to capitalise on what she had done to him now, to express his feelings whilst still possessed by the excitement she'd inspired in him. So, he dashed off a short note and wasted no time in calling his valet to urgently dispatch it to Orchidea's hotel. It was brief and to the point.

****

Dear Orchidea

What a wondrous surprise it was to be introduced to you this evening. Excuse my impetuosity, but I just wanted to say I found you utterly adorable. There, I have expressed it out loud!

I am not prone to such impulsive actions as a rule, yet life is too brief to dither. If a second meeting is something you desire as much as I do, please reply to this short missive. Anyone whose life has been enlivened by my humble jottings matters, believe me.

Your servant
Jeremiah Meadowbrook
15 Trinity Terrace

****

Orchidea became aware of the note when she was poised to depart the hotel early the following morning. She hastily wrote a reply, mirroring Meadowbrook's sentiments. Indeed, life *was* too brief to dither, though her return home could well serve as the most deflating of wake-up calls from an excursion that had been perhaps even more life-changing for her than for the man whose impact on her superseded hers on him.

Neither expected what had happened to happen. But it had.

Mother's Keeper

If I want to eat, you will not let me do so free from interruption. If I want to read, bathe or sleep, you are always there demanding my attention. I have sacrificed myself to be your permanent appendage. You are my malignant shadow, my punishment, my curse. I resent you, but I love you.

You are a part of me I gave birth to and you will never leave me. The umbilical cord is unbroken. You are familiarity. You are security. You have shaped my world so that a world without you in it is even more terrifying than the one I share with you. I have arranged everything around you for so long that the routine has become me. Take that away and I would struggle to survive. I would be lost and scared at having nothing to cling to that defines me because *you* define me. Without you, I do not know who I am.

I return home and you are angry because I left you in the care of others overnight. You roar, you claw, you lash out and greet me with a bite. I have to entertain you within a minute of my arrival. I have to accompany you outdoors for hours and hold your attention throughout as it wanders and wavers. I throw sticks for you that you chase but never bring back. Once you grab it, you are bored with it and I have to search for another stick in order to repeat the gesture, over and over and over again. It is the repetition that is so exhausting and so draining.

There are some distractions that have proven durable for days, but then you are abruptly bored with them and the brief sensation of salvation I experienced has gone again. I vainly depended on them as magical – if momentary – cures and then I am forced into finding others. Every time I think I've found the answer, boredom kicks in once more and you want some new stimulation I've yet to concoct.

At one time, balls would work. I'd throw them so far and with such speed that I could have been selected as a spin-bowler for the county. I honed the skill to perfection and you responded with a run that reminded me what a graceful, magnificent creature you can be in full flight. It would be a joy to observe you, but how short-lived joy can be. You'd reach the ball, pick it up, shake it about and then stand there snarling at me. You wanted another ball. In the end, I had to be accompanied by a handmaiden and between us we had to carry sacks with around half-a-dozen balls in each of them.

I've tried balls since and you frustratingly don't want to know anymore. I throw one and you just stand there, watching it fly through the air and then bounce on the ground. But the impetus to chase it has left you. There is absolutely no desire to follow the ball's trajectory and catch it before it lands. You look at me with an unimpressed air and demand something else with a menacing growl. This is when I resort to sticks. For now, they work. But for how long?

I engage in this for what always feels like forever and think of nothing as I do it. My mind is blank because your demands have emptied it of all other concerns. Other concerns have never been given the time and space to develop and mature into interests. You will not allow it. I am here for your benefit, not my own or anyone else's. How dare I devote even the smallest part of myself to something that does not include you? I must place you before everything, thus reducing everything to nothing.

Your temper can be incendiary and unpredictable.

Even after all this time, you still possess the capacity to catch me unawares with a random roar and swing of the paw. When you were a cub, you were no less demanding, but you were small enough to handle – and cute to look at. Recruiting handmaidens to aid your round-the-clock care was easier then. They'd be introduced to you and think you no more of a handful than a badly-behaved kitten. However, now you are bigger and so much bolder. Your sharp awareness of your dominant role in the household has grown to complement your increased size, and the only staff members I can rely on are those who have watched you grow and have learnt how to appease you when you choose to be difficult.

Impatience is a virtue for you.

When you are hungry, you will not wait for your food to be delivered and you roar with rage until it arrives. When you want to go outdoors, you will not acknowledge that I have to dress for the excursion and that this takes a few minutes. When nothing I offer you serves to entrance you, you blame me for your boredom. When you are tired, you rally against the onset of slumber and take out your resentment at having to succumb to sleep on me. You are angry that I will not be there to entertain you in your dreams.

I retreat to the library on tiptoe when you eventually drift off, leaving a handmaiden to watch over you in my absence. My collection is securely behind lock and key to keep you from destroying the one thing I have that you do not control. This is my oasis, the only section of the house in which the decor is not bare and sparse to suit your savagery – an aesthetic factor that renders the house even more of an ugly prison for me.

Here in my precious oasis, however, I can almost pretend there is no you, that I am as others are and have the luxury of relaxation and intellectual stimulation. It is a lovely fantasy. Depending on how long you sleep, however, I can sometimes plunge into a novel and lose myself in it so successfully that time is a redundant, meaningless concept and I really am just another reader enjoying the fruits of an author's labours.

This is the closest to bliss I ever get.

It is no wonder I have formed long-distance attachments to authors. They have become like Gods to me, supernatural beings that inhabit a world as fantastically unreal and detached from mine as the ones they create in their books. Of them all, Jeremiah Meadowbrook was the one who spoke to me with the greatest intimacy, the one who lifted me out of my life and onto a plane so high that I daren't look down.

Unlike the rest, I relented from corresponding with him. I adored him so much that I felt unworthy of his company. Why on earth would he be remotely interested in me? I confessed this in a letter to the playwright Jasper Hampshire and he replied by informing me he'd been invited to the inaugural performance of a play written by Meadowbrook in which the great man would be in attendance. Hampshire enquired if I'd care to accompany him to not only the event, but the private after-show reception as well; I could hardly imagine such a dreamlike scenario. But even though I would ordinarily have politely declined due to *you,* the tempting prospect of being introduced to Jeremiah Meadowbrook was too great to resist. If I didn't take this opportunity, it may never come around again.

I accepted Hampshire's invitation and then immediately regretted what felt like a foolish fancy. How could I leave you overnight? It would have to be overnight, too; there was no way I could make it there and back on the same day *and* sit through a play as well as meeting Jeremiah Meadowbrook afterwards. Then I realised there was one way I could leave as late as possible and not risk missing the play – the balloon. A felicitous purchase only enjoyed on the odd occasion, allowing me a short break from your tantrums as I soared above them, I could finally put it to good use if the wind was favourable on the day.

Come the day, it *was.*

This was an unprecedented occasion fraught with complications, but I had to do it. Every provision for your awkwardness was considered with meticulous thoroughness beforehand; nothing was left to chance. This would be the longest you and I had been apart since your birth, so I couldn't brush aside any potential disaster in my absence. I had to plan for every possibility.

Yet when the moment arrived for me to step into the basket, I had to delve into the deepest recesses of strength I still had in me to go through with it. I was terrified. So many years had passed since I'd socialised like a normal lady, I was convinced everyone would see through the charade of normality I'd have to adopt.

Thankfully, the journey took the fear from me, at least for its duration. I could never tire of this glorious method of travel and it was a shame I had used it on so few occasions, for I had forgotten how much I loved it. The fact we had the sky to ourselves served as a reminder that it remained a vehicle for the few rather than the many, which is a shame. More people should be able to experience it. Seeing the landscape mapped out so far down below elevated me above so many of the earthbound fears that consume us, almost diminishing their importance by distance. Only when the time arrived to touch down did they return to my head.

I would've liked to have arrived unnoticed, but a balloon is rather conspicuous and there was a small, understandably curious crowd that gathered as we came in to land. They assumed me to be some famous figure, bombarding me with questions I felt almost embarrassed not to have the correct answers to; but with assistance of my invaluable manservant old Sam, I managed to wade my way through them straight to a waiting cabriolet I provided with the address of the hotel Jasper Hampshire had arranged for me in advance. And yet even after all this unaccustomed exhilaration, I still couldn't help but wonder what you were up to right at that very moment. I had temporarily lost my shadow and it felt strange.

Jasper Hampshire met me at the hotel a few hours later and then escorted me to the theatre. He was a charming flirt, but wasting his time if he imagined we could extend our correspondence beyond what it was. He had no idea about me at all. The play itself was a pleasure to watch, even if the limited concentration that being at your beck and call for so long has engendered made it occasionally uncomfortable to sit still; but the exclusive reception afterwards was when nerves really returned. The thought of meeting Jeremiah Meadowbrook, a man whose talent I was so in awe of that I cared deeply as to what impression I might make upon him, was nerve-wracking.

I had seen a portrait of Jeremiah Meadowbrook in one of his books, so I had an inkling of what he looked like, and the impression given by that engraving had been that here was an extremely handsome albeit vaguely arrogant individual, cocksure and confident in his own skin – an alien concept to me. How wrong I was. In person, he reminded me a great deal of a picture I once saw of Franz Liszt; he has the same long dark hair hung around a striking pale face with prominent cheekbones. But there was no arrogance about him at all.

To receive that note from him, expressing sentiments that entirely echoed my own, couldn't have prompted any other response than the one I gave. He had laid his cards on the table, so I had no need to hide behind coquettish diffidence.

'It was lovely to meet you,' I wrote. *'I have read and loved your books for a long time. They have kept me going when life has been at its bleakest. I would indeed like to meet again.'*

I kept it brief, for I didn't have the time or the nerve to pour my heart out on the page. That was *his* job, and the fact he told me he found me adorable meant I was already walking on air even before the moorings of the balloon were severed and I was back sailing across the sky.

And now I am here again – back to reality. Yet, I have seen an alternate reality that has shown me it has the potential to be more than mere fantasy. Yes, you are watching me as you chomp on that gristle in the garden. You are always watching me. But I evaded your eyes for one night. I can do so again if I draw strength from the adventure I embarked upon. I have proven that I don't have to confine myself to this prison all day every day. I can enjoy a break from the grind. As long as I make the same arrangements for your needs as I made for that one evening, I can repeat it. I *can*.

I intend to build upon this. I *must*. I shall send Jeremiah Meadowbrook a token of my appreciation for allowing me to see the opening night of his play and for giving me a seat at his table afterwards – a small token, nothing too elaborate. A bottle of cherry brandy he can mix with laudanum, perhaps, and a pipe, both to be delivered to his door. And I shall write to him. If I suggest a date a couple of weeks hence when we can reunite, it gives us both plenty of time to make our respective arrangements – and I certainly need the time to make mine.

Yes, I am here once more, appeasing you and arranging my day around you and your demands. You still have me in your paw, as you always have and you always will. But I have seen a glimpse of a different life and I want more. I will not spurn this gift from the Gods. And you will not make me.

The First Day of Spring

The collective feeling on the eve of peace is not as explosively emotive as the collective feeling on the eve of war. The former comprises weary relief born of exhaustion, lacking the tense adrenalin rush of the latter. If one could encapsulate the feelings of the eve of war – that exciting, instinctive awareness that the world is poised to change forever and all that has been will be no more – and substitute the awful onset of conflict with something truly beautiful, one would have the shared sensation of Jeremiah Meadowbrook and Orchidea in the immediate aftermath of their second encounter. They both recognised this was a major game-changer. There was absolutely no doubt.

Meadowbrook was instantly convinced of the magnitude of the change. As far as he was concerned, he had awoken in a new century, a new epoch. After all, there are only ever really days. If they should take the shape of decades when we are distracted, so be it. Overnight, Wilde was disgraced, imprisoned and exiled as Victoria passed away in her regal repose. But none of that mattered.

All external events were erased from his field of vision as effectively as Conan Blackcastle and Jasper Hampshire had been during that first meeting; and the same hypnotically addictive light that blacked out its surroundings with such luscious luminosity that evening was responsible again. Without his knowledge, a lamp may as well have fallen into Meadowbrook's lap from which one casual rub had produced a puff of smoke that then took the physical form of the most desirable, ethereal genie that human eyes had ever settled upon. Where the hell did she come from?

For her part, Orchidea was shaken, stirred and overwhelmed by a full body and soul massage that the reader, like the author, generally just imagines; but the imagination comes nowhere near the glory of reality. In the dreamlike shadow of its aftermath, she remained travelling by balloon for days, gliding through the clouds as her feet became immune to the earth. The whole experience to her had exceeded the will of the wind, for she was no longer dependent on the elements to fly as a feather.

The thrill of her literary hero merely noticing she existed had been superseded by a scenario unimaginable when she had emptied her head of everything in order to go through the stick-throwing motions for Biba. So, there *was* another life out there for her after all. She didn't have to restrict herself to the sole role of lion-tamer.

Meadowbrook's situation was in no way comparable to Orchidea's – though, to be fair, few situations were; but nonetheless, he too had spent several years in which his being had been severely starved of emotional nutrition. The death of his wife had encased him in a casket of ice that success as a novelist had failed to thaw. For all the materialistic comforts best-selling books had brought, the actual composition of those books had largely been an evasion of emotions than a reconnection with them. Even the novel that made his name and provided fame, one which told the tragic tale of that doomed romance, was not a cathartic exercise that served to cure him of grief; it simply enabled him to make a decent living out of a good story. And he now knew that wasn't enough.

Meadowbrook needed Orchidea as much as she needed him. He may have been the one who made the move, but only because he had confidence in himself in one area – as a celebrity – whereas Orchidea had none at all. She had already responded to that celebrity by accepting Jasper Hampshire's invitation, so he used it to both their advantage.

Correspondence was quick to establish itself between them. Orchidea did indeed send a bottle of cherry brandy and a pipe as a thank you for that inaugural evening; then twice (often thrice) daily letters began to be sealed and dispatched with the ink still bearing the feverish freshness of a new passion as it splashed onto the paper and barely had time to dry before a sequel was scribbled.

A reunion was arranged for a fortnight after their initial encounter, though there was a curious, somewhat juvenile excitement in keeping their plans secret from Meadowbrook's circle. She said nothing to Jasper Hampshire, and he didn't even inform Conan Blackcastle of his intended liaison. Perhaps Meadowbrook figured any male acquaintance might prejudge Orchidea as just another disposable conquest, so he only shared the news with Lady Sarah Stabinbach, whose first reaction was one of genuine joy that her Jeremiah appeared to have found someone a cut above the harlots the rest of her bachelor artists settled for.

As a widower, however, it took a cut above to catch the eye that had always looked to the stars for romantic inspiration rather than the gutter.

Having made the brave step of journeying to meet Jeremiah Meadowbrook in the first place, Orchidea finally knew she had it in her to organise the small semblance of a life outside her prison walls. She had become so accustomed to her unnatural existence and had normalised it to such an extent that she neglected to acknowledge the extraordinary amount of strength and resourcefulness she possessed in order to live the way she did. Here at last was an opportunity to utilise those qualities for a different and wholly positive purpose.

She made all the arrangements with the same meticulousness as before, but was terribly afflicted by anxiety as the designated day approached. This time, she would be travelling to town by the more conventional method of her personal coach, which required an earlier start and a longer journey; but it was not so much the prospect of the travel that provoked nerves as the thought that Jeremiah Meadowbrook would somehow find several hours alone in her company to be a dire disappointment. Her self-esteem still languished so low that she was tormented by such nightmarish images of her own failure as an attractive and interesting woman despite being confronted by an individual who amazingly appeared to contradict her opinion.

These anxious premonitions of disaster plagued Orchidea throughout her lengthy journey, causing her particular trauma halfway, when the horses were changed at a coaching inn and she had to twiddle her thumbs for an hour, unable to eat or drink despite desperate entreaties from her driver. She was carrying a hamper of edible goodies to present Jeremiah Meadowbrook with and couldn't even bring herself to sample them en route, fearful she'd end up throwing up and disgracing herself in the process. When they finally resumed the trek, she retreated to the carriage and continued to fret over endless potential disasters when there was little evidence to suggest any of it would end in tears.

By contrast, Jeremiah Meadowbrook approached the prospect of an evening in the company of a woman who had been the first to provoke any sign of feeling in him since the death of his wife with a calmness that reflected his attitude towards matters of the heart after that devastating blow. He recognised something special was taking place, but he knew that the build-up to a new dawn was to be embraced, not feared; how could it be compared to the emotional maelstrom that comes with the death of one's beloved? No, it was a joyous occasion and there was nothing to be scared of at all. He was calm and composed, confident all would be well.

Why wouldn't it be?

The same hotel Orchidea had been an overnight guest at during her previous visit was again booked in advance, and it was arranged that Meadowbrook would meet her there at a prearranged time before escorting her to his own home for dinner and discussion. There was no question of her spending the night under Meadowbrook's roof; neither was hampered by moralistic etiquette, yet neither wanted to appear presumptuous to the other. Yes, both knew it was inevitable that they would eventually end up sharing a bed, but perhaps it was best not to prematurely leap ahead of the blunderbuss.

****

My nerves evaporated the moment he emerged through the fog. I knew then that all the anxious fretting that had consumed me during the dreary journey from home to town was unnecessary. Just the sight of that beautiful man making the effort to meet and greet humble little me put me at ease and made me feel that I had slipped into safe hands. I knew he would take care of me for the evening, that he would be gentle and kind, and that he would not be a bastard rake intent on ravishment and rape.

There was a melancholy graciousness in his eyes that moved me and told me he would not treat me with disrespect. The tragedy of his marriage was writ large on his gorgeous countenance. I instantly knew he had a high regard for the fairer sex and would not exploit my perceived vulnerability in his company. I consented to be led to his abode and was immediately confident I would be led back to the hotel several hours later without what remained of my virtue having been soiled or stolen.

I took the decision to stroll to the hotel rather than summon the carriage. Nerves I had none, but a walk would clear my head of them should they see fit to materialise. Nevertheless, she had agreed to come to me without the need for any tedious prolonged pursuit, so what cause had I to be stricken by anxiety? I had no doubt my attraction to her was reciprocated due to the haste with which she had suggested a second rendezvous. It was evident to me that she desired the same eventuality as I did, though I was not determined to accelerate that eventuality this evening. I was content to let events unfold at a pace of fate's choosing.

Anyway, when I caught sight of her in the hotel doorway, I knew she was mine; and I felt a humbling sense of honour that I was her chosen one. Fortune had finally favoured me in the shape of this divine visitation I yearned to hold. That sight was the culmination of every yearning that had consumed my adult life. We kissed and I took her by the hand to lead her home. The century was drawing to a close.

His "lair" was exactly as I had visualised it in my head, based upon the portrait I had painted from exposure to his writings – the rococo refuge of a true artistic individual immune to fad and fashion. I instantly absorbed his personal aesthetic and knew how I could embellish it with the occasional object I'd present as a present. He had arranged a meal far in advance of our arrival, and the hamper I brought with me served us well with snacks both before and after the food being delivered to the table.

He was the perfect host, playing the gentleman throughout the prologue to our post-dinner withdrawal to the chez-longue. As the evening progressed, any notions of virtuous modesty seemed silly and irrelevant when in the hands of someone I quickly realised not only lived up to, but exceeded, my expectations.

The chez-longue seemed the ideal item of furniture upon which we could retire for a post-meal recline, being as it was midway between settee and bed. The main topic of discussion to date had largely been my literary canon, and I'd been happy to go over all that with Orchidea, knowing she was such a fan. But she remained sufficiently mysterious to stoke my curiosity when I'd exhausted my own life story and was eager to hear hers. I at least received a sample of snippets as I edged closer to her on that subtly sensual seat.

Few words expressed our joint urges that night; it was mostly all about actions; and as I slowly instigated a union of our respective thighs, I surmised the meeting of them would have provoked withdrawal on her part had she objected. There was no withdrawal. I had gradually eased my person within the intimate boundaries of her own in order to test her response; when she allowed me to encroach upon her territory without resistance, I knew I was making the right move and I derived as much pleasure from that intimacy as she must have.

I had a pretty accurate idea as to what was in his head on that chez-longue and I was content to let him progress because I lacked the nerve to do likewise; I was more than happy for him to articulate something we were both feeling; one of us needed to, and it wasn't going to be me, alas. When I felt the warm, soothing softness of his thigh press against mine, I was relieved he had done so. That slow, subtle move gave me the confidence I'd lacked all day and finally confirmed my suspicion that this connection wasn't one-sided. I knew for certain then that we undoubtedly shared the same aims and intentions.

I cannot say precisely what he experienced at the moment of contact, but I relished the electrifying sensation that sent a delicious shiver through my entire body. Nobody had touched me like that in years – and nobody I really wanted to touch me like that had ever done so.

Thigh-to-thigh, we continued to chat for a little while before I threw caution to the wind and abruptly announced how adorable I thought she was, saying out loud for the first time what I had expressed in writing via the note I'd dashed off following our first meeting; she responded with touching coyness, peering at me through the silky security of that lemon curtain of hair like a child engaged in a game of hide-and-seek. This coyness was something I found quite endearing rather than off-putting; it said to me that she wasn't opposed to my sentiments. And when I apologised for embarrassing her, she immediately retorted with a declaration that she *wasn't* embarrassed; within seconds we were engaged in a passionate kiss of the kind I had previously imagined in prose without having experienced so satisfactorily in reality. The last barrier to our unspoken desires had been breached and there was no turning back.

We kissed and he speedily suggested his bedchamber might be a more conducive and comfortable environment in which to continue our conversation. Quite frankly, I cared not whether chat ploughed through the past; the present was far more invigorating for me, and I held out my hand for him to lead me upstairs. There was no suggestion we would disrobe, and I was pretty certain I'd object to that. I simply wanted to be held, and there was no one else on this earth I wanted to be held by more than him.

The fact she didn't object to my suggestion suggested my desire wasn't an offshoot of the ego that swells with professional success, but was instead the airing of a mutual craving. The fact we laid *on* the bed and fully-clothed rather than naked *in* it didn't matter. Yes, I wanted to make love to her, but to just hold her was enough right there and then. She was so lovely and warm to the touch and smelt so nice. I had forgotten both those things; it had been so long since I'd clutched anyone so close to me. I had forgotten how much my neglected frame had missed physical intimacy and the therapeutic healing of embracing. Being aroused alone by an erotic lithograph just didn't compare.

But it wasn't just holding her or being close to her that affected me; there was more to it than that. There was a very clear awareness that a quest had come to an end; I'd reached the peak of the mountain I'd spent a lifetime climbing, and what I'd found there made every agonising moment of that tumultuous ascent worthwhile. This was what I'd always been looking for; I just didn't know that until I'd got my hands on it.

Of course, I'd been held before, but this was different. The feelings running through me as he wrapped himself around me were unique. I didn't really know what was happening; it felt as though I had drunk or digested something that had affected me in a profound and unprecedented way. Something had changed in me at that moment, above and beyond the simple excitement of lying beside a man I thought beautiful. I'd hoped this scenario might come about, but now it had I was utterly unprepared for what it provoked in me.

I was overcome with an indescribable inner peace, a languid calm that sedated my entire mind and body. It felt as though I'd been waiting my whole life for this moment, to be cradled by this man – as though every other man who had ever held me was merely an apprentice and I had finally found the sorcerer. All the hellish trauma of the last few years, and every mark it had left on me, simply vanished. I was being cleansed of everything bad that had ever happened to me. There was nothing and no one but the two of us – Yin and Yang united at last. A matching pair that had always been incomplete without even knowing it now realised why everything suddenly made sense. We had been designed from day one to slot together; we hadn't realised this fact because it had taken this long for us to meet.

When someone has been engaged in some distracting activity or other and they say they lost track of time, it's generally an exaggeration on a par with declaring one is starving when one is simply hungry. But when Orchidea and I were laid on that bed together, I really did lose track of time. In effect, time ceased to exist as she and I drifted off into some timeless dreamland where nothing mattered but us. What are clocks there for, anyway, but to inform us of external events we have been conditioned to acknowledge? We can see the hours pass merely by observing the daylight. We don't need clocks to tell us what nature displays on a daily basis.

And clocks were rendered utterly irrelevant by nature's greatest gift there and then – a partner. I heard occasional chiming on the landing outside the bedchamber, but I had no idea how many times because it no longer had any meaning. Only she mattered, and I had merged with her. We were one and the same – Siamese twins separated at birth and belatedly back in one piece, just as we should have been all along.

We read each other like we were both engrossing novels we couldn't put down – and we did so without saying a word. We just looked into one another's eyes. And every once in a while, we'd laugh, a laugh that said what we were simultaneously thinking – What the hell is happening? How is this happening? Can something that feels this good be real? And can it really happen to us? Isn't this the sort of thing the poets write about when they've taken too many hallucinogenic drugs?

It felt so bloody wonderful that it was unlike any sensation either of us had ever experienced, drunk or sober. This was a completely uncharted realm of experience we were in, and it was scary; but scary in a good way. It was invigorating. I felt like every cell in my body was regenerating, and the regenerative energy was passing between us, going backwards and forwards as it slowly sealed us together like an adhesive and we could no longer move. We were paralysed by unshakable attraction.

The events prior to this moment already felt like a thousand years ago. I could believe we had always existed as we were right then – always wrapped around each other on that bed. Walking over to her hotel, walking back home with her, dining and drinking, even sitting on the chez-longue – all of it seemed so distant from where we were that it didn't seem like it had happened just a few hours ago. Had life existed at all before this moment? The telepathic realisation of what was happening to us was immense. This was it – the Big One. We knew even without saying it that we were in it for the rest of our days. This was our destiny. From now on, we were Us.

These incredibly rare occurrences only happen once in a lifetime – hell, for so many people, they never happen at all – and when/if they happen, you appreciate their significance in an instant. You know why they have happened and you know they are meant to be. You recognise this without question. The meaning of life is no longer an elusive riddle. It has been revealed at last.

How many hours? How many days? How many weeks or months or years passed us by as we lay there? How many empires rose and fell? How many kings and queens were crowned and deposed? How many wars were won and lost? I didn't care because we had each other. Let this be the way things will always be, I thought; let nothing end this bliss. To take this from me now would be unendurable cruelty. I cannot be given this gift only for it to be stolen away. Better to have never been so blessed than to be robbed of this prize. But I had earned it. I had suffered enough. Perhaps that suffering had been a necessary rite of passage leading to this moment. If so, every awful second of that suffering was worth it. Just look at where it had eventually brought me, on this bed with this man – my man. I was holding gold.

I didn't want to move, but I wanted to take this remarkable sensual harmony to the next stage. After a few hours of static serenity, I suggested it several times, but she was admittedly anxious at the prospect. She said she hadn't shared a bed with anyone in years; I told her I hadn't either. Nobody else would have believed me if I'd confessed I hadn't touched a woman since the death of my wife. Surely the big literary sensation, the toast-of-the town with a bevy of fanatical female followers, surely he must regularly get his leg over? He wouldn't have to try hard, after all. No, he wouldn't.

But maybe he wanted more than regularly getting his leg over with whichever ravenous slut was throwing herself at him – and a fair few had. For the first time since becoming a widower, a woman had entered my orbit that I really wanted to be intimate with, and the absolute conviction we shared that what was happening to us was utterly right and proper said to me that we should immediately progress to what inevitably came next. The astounding speed of this coming together was such that it wouldn't have been out of place to move it on before the next day dawned.

Yes, I wanted to – of course I did. But I wanted to catch my breath before that eventuality. I wasn't sure my body could take another sensuous shock on the same day as this internal earthquake. I was already tingling all over from just being held, and I didn't believe I had the physical strength to do more. I was delightfully exhausted and blissfully sedated by one stunning sensation, and wasn't certain I could handle another.

Even though I could feel his unmistakable arousal when we slipped into the spoons position, I liked the feel of that arousal against me as it was. I didn't have the desire or urgency to take it further right there and then. I wanted what we had to remain preserved just like that for a while longer. It was so wonderful that the deepest yearning in me was simply to prolong and not progress – not yet, anyway. I wanted us to be two conjoined souls petrified in aspic, reclining in sublime stasis. I knew there would be plenty of time for everything else. Just let us stay this way for now.

I pleaded half-heartedly, but didn't press her when she resisted my entreaties. She, like me, knew that there would be a next time and she promised that we would indeed take the next step then. I accepted her reasoning and we resumed the intimacy we had established for even more hours. I've no real idea how many. There was a clock in the bedchamber and I only acknowledged the time it told when she herself did and then alerted me to it. She was concerned the hotel doors would be locked if she lingered any longer, and though neither of us wanted to bring this dream to an end, we reluctantly awoke. She had a little personal work to attend to before we made a move, however.

The lascivious locks of her unbound hair gave the impression she'd been willingly dragged through a hedge, and she believed anyone seeing us leave the house would instantly jump to the conclusion that we had indeed been doing what we'd never actually got round to. Our clothes were crumpled and creased, but mine had absorbed her scent so successfully that I didn't want to change – ever. In her absence, I could smell her and feel she was always clinging to my person. I wasn't to know then that for days afterwards I would sense the presence of her body next to mine in the same way that someone who has had a limb amputated often claims they can still feel the lost limb even when it's long gone. I now couldn't remember a moment when she hadn't been in my arms. It seemed unnatural for her not to be next to me, so the prospect of parting was unimaginable. But it was about to happen.

It would have been so much easier to have said to hell with the hotel and instead remained where I was until sunrise. But we both knew there would be many more next times to come – there was no disputing that – so we prepared to depart with the most sluggish lack of enthusiasm imaginable. He pointed me in the direction of a looking-glass so I could ensure I would leave his residence in as respectable a state of dress as I had entered it. But it was impossible to look exactly the same, for everything that had happened was imprinted on my face, and I undoubtedly looked very different as a consequence.

I had known traumatic events of the worst kind could be mirrored on one's countenance; they could add lines and wrinkles and streak one's hair with silver overnight; but I hadn't realised the opposite kind of events could also leave their mark. That was a joyous revelation. I thought I had shed a dozen years. I hadn't seen that face in a long time, and it was lovely to reunite with it – the face of a happy, carefree girl without a worry in the world. Right here, within the walls of Jeremiah

Meadowbrook's home, there were indeed no worries, and for a few hours I had forgotten all of them. I had drifted outside of time and space so that nothing beyond his body and that bed existed.

That walk back to the hotel could have been like a march to the gallows, but two things rescued it from that ominous prospect. The first was that we both knew we would reunite soon, so it wasn't a goodbye; the second was that her hand slipped into mine when we set foot outside and remained there until we reached the hotel doorway. The most simple of loving gestures can often move one more than the grandest, and the sensation of her hand holding mine for that short journey was as glorious a feeling as any I have ever experienced. I can say with absolute certainty that I don't believe I have ever found such contentment and pure happiness as I did when we strolled hand-in-hand along those streets. I was convinced this was the first day of the rest of my life, convinced that life from that moment on was going to be good because I had Orchidea.

The route to the hotel was remarkably lively for the time of night, but many taverns were turfing out their patrons. Yet, we passed through the multitudes as if we were floating above them; we were wearing blinkers that removed everyone from our vision but each other. And even when we finally parted with a kiss and an embrace on the hotel doorstep, it didn't feel final. It was the beginning of something, not the end.

Even the return home the next morning didn't sour my mood. I bore the journey with stoic resignation, but not depression. I was too invigorated by what had taken place the night before, feeling his arms around me all the way home; purely on memory alone, I was soaring even higher than I could have if I'd taken the balloon instead of the coach. That sensation was still too present on my person for it not to affect my mood and sustain the heights he'd lifted me to even though he wasn't actually there in the carriage with me. Yes, once back with Biba and all the attendant headaches that accompanied life with a lion, events in the lair of Jeremiah Meadowbrook had the hazy radiance of a half-remembered childhood incident recalled as something so out of the ordinary that it felt more akin to an event dreamt than lived. But this was real.

I wrote to him within two hours of arriving home and did so again the following day before even receiving his reply. At least the constant correspondence between us made it seem as though he was much closer than he actually was – not quite my next-door neighbour but equally not my long-distance paramour. Anyway, he was so much more than paramour. He had taken me and shaken me out of a coma, and my gratitude for this heroic act was manifested as my tumbling head-over-heels in love.

****

Letters flew from one address to the other, back and forth for a fortnight until Orchidea and Jeremy Meadowbrook reunited again. The evening that was arranged as their next get-together unfortunately happened to coincide with a salon held by Lady Sarah

Stabinbach – the kind of social occasion that would normally have had the name of Jeremiah Meadowbrook at the head of its guest-list. Meadowbrook explained his situation and Lady Sarah excused him from the event. She recognised something significant was happening and didn't want to spoil his first sighting of happiness in years. He promised he'd try and stop by for an hour or so, but his main priority that day would be Orchidea.

Yes, one or two empires had risen and fallen; one or two kings and queens had been crowned and deposed; and one or two wars had been won and lost. And two lost souls who had known no love for so long that they'd forgotten what it felt like had found each other – at last.

An Invitation to Play

Note to Self – *I've just started seeing a guy who is something of an eccentric outsider, and I'm smitten! I won't be so corny as to claim it was love at first sight, but it was! I can't stop thinking about him, and he can't stop thinking about me either! I feel like I've made a connection with him like no connection I've ever made with anyone before. Am I living in a fantasy or does this sound like the beginning of a beautiful friendship?*

Self to Note – Well, it depends on what you mean by 'eccentric outsider'. If this guy is a contrast with the sort of man you're used to, he's bound to seem like a breath of fresh air. It also depends on how he makes you feel, especially with regards to how you see yourself. The more conventional 'husband material' tends to flatter you in pursuit and then suppresses any instincts in you that might threaten his idea of what a wife should be once he's captured you.

Guys who operate outside of this pattern are more of a long-term risk, though if what you're in need of is some exciting, knee-trembling fucking of a kind you only ever read of in erotic thrillers before and never believed you'd ever experience, i.e. the kind of life-enhancing lovemaking that lifts you higher than any illicit substance on the (black) market and is centred on pure pleasure as opposed to propagating the species, you could do worse.

Much better to become involved with a guy on the outskirts of society who can have such a seismic effect on you than be chained to some boring bastard conformist control-freak – the type of aesthetically vacuous, materialistic wanker who measures people's value by how many possessions they have. That kind of dickhead might be able to provide you with security of a financial nature, but you'll find your life-force draining away from you with each passing day.

If being permanently dead from both the neck up and the waist down is the sort of future you're looking forward to, don't get involved with this 'eccentric outsider' who sounds to me like he could be The One.

I guess it's down to how much importance you place on things like love and passion or having finally found your soulmate after decades of dalliances with incompatible arseholes whose negative attitude towards you has shaped your notion of self and what you're actually worth. If you feel you're not worthy of being worshipped by a man who will always adore you and value you as an intelligent, sensual woman, and sees in you so much more than you see in yourself, I suggest you remain in denial and instead stick with some regular dullard who plays it safe and treats you like part of the furniture. It's your choice, love.

****

She recalled the rotten route to that dismal dungeon with a shudder. It had been an upsetting experience, cuffing and blindfolding a girl she'd once been so fond of, and having to lead her down those chilly stone steps in the dark. The ill-lit cavernous depths of the destination were such a dramatic contrast with the dazzling vivacity of her victim, a girl whose unquenchable summer spirit had carried them both through wretched winter days with such an exuberant lust for life.

But the woman didn't provide any sort of explanation or answer the girl's understandable questions; she just did it. She pushed her into the cell and locked it without looking back or saying a word, blocking her ears to those confused pleas that reverberated from wall-to-wall until they could be heard no more.

Unfortunately, it was a necessary evil, as much as the woman regretted her decision to bury the girl alive. The plan was that she'd never have reason to see her again, even if she couldn't help but occasionally remember her with affection. If she hadn't acted when she did, the girl's frustration with the altered situation and her thwarted ambition would have boiled over and done neither of them any good. The girl came to be viewed as an anachronism and an embarrassment – someone somewhat incompatible with changing circumstances. She wasn't capable of modifying her thoughts, emotions and actions to the new landscape the woman had relocated to, so she had to be incarcerated with an indeterminate sentence, possibly one stretching to life.

Orchidea's progression from feral beggar to lady-in-waiting, battered wife to feral beggar (again), then respectable housekeeper to wealthy woman of independent means meant there'd been no place for this bohemian aesthete in the bigger picture for a long time. And once Biba appeared, any lingering hopes of an appeal leading to an early release were dashed, presumably for good. Yes, she missed her; but she was scared of what she represented – something she'd consciously suppressed out of necessity.

And then something utterly unexpected happened.

The day after Jeremiah Meadowbrook had dispatched his valet to deliver a brief note to Orchidea's hotel Orchidea was composing her reply and thought she could hear a familiar voice in the far distance. The unmistakable *A cappella* melody of the old folk-song, 'She Moves through the Fair' was distinctly discernible, though Orchidea knew not from where it emanated; she surmised there must have been some street-corner siren in operation, despite the early hour. When stepping outside the hotel, however, there was no sign of any optimistic and opportunistic pavement diva. Orchidea travelled home and thought no more of it.

In the run-up to her first reunion with Meadowbrook, Orchidea's ears again detected the distant singing of that song; the realisation that it might just stem from a certain dungeon was worrying, but Orchidea tried her best to mute the voice. It didn't make any difference.

What actually awoke her from the languorous interlude in Meadowbrook's arms was that bloody tune drifting into her consciousness; it prompted her to pay attention to the clock and then declare it was time to head back to the hotel before the doors were bolted. She said nothing of this to her love, but it proved to be an unavoidable issue when she gazed into the looking-glass of his bedchamber and was face-to-face with that girl for the first time in over a decade.

Amazingly, she was unchanged, with that beautifully buoyant persona once again imprinted on her every feature, bearing no scars of incarceration at all. And those exquisite features were the same – still sharply-defined, yet simultaneously *softly*-defined, like her countenance had been carved from soap. Of course, there was an immense overdose of guilt to endure on Orchidea's part when the two looked each other in the eye, but Orchidea returned home with a refreshed perspective on her role as judge, jury and executioner. Could she really quash that sentence after all these years?

On the eve of Orchidea's second get-together with Meadowbrook – the one that would climax with the pair disrobed and beneath sheets rather than fully-clothed above them – Orchidea knew she had a dreaded duty to attend to, one she thought she'd never have to embark upon. At the same time, she couldn't deny that the inevitable trepidation mingled with invigorating excitement; she understood what releasing the girl would mean. And though Orchidea realised that release was as much a necessity in taking her forward as imprisoning the girl in the first place had been, the prospect of letting her out (and the possible consequences of that decision) remained one she approached with anxiety. Then again, all momentous moves in life come with the same emotionally fraught package, whether good or bad. Leaps into the dark are rarely accompanied by a lantern.

Orchidea sighed and descended a staircase that hadn't been graced by human feet for so long that the slimy patina formed in her absence made each step a slippery slope to an unknown outcome. As she moved deeper down the helter-skelter that song could be heard again, but with such amplified intensity that by the time Orchidea produced her keys and prepared to stick one in the rusty lock, the rendition of the standard was scaling a peak of unbearable sonic torture. Mercifully, it ceased when the door opened.

'I wondered how long it'd take you to come,' said the girl, who was remarkably calm and composed considering her lengthy incarceration; then again, she'd been expecting Orchidea.

'I suppose I didn't have much choice but to come,' replied Orchidea. 'I need you.'

'Well, is this it, then? Am I reprieved?'

'I guess so; if it stops you singing that bloody song, I'll happily let you out.'

'You heard it?'

'Of course – ever since...well...I...'

'That morning in the hotel?'

'How did you...'

'Come on; we're one and the same, you and me – even if you've been in denial all these years.'

'Yes, I realise that now; I just thought I'd never have need to call on you again. I'd convinced myself I never would.'

'You and me both, darlin'. But then, I had no idea you were going to be made aware you were a desirable woman after such a lengthy spell in suspended animation.'

'Me neither.'

'Well, let's make the most of it while we can, eh?' cried the girl excitedly as she stepped out of the cell. 'God, it feels good to be out again! Bloody hell, I can't wait to ride that Meadowbrook member!'

'Please!' Orchidea exclaimed with an exasperated blush sweeping across her cheeks. 'Let's not lower ourselves to that level, you silly sausage!'

'Sorry,' replied the girl with a wicked grin. 'I forgot you were such a *lady*. But, hell, we've been given a licence to be licentious. Let's enjoy it while we can!'

'If you say so; I mean, I *want* to enjoy it, but I can't help but confess my nerves are all over the place.'

'Why?'

'Because I think he's amazing – and that I'm not worthy.'

'Bollocks! He's as enamoured of you as you are of him. Why can't you see that?

'Me? I'm just a nondescript nonentity with the kind of...er...handicap to happiness that's pretty unique, shall we say. I can't help but feel I'm just not worthy of sharing his artistic space.'

'What? Just wait till he sees you in that velvet bodice and those silk stockings you ordered yesterday without telling him! He'll be so fucking hard he'll have your eye out!'

Orchidea laughed and looked away. It had been so long since any man had viewed her as a sexual (let alone interesting) being that she'd struggled to visualise herself as one. But she suddenly felt she could believe it again.

'I don't get the problem,' said the girl. 'You're bleedin' gorgeous – in your prime of sensual life! As far as I can see, there's nothing to worry about at all. You never worried in the past – back when you and me was thick as thieves.'

'Yes, well,' replied Orchidea, 'that was a long time ago. I was younger then; we both were – a hell of a lot younger.'

'Ah, what's age but a collection of meaningless numbers after yer name, eh? It don't bother him that you're over twenty-one and you've got a history, do it? And it's not as if he's some naive young buck, is it? He's a bleedin' widower, for Christ's sake. He's been around the block as well, y'know. Neither of you is virgins, madam.'

'Well, when you put it like that, I...'

'Come on – after what you and him experienced on his bed, how can you doubt what you both feel for each other, eh? Listen, luv – the basic inescapable truth is that he wants to fuck you and you want him to! There's no doubt on either side when it comes to aims and ambitions, so why piss about? Slip into your sexy costume and let me take over for the duration. I've been waiting for this for bleedin' years! I thought you'd never let me loose again. You suppressed every horny thought I could've had. It was like you didn't want us to *feel* anything anymore, like you'd castrated us.'

'Yes, that's exactly what I did. Eradicating all urges seemed the best way of dealing with them when I had no outlet for them, and very little prospect of an outlet.'

'Well, you got an outlet now – and you ain't past it, okay?' said the girl as she put her arm around Orchidea. 'I might have been an embarrassment to you when you were being courted by those inbred chinless suitors from the gentry; but this ain't like that. Meadowbrook didn't have a clue about your finances when he met you, and I doubt he gives a shit now. He wants you because he adores the important elements of the package – your body and your intellect. You give him the horn and you stimulate him in conversation as well. Ain't that the perfect combination? Your bleedin' income ain't important to him at all. And it shouldn't be a factor of attraction; if it is, you're attracting the wrong men.'

'I haven't been attracting *any* men,' replied Orchidea, 'not since I locked you away. This is why I've been so thrown off-course by what's happened. I didn't see it coming at all.'

'That's been obvious in the negative signals you've been sending out there, sweetheart, hiding yourself away and avoiding all contact because you reckon your circumstances are so weird that they'd put off anyone remotely decent. But you had the good fortune to meet a geezer smart enough to pick up the faint traces of me still left on you. He saw something no one else could 'cause he's a cut above all the wankers you were trying to impress before – the ones who could only see your fortune. I suppose the potential problem now is that if you keep me free and don't stick me back in that bleedin' cell, I may well start attracting other fellers on your behalf. He'll have competition before long, whereas at the moment he's got you all to himself. Do you wanna take that risk, darlin'?'

'I can't see that as a risk right now, trust me. I don't want any others at all; I just want *him.*'

'And he just wants *you,* darlin' – that's why this is gonna be a piece of piss. You've already won his heart; now you just need to get a grip on his libido. All you've got to do is get a silken skin on that beautiful body and he's all yours. No worries. It's a done deal.'

'But I'm just so bloody nervous. It's been so long. I'm no bloody virago. I can talk the talk in jest, but when it comes down to it I'm terrified. Maybe he's expecting something I can't deliver.'

'Darlin', you'll deliver – trust me. Anyway, he hasn't slept with anyone since his wife died five years ago, or whenever it was. You never know; he might be pretty nervous himself.'

'Christ, I hope not. At least one of us should be in control.'

'Well, were you both shaking with nerves when you were laid on the bed together all those hours? No! You were never so relaxed in your whole bloody life. Why should sleeping with him be any different? It's just the next logical step, and it'll be wonderful, better than anything you've ever experienced before, believe me.'

'I do. You always oozed such confidence. And I need you again. I feel more like a virgin now than when I lost my virginity.'

'Jesus! Come on, we've got work to do. And the first item on the agenda is to get the hell out of this bloody dungeon and then close it off to us both forever, okay?'

'Hah! Yes, let's do it.'

'And there's always Biba, of course,' said Orchidea as she slipped into the silken skin and experienced one hell of a thrill when she saw the girl as delectable as she ever was. 'But I don't want what we have to be tainted by Biba. I want to keep all that separate from me and him; I want us to have a life outside of those concerns. I want this to be my escape from it. I need an escape. And he's giving me that escape, the escape I doubted I'd ever have. Biba and me; Jeremiah and me – two lives for one woman; and never the twain shall meet.

'In fact, I've just realised that when you're here I can't even hear Biba. That's usually a bad sign because it means he's quietly destroying something somewhere in the house; but even then I'd be able to hear something being ripped and torn and hear the odd snarl or growl. Yet, I can't hear a thing right now. And all kinds of thoughts...*artistic* thoughts...are flooding through my head again. I'm being bombarded with images of paintings I can purchase and sculptures and ornaments I can buy to complement his home, and how I can enrich his life with them, and mine at the same time; and...and...oh, I'm *back!*'

Changing of the Guard

Some of Lady Sarah Stabinbach's society rivals sneered and nodded knowingly whenever their nemesis occasionally withdrew from hosting a high-profile salon; the reason given was that it was due to a recurring illness, one Lady Sarah never named or referred to other than as 'an attack of the vapours'. Her bitchy competitors, however, always claimed it was syphilis, a legacy of Lady Sarah's lively youth and fairly active middle-age. They pointed to the scabby lips some of her favourites sometimes struggled to powder into invisibility as evidence this particular curse remained an ongoing thumbprint of the past.

Thankfully, this evening had nothing to suggest such disreputable rumours would resurface. Lady Sarah was scheduled to play hostess at her plush palace of a residence again, and it was hailed as the hottest ticket in town once more – at least by those whose names were on the guest-list. The rest just dismissed both it and the hostess as a redundant relic of an age already on the way out.

Lady Sarah was aware of Jeremiah Meadowbrook's prior commitment, though he had promised to pop by in order to introduce Orchidea to his patron. Lady Sarah expressed pleasure to the man himself that he appeared to have located love again; when she first made his acquaintance he was still in the deep throes of grief for his wife, something she had encouraged him to write about. Her encouragement, coming at a time when he remained resistant to revisiting that tragedy in prose, eventually resulted in Meadowbrook's breakthrough book, one he dedicated to Lady Sarah, without whom (he felt) his phenomenal success would never have come about.

Alice, his bride, had died in a fire that destroyed their home and their life together, but this was an incident that had plunged Meadowbrook into a dark place that Lady Sarah had only partially retrieved him from; the same applied when it came to the best-selling status of the novel he based on the story. The whirlwind that transformed his fortunes in the wake of its publication meant he didn't have to worry about the tallyman at the door anymore, but he was still internally dissatisfied with life.

Yes, he mined the material benefits of literary success, buying his own home after vacating the premises loaned to him free of charge as part of Lady Sarah's patronage, and he continued to honour Alice's memory (her portrait dominated the space above his fireplace while her grave was still a weekly port of call); but there was a void at the heart of his existence that nothing appeared capable of filling. Until now.

Lady Sarah's conviction that she was the central female in the lives of those upon whom she bestowed her patronage was perhaps reflected in the fact that all the ones she favoured were bachelor boys. Even Conan Blackcastle, the man Jeremiah Meadowbrook inadvertently usurped as Lady Sarah's chosen one, had still to become attached to a permanent sweetheart. Meadowbrook being a widower meant he was slightly different from the beginning, so perhaps Lady Sarah cut him a little slack as he confided in her that he believed he had met the love of his life.

The often bitchy gossip that flourished in the cauldron of literary circles was something from which he sought to spare Orchidea – in many ways, just as Orchidea was keen to shield him from her own unique domestic dilemmas; and this was one of the reasons why he didn't announce his abrupt involvement with Orchidea to all in his circle, initially reserving the news for Lady Sarah alone. By the time the salon was approaching, however, Meadowbrook had come clean to Conan just as Orchidea had done likewise with Jasper Hampshire.

Unconditional loyalty expected even from those she hadn't seduced was one of Lady Sarah Stabinbach's unspoken conditions of patronage, and whilst Jeremiah Meadowbrook never ceased to sing her praises and promote her part in his success, he didn't see how his relationship with Orchidea could have any effect on his relationship with Lady Sarah.

Yes, he *had* once shared her bed early on, but nothing physical had occurred between them on account of laudanum doping them both and Jeremiah not being that keen anyway; Lady Sarah had never been his lover and never would be. Therefore, Orchidea's appearance shouldn't contradict or threaten Lady Sarah's purely platonic patronage at all.

Like many a lady of her advancing years, however – and just how far those years had advanced was never revealed – Lady Sarah Stabinbach housed a considerable surfeit of delusional vanity; no, she didn't sleep with every artist she patronised, but she seemed to believe they all regarded her as the ultimate embodiment of feminine desire. She convinced herself none of them would ever be able to marry because they would never be able to shake off the feeling that any wife would only really be a substitute for the woman their hearts would always belong to, Lady Sarah Stabinbach.

Her ego was kept pampered by the power she wielded over her boys, and those she chose not to invite into her boudoir were still expected to avoid matrimony. She wanted them to want her even when there was no possibility of getting her, and somehow expected their libidos to be satisfied with no more than a whore when her own bedchamber door remained locked to them.

Lady Sarah perhaps preferred Meadowbrook in his original guise as the broken-hearted widower; after all, a dead woman was no competition, and she felt secure in the land of the living when it came to his affections. Then suddenly, another woman arrives without warning. A devotee of his writing, apparently; but it wasn't as though there weren't plenty of them already. Meadowbrook had met many and had never given his patron the impression that any of them inspired feelings comparable to those he still had for his late lamented Alice. What made this newcomer so special? Lady Sarah was puzzled. She imagined Meadowbrook as the eternal loner in matters of the heart and hadn't anticipated this turn of events. Then again, neither had he.

****

For her third – and perhaps most pivotal – journey to Jeremiah Meadowbrook's town, Orchidea chose to take the train.

Old Sam, the manservant who had steered her balloon and driven her carriage now only accompanied her as far as the station in order to carry her luggage onto the train, for Meadowbrook would be meeting her at the other end. Although she called Sam her manservant, he performed several functions on her estate that required the kind of brawn her handmaidens lacked. For any job that needed physical strength absent elsewhere amongst her domestic staff, she called on Sam.

He claimed to have been a bare-knuckle prize-fighter in his youth and (so he said) had once gone fifteen rounds with the great Tom Cribb; but though his pugilist past was long behind him, old Sam still possessed a fair amount of muscle beneath his broad shoulders and could be relied upon to do everything bar cope with Biba. The lion had never taken to him and the suspicion was mutual, so Orchidea (partly fearing for Sam's safety) spared him all contact with Biba.

Orchidea had a first-class compartment all to herself on the journey and although nervousness returned to periodically torment her throughout, she actually found the method of travel to be more to her taste than both the balloon and coach had been. She felt that trying to focus on the potentially positive outcome of the evening ahead was a more conducive exercise when comfortably viewing glimpses of greenery through the occasional gap in the clouds of steam billowing past the window. It had a strangely calming effect on her overall mood than she had realised it would beforehand; it lacked the heightened drama of the hot air balloon and the bumpy rhythm of the coach and instead felt more like being propelled forward at high speed whilst reclining in a drawing-room easy-chair.

Orchidea decided to use the railway as her main mode of transport to town from this moment on.

For his part, Jeremiah Meadowbrook retained his relaxed composure prior to Orchidea's arrival, even though this was to be the night they were intending to venture into the bed instead of settling for holding each other on top of it. But just the mere thought of Orchidea put him at ease rather than inspiring anxiety, and this day was no different other than it contained the prospect of genuine, exhilarating adventure ahead.

Now that Conan Blackcastle and everyone else was aware of the relationship, Meadowbrook was also looking forward to entering a society event with Orchidea on his arm; the pride he knew he would feel when strolling into a crowded room with such a beauty beside him improved his mood no end.

Although it would be difficult for him and Orchidea to wrench their hands off each other after a couple of hours together, Meadowbrook planned to call at Lady Sarah's salon at a fixed point into Orchidea's visit and he felt he couldn't alter it now. He had seen Lady Sarah herself the day before and everything was arranged. She convinced him she was eager to meet Orchidea, though she gave the impression she'd be sizing her up in the same way an ex-wife sizes up her replacement. Meadowbrook didn't really think anything of it there and then, even if it should have struck him immediately that Lady Sarah had no real right to judge Orchidea in that way at all.

Tellingly, Lady Sarah Stabinbach lived in a different neighbourhood to her 'boys'; maybe a little distance enhanced her mystique – mystique that could perhaps have been slightly diminished it if she'd been constantly bumping into those claiming her patronage, forever encountering them in mundane surroundings whenever they ventured outdoors. They always had to travel to her – never the other way round. And when it came to her salons, Lady Sarah really pushed the opulent boat out.

The fact she was able to put on such an ostentatious show was solely down to an opportunistic marriage with an ageing aristocrat to whom she'd been the mistress for mere months; his death less than a year later provoked many a predictable rumour, but Lady Sarah cared not a jot. As far as she was concerned, she was constantly putting her fortune to good use in the name of the Arts, and only splashed out on frivolities when hosting an elaborate evening for the great and the good, rather than indulging on a selfish daily basis like her society rivals.

An unwelcome downpour drenched the town in the hours before the entertainment was intended, but the inclement weather didn't dissuade any of Lady Sarah's guests from making their way to her residence – including Jeremiah and Orchidea. But their arrival would be later than most of the rest. They had more important things to them on their minds and popping in at the salon was just a matter of showing their faces from Meadowbrook's perspective. He'd say hello, introduce Orchidea to everyone he wanted to meet her who hadn't yet met her, and would then escort his beloved home for a far more invigorating evening.

It was indeed frustrating to have to halt proceedings with Orchidea at the point when passions were beginning to run very high, but Meadowbrook felt obliged to make an appearance whereas Orchidea was keen to meet her man's patron – even if it was a further source of potential anxiety to her. Anyway, they made a reluctant move and boarded Jeremiah's carriage just gone 8 o'clock.

It was still raining heavy and the road was reduced to a murky mix of mud and manure, a factor that added time onto the journey, but at least gave the lovers more private moments together before their grand entrance into society. When they neared their destination, the constant stopping and starting because of the appalling condition of the road surface prompted Meadowbrook to hammer his cane on the carriage ceiling and request that his driver turn the vehicle around. He announced he and Orchidea would travel the remaining distance on foot. By now, the rain had more or less stopped and they were able to avoid the worst of the weather as they disembarked from the carriage and joined hands.

Meadowbrook knew the way well enough, but he prolonged the walk with Orchidea to show her a few familiar streets and sights before turning the corner that led to the Stabinbach residence. En route, she displayed her big heart via an impromptu monetary gift to a beggar and his ragged dog in a doorway; Meadowbrook kissed her affectionately following this kind gesture. Then they were there, confronted by the sort of stark contrast this town specialised in.

Lady Sarah's grandiose Palladian homestead was hidden from the road and the riffraff of the road by a high, imposing wall, behind which were sprawling grounds that took the best part of ten minutes to cover on foot before the visitor reached the distant mansion; the congestion of stationary carriages along the way suggested all those on the guest-list had already arrived, and Meadowbrook strolled inside confident his patron would greet Orchidea with the respect she deserved.

There was no footman on hand to announce the entrance of Meadowbrook and Orchidea, which was unusual, though he put it down to the fact they were late arrivals. It was certainly crowded once they weaved their way into the drawing-room, but the atmosphere seemed somewhat dead, if not a little desperate – lots of people making a grand show about having a good time rather than simply having one. Meadowbrook nodded to a few faces he recognised before he was accosted by Conan Blackcastle, who informed him Lady Sarah had suffered 'an attack of the vapours' and would not be attending her own salon. This was odd. Whenever she was ordinarily stricken with the sickness, the event was cancelled; she wouldn't have let it go ahead because she adored playing hostess.

As Orchidea then shared a few words with both Conan and Jasper Hampshire, Meadowbrook spoke to the prominent albeit slightly inebriated QC Sir Marius Jarvis, who took the conversation away from the subject of the absent hostess and on to the current standard of contemporary literary fiction. The chat was interesting, but Meadowbrook was more concerned with Lady Sarah Stabinbach. She knew this was a special evening for him and now she had again become the centre of attention by not turning up – as had almost been the case on the opening night of Meadowbrook's play until Orchidea captured his eye.

Meadowbrook and Orchidea stayed at the Stabinbach residence for a good hour, but both were itching to get back home – and to bed. With Lady Sarah not even being there to be introduced to Orchidea, there didn't seem much point in hanging around; they'd done their social duty, after all; it wasn't Meadowbrook's problem that Lady Sarah had excused herself from her own event. Meadowbrook took Orchidea by the hand and suggested they depart without making a big fuss.

'Let's just slip out,' he said. 'We've shown our faces, and Lady Sarah isn't even here, anyway. We can hail a cabriolet after a short walk, eh?'

She agreed and they were gone before anyone noticed. It wasn't as if Lady Sarah expected Jeremiah to step into the breach and play host on her behalf, was it? Nothing of the sort had even been suggested.

****

Only later – much later – did Jeremiah Meadowbrook conclude that the timing of Lady Sarah's disappearing act was too coincidental considering the sudden change in his circumstances. It was the beginning of the end of her patronage. She stopped replying when he left his card at her home, she ceased writing him letters or extending invitations to visit, and she never added his name to the guest-list of any salon ever again. Far worse than all this social snubbing, however, was that she started to badmouth him around town to anyone willing to listen.

Interestingly, when her poison tongue asserted itself and aimed its malignant missives in his direction, many who (like him) had been amongst her most loyal supporters also began to see her in a different light. She hadn't anticipated what a misfire this would be.

Before long, she was bedridden and bitter towards anyone who had ever sung her praises. Bizarrely, as her bachelor boys began to desert her in droves, she cultivated the friendship of all the old hags who had long been her society rivals. They soon became the only regular visitors she received as a house that had so recently throbbed with the joyous exuberance of glamorous youth rapidly descended and decayed into a gloomy mausoleum of rack and ruin, mirroring the hasty decline of its inhabitant.

But perhaps her bitchy sisters were now the only people she could relate to – as vain, nasty and in denial as she was. Jealousy had combined with deluded notions of her own invincible charisma and caused her to embark upon a suicidal campaign of character assassination and self-destructive defamation.

It didn't take much more than a year for death to claim her and bring the curtain down on an eventful life that had unnecessarily climaxed with anyone who had ever genuinely cared about her having abandoned her. Suspicions of syphilis were confirmed, and the madness the disease spreads in the heads of its victims was blamed for her dramatic transformation into a hateful banshee. Perhaps the syphilis didn't help, but Jeremiah Meadowbrook sensed it merely exacerbated something latent in her that was just waiting for a cue.

The vicious manner of her about-turn shook him considerably, but he was supported throughout Lady Sarah's assault and its aftermath by someone whose priceless presence was an immeasurable comfort – Orchidea.

The Great Adventure

Hold my hand. We're going for a walk like lovers do. We'll kick our way through marmalade leaves crackling in a misty sunset before pausing beneath the branches. You tremble, but I am solid and steady without sacrificing the gentle touch. You'll be safe with me. Absorb my strength when I pull you to me, lose all anxiety and nervous preconceptions as you feel the confidence flowing from me to you in a tender transfusion. I am a romantic who's been starved of romance; you are a ballerina who's forgotten how to dance. In your eyes, I see me and I empathise, for I recognise the symptoms. If you are scared, I will sooth you. If you are shy, I will cure you. If you are cold, I will warm you. If your wings are broken, I will teach you how to fly again. We shall soar together.

In the midst of the energising embrace, you say you will never hurt me; I will never hurt you, my love. I could never hurt you just as I could never *hate* you. You are my precious, preordained gift from the Gods who have long observed my misery and taken pity. We wouldn't have entered into this adventure if we didn't both know we were destined to do it. We are fulfilling that destiny and embarking upon something neither of us expected to experience – which makes it an utterly fearless enterprise, free from all the angst and anguish that stained and scarred our past dalliances with the undeserving. Remember that as we clutch and cling.

I am here to deliver you to the doorstep of Nirvana.

But the power to heal is in your hands too; this union is mutual and your instinct senses needs in me you are happy to satisfy. Legs locate my lap and the implication is unspoken; no words are required, for the gesture suggests an invitation I accept. You give permission for the exercise of ambition, and the permission given is a Godsend to one who has long anticipated objections to the progression of the palm skimming the surface of the sheen that shields the shin from the elements. Combing those contours was an offence in the imagination, provoking protest and condemnation, yet now the limitations are lifted and the hemline is no longer a barrier to yearning.

Why the secret stretch between toe and thigh possesses such amorous appeal is a mystery, but it does, and the knee beneath the bustle no longer hides its ability to inspire electricity when contact is made. Of all the anatomical treasures housed within the feminine goldmine, the knee is the first significant gem en route to the more celebrated prizes, and to stroke that delicious dome when wrapped in the weaver's woven fibre is to trace the texture of Venus. It transmits the initial signal that stirs the inert sleeping giant from slumber and stokes the appetite for ascendancy that follows.

The land beyond the silk divide, the one that spans the top of the stocking to the tip of the hip, is a sacred plane of pleasure for the ecstatic explorer, a glossy expanse of a succulent vista that the recipient savours in slow motion. Back and forth the fingers follow the trail, eager to prolong a sensation that improves with repetition. Perhaps awareness that twin destinations of imminent gratification await on either side of the location enhance its erotic potency, but to venture there when its delights remain obscured from the eye and all visuals are visualised by the simple power of touch alone is sufficient preparation for the moment when the area is uncovered and awaiting inspection.

That moment will not be long in coming, for the petting grows heavier and the hunger is becoming too insatiable to resist. The exploratory overture has served its purpose; the territory is ready.

You clad yourself in black and I've opted instead for red. Serendipity has selected our lucky colours and we shall memorise their magic. Like the silken skin unveiled in modesty with the minimum of ceremony, the clothes maketh the moment, and the effort to strike the right sartorial chord is not unnoticed or unappreciated. I know what it took to achieve the look and the fact you did it for me displays your commitment to this glorious cause even at your most anxious – though it only intensifies eternal adoration in the process.

Each item designed with stimulation in mind constitutes the sumptuous icing on a cake already baked, giving additional flavour to a recipe prepared earlier. And now it is time to dine. I am your feast and you are mine.

It doesn't matter if you haven't ridden the bicycle or strummed the guitar or swum the lake in years; you'll find it's not been forgotten, and what may have challenged and frightened in thought is easier than imagined once in action. We can take it slow and take our time. There is no hurry; we have waited years to get here, so let the tempo return at its own sweet pace. Don't force it; let it infect you and it will be fine. Before you know it, amnesia will be banished. Remember the moves as they come flooding back; reunite with the rhythm and enjoy the revelation of the new dimension that merges love and lust in one intoxicating brew.

And love is our extra ingredient, one that elevates the physical into the rarefied realm of the spiritual. I could go through the motions with one I could never love, just as you could lay back and think of England. But what would remain once the rush of the climax had passed? Very little that lasts or lingers. What *we* have has meaning above and beyond the admittedly (if momentarily) enjoyable thrill of the basic consenting exchange, and this rendezvous in fresh sheets is merely another enchanting chapter in a saga scheduled to last our lives.

Hand-in-hand, we cross the next bridge on our joyful journey, knowing this is the first of many. And it will indeed be the first of many such journeys – many memorable meetings that will grow in their greatness as familiarity breeds ease.

Incurable craving and inquiring curiosity will quickly breach the barriers of nerves, and your body will become as much mine as mine is yours. I will grow to know it as a cartographer knows the land he maps. I will grow to know each and every inch of delicate perfection as I survey nature's exquisitely embroidered tapestry up close, inhaling and tasting the land I claim in the name of love.

There will be times when its staggering beauty provokes a gasp, a head-shaking intake of breath, almost as if I have forgotten just how beautiful it is and how lucky I am to have been gifted with the freedom to roam. I would prove to be a wise man were I never to neglect my good fortune or take it for granted; this honour is the kind I have rarely had handed to me, and to be deprived of it now I have savoured it would be as cruel a blow as receiving it was a major miracle. It is my hometown.

This is bliss.

Bliss it is to varnish the surface. Bliss it is to slide inside. Bliss it is to kiss and cup those curves. Bliss it is to nestle in that concave cauldron. Bliss it is to feel your legs shiver. Bliss it is to hear you voice your joy when words fail you. Bliss it is to love you from above. Bliss it is to love you from below. Bliss it is to love you from behind. Bliss it is to love you side-by-side. Bliss it is to fall asleep with you. Bliss it is to wake-up with you. Bliss it is to lay with beauty and be permitted to examine it without a time limit or being admonished or punished for looking or touching.

This is bliss.

Soon enough, *you* will become the confident one, enthusiastically seizing upon anything that will extend the adventure and carry it into unprecedented avenues of pleasure. You will spring from the shadows of premature retirement into the bright light of our Indian summer with the addictively infectious zeal of the newly-converted. Everything I have hesitated about expressing in the beginning will be quickly overcome by your vivacious appetite for adventure as you are to be possessed by the ravenous desire for the uncharted and unexplored. Each proposal still aired with optimistic trepidation will be excitedly embraced with a refreshing absence of caution within seconds of suggestion.

Ever tried that before? No. Want to give it a go? Yes! Before long, there will be little we haven't done.

Once between the linen, you will be wild and willing – even if the lady shall linger for the odd arousing cry of knowing *faux*-probity, expressing arch outrage and shock at the fact she loves it with a passion. Unleashing the beast as the crouching tiger awaits the hidden dragon, I will be the animal you kneel in wait for, the one whose claws force you onto all fours before thrusting you into the stratosphere. And after the storm, exhausted from our exertions, we will collapse in an uncontrollable chorus of laughter as the rasping gust gatecrashes the potentially solemn post-coital serenity. Moments such as these are what solidify a union as much as a held hand.

And then there will be numerous occasions when we transcend the saucy seaside postcard, entering a miasmic erotic underworld that extends the years of our intimacy so that we pass from Victorians to Edwardians to Georgians again. We will jointly generate an energy that encircles us in our own impenetrable time-zone, one we travel through in a trance; and in the middle of that trance, you will tilt your head over your shoulder and kiss me before resuming the rhythm for the best part of an aeon. In that action, I see the woman I will always want – the *only* woman I will always want. I will be a part of that woman's internal body and soul; I will permanently inhabit her interior; I will always be a physical presence, setting up home and laying down roots within her warm walls, finding my rightful place in the heated cocoon of her beckoning nest and releasing the glue that binds us together as one. I want her to think of me and declare 'I *am* Heathcliff', so inseparable will we be, so unthinkable will it be for us to exist without the other. When I am inside her, we are complete.

How blessed I am.

The phantasmagorical Goddess who haunted my dreams for decades has finally taken the flesh and the blood of woman; and she is here in my arms. This is the Goddess with the entrancing colour in her cheeks, she of the flushed face framed by the shimmering and glimmering droplets that dampen the tresses clinging to the luminous brow, the one with the lazy, hazy smile that has been painted by hands which I never realised were capable of such creation – *my* hands.

Oh, my love! How I relish and cherish my beautiful prize. You must always be mine. That look you will give me over your shoulder can never be given by anyone else and should never be given *to* anyone else. It will make you mine for life. Any fragments of distant doubt will be gone in that moment. It will seal it. You are bliss embodied, a mirror on my own ecstasy. I have never felt for anyone what I feel for you right now. *Nobody* has ever felt for anyone what I feel for you right now.

We are dual beneficiaries of an unbreakable spell cast by ancient alchemists whose mystical mix is a clandestine potion exclusive to us. After this, we will be sworn to ourselves for the duration. How could we *not* be? When I have burrowed so deeply and you have drunk me completely, we have bared bodies and souls in intimate ways that bind us for keeps. We can never consider passing one another to the hands of a stranger now. That'd just be so bloody *wrong*.

I can no more picture you writhing with another man any more than I can picture me writhing with another woman. Such sickening sacrilege is utterly inconceivable. No, this is ours alone. It cannot be shared with any individual, never mind the rest of the world. It is the sweet secret we guard with our lives, like a drug addict hides his habit or an alcoholic hides his bottles. But the difference between us and them is that *our* secret is something that makes us better than who we were before.

This signs the dotted line of the deal, for it doesn't get any better than this. How could we ever see a future without each other after it? The love that germinated when we just held one another has flowered and bloomed into something neither of us thought possible. We have ascended to the stars...

RECIPE: BROCCOLI PASTA BAKE

Penne pasta (400g)
Amorous lover
Chopped red onion
One glass of absinthe
One vegetable stock cube
A musical box
Grated cheddar (100g)
Suggestive innuendo
Chopped parsley leaves
Fresh white breadcrumbs
Affectionate groping
½ Teaspoon of dried mixed herbs
One cigar
Broccoli (250g) with chopped stalks
Regular cuddling
Fresh cream (200g tub)

1 Boil the broccoli, onion and pasta together in water for 10 minutes. Clutch cook's breasts and buttocks whilst waiting for water to come to the boil. Save around 400ml of water when draining veg and pasta.

2 Place saved water back on the boil and dissolve stock cube in it before adding fresh cream. Add the drained veg and

pasta, stirring them into the mix along with the parsley and half of the cheese until cheese has melted. Kiss back of cook's neck as cook stirs.

3 Pre-heat the grill for around three minutes and then empty contents of pan into oven-proof dish. Mix together the rest of the cheese with the herbs and the breadcrumbs, sprinkle over the top of the concoction before bunging the lot under the grill. Lay the table and set up the magic lantern ready to view after the meal. Kiss the cook again.

4 Give the grill another three minutes to work its magic, but keep an eye on it to make sure once the surface is brown it doesn't harden too much. Remove from oven and stand for a further five minutes before scooping up into matching dishes. Serve along with vintage wine, then sit down to eat, followed by viewing a private magic lantern show with a beautiful woman who also concocted and cooked the feast.

Bon appétit!

Domestic Bliss

There was a tender gentleness to Orchidea, a fragile delicacy that touched and moved Meadowbrook, as though she was a beautiful, slender flower that an especially angry bastard wind could easily scatter into a thousand petals. He couldn't help himself from feeling protective towards her. She just brought that out in him. Yes, her struggles with Biba required a steely, stoic resilience that was undoubtedly a core element of her character; but the Orchidea Meadowbrook fell in love with was an Orchidea he felt was reserved for him; and he recognised how privileged he was to be given a gift Orchidea had rarely presented to anyone. She revealed a side of herself to him that he believed to be the side few others saw because it was too vulnerable, too naked – and too dangerous to be exposed to a wider audience that might see fit to exploit it.

At the same time, he was also honoured to be the sole beneficiary of another even rarer Orchidea – that deliciously secret and salacious incarnation, the wild, unrestrained sexual animal, an erotic joy to both behold and hold.

Orchidea possessed an empathic understanding of those who most needed empathy, and equally saw through those demanding it on false pretences. The latter quality was a handy one for Orchidea to have in a world where openness could easily be manipulated with malevolence, but it needed to be kept in check. Unchecked, it could morph into a harder, cynical and pessimistic perspective on mankind born of past traumas

– and if not for the gentler, warm-hearted Orchidea, there was always the possibility that this angry, self-destructive trait could take control if life offered her little evidence that it could be good.

Meadowbrook felt, not unreasonably, that their blossoming relationship was counteracting this negativity in the most positive and beneficial way. It allowed the Orchidea he loved to show him what he regarded as her true and most enlightening colours; and she again exhibited just how lovely this aspect of her persona really was (when she allowed it to define her) in her attitude towards his late, lamented wife.

Alice Meadowbrook's grave was a simple affair, but Jeremiah always ensured it looked pretty by laying the right flowers when he made his weekly visit. Alice's own tastes had been simple enough, as had his at the time; but both were forced to economise with everything back then, including aesthetic expression. Their clothes were as threadbare as their furniture. The earnings of a struggling author can never be stretched very far, and Jeremiah Meadowbrook's status during his short marriage didn't make for particularly comfortable domestic arrangements, especially when his young bride had grown from being 'a sickly child' into a perennially ill and physically weak adult incapable of contributing to the household's meagre income. Often seeking solace in laudanum, Jeremiah believed Alice had stumbled into the candle that set fire to their home when affected by the drug; but he would never know for sure. He wasn't present when it happened.

Guilt had extended Jeremiah Meadowbrook's grief over Alice's death and retained its grip over all thoughts relating to her along with a sadness that would never leave him. He felt guilt over the fact he had taken her away from an unhappy family situation that was nevertheless financially stable, and had then plunged her into penury; he had believed love would be enough to sustain them through their struggles. But it wasn't.

What made things worse was that Alice naively placed her faith in him to deliver, and he failed to do so in her lifetime. When he eventually became a successful writer, he felt guilt that he now had the kind of income that would have made Alice's life so much easier and so much happier, but it had come far too late for her. She wasn't there to share it with him. And, of course, he felt guilt over the fact he'd been out when his home burned down and killed his wife.

They hadn't been married very long and she had been a good few years younger than him; but there had been love there, just different to what he now felt for Orchidea. Tellingly, there was no conflict or guilt in him when it came to the two women, which was an encouraging sign. He'd always wondered, should anyone else ever capture his heart, if he'd feel as though he was betraying Alice's memory and thus letting her down once again; but it didn't feel that way at all. Orchidea certainly never expressed any sense of competition for his affections regarding Alice. She said the book he'd written about Alice had moved her to tears, so she was already sympathetic to Alice's place in the scheme of things. Indeed, accompanying Meadowbrook to Alice's grave, something she suggested, was confirmation that she recognised the importance of continuing to honour the memory of Alice.

Meadowbrook would speak of Alice if prompted, but he usually felt he'd said all that needed to be said on the subject in his book, and with Orchidea having read it there didn't seem much point adding anything else unless she asked. As for Orchidea's own past lives and loves, Meadowbrook had obviously known nothing before they met. That was one of the advantages she'd had over him when they first became acquainted; she was already quite well-informed via his works and his fame. Orchidea therefore had far more stories to tell than the storyteller.

The slow opening of Orchidea's book was something that unfolded over several visits. Sometimes, they'd go riding together and would often dismount by some woods they'd stroll through for a good couple of hours, with Orchidea comfortable enough in Meadowbrook's company to answer any questions he put to her. They had a little more breathing space on the occasions when Orchidea's growing confidence in her newfound passion enabled her to extend her absence from Biba to a couple of days rather than merely overnight. These were the occasions when both began to develop a clearer idea of what life might be like if they themselves were man and wife. And it was a wonderful picture they shared the sight of.

Their time together may have been too brief for either's liking, but they appreciated they had to make the most of what little they had. Considering the limitations on this time, the speed with which they developed as a true twosome matched the speed with which they had moved from first meeting to first intimacy. Orchidea had taken instant mental notes of Meadowbrook's aesthetic tastes in terms of interior decor on her debut visit to his abode; she immediately knew what he would like and what would work as complementary additions to the house; she did likewise when it came to his clothes, presenting him with everything she could that didn't require a tailor's intervention, such as hats, gloves and neckerchiefs.

On Meadowbrook's part, he noticed Orchidea's fondness for items of jewellery and made it his mission to visit every jeweller in town in order to personally decorate her. Both subconsciously gifted presents of this nature as a means of lovingly branding one another as their respective property.

Another factor that helped solidify their bond was the intellectual stimulation they derived from conversation and debate. Meadowbrook had spent so long playing the superficial society wit that the chance to discuss serious issues in depth without having to churn out waspish one-liners about rival authors was one hell of a refreshing relief. In private with Lady Sarah Stabinbach he had talked politics a lot, and she had at least begun her salons with a political bent before age and vanity gradually pushed them into a more frivolous arena, with regards to both conversational topics and the people she invited; but Lady Sarah's abrupt disappearance from his life created a vacuum that Orchidea filled in an instant.

Orchidea had been starved of such discussions for far longer. As a spinster of independent means, she had been courted by some of the dimmest and most intellectually vacuous cretins on the marriage market, and as soon as

Biba appeared the sudden absence of any visitors put paid to talk altogether. She tried her best with her domestic staff, but they weren't on her payroll because they'd been President of the Oxford Union, and invigorating chat was fairly limited. Her mind had mainly been fired in recent years through reading, and though she put her thoughts down on paper when writing to authors, engaging in a two-way debate on subjects that interested her was something she'd been denied for decades. With Jeremiah Meadowbrook, she could finally find inspiration in conversation again.

They didn't agree on everything, which made their conversations even livelier.

Orchidea still believed the main threat to peace in Europe came from the French, whereas Meadowbrook was convinced the Germans were the ones that needed watching. Meadowbrook favoured Home Rule for Ireland, whereas Orchidea reckoned it would be the undoing of the Empire, setting a lethal example to other colonies. Orchidea had an aversion to the fight for women's rights, seeing it as less motivated by a desire to emancipate working-class women and more another evangelical example of middle-class patrician, paternalist thinking, whereas Meadowbrook approved of militant action as the eventual way forward if the male powers-that-be continued to be resistant to equality between the sexes. Meadowbrook still regarded Gladstone as the best man to lead the nation, whereas Orchidea opted for Salisbury.

Not all of their conversations concerned heavyweight political issues, however. They shared a love of Edward Lear and Lewis Carroll, 'Punch' magazine, bawdy old songs and the equally bawdy old satirical cartoons of Gillray and Cruikshank, many of which Meadowbrook owned as framed prints. And their humour quickly developed its own language, a clandestine lingo that they only spoke to one another, cracking jokes that only they got the punch-lines of and adopting silly voices as they recited quotes by their favourite comic characters from literature – silly voices nobody but them would probably have found funny. But, in a way, that was the point.

All of these things belonged to them, no one else.

Following the rather unhappy outcome of their brief call at the salon of Lady Sarah Stabinbach that eventful evening, Meadowbrook and Orchidea withdrew from the notion of being society animals and found they preferred a world in which their own company sufficed at the expense of society. The experience with Lady Sarah spawned a lingering bitterness in Meadowbrook over the facile frivolity of society, anyway, and Orchidea was never happier than when in her lover's arms, so it made sense to entomb themselves in the Meadowbrook residence rather than feeling obliged to be seen at some tedious gathering. Sod society.

The two people who saw the most of Jeremiah and Orchidea together were Meadowbrook's sister Verity and her violinist husband Kingsley Hope (who made a good living from his membership of a popular orchestra). Although Meadowbrook didn't have much contact with his parents, he had always been close to his sister and had encouraged her to move to town when he enjoyed his first success as a writer, offering to buy her an artist's studio so she could become the professional portrait painter she indisputably possessed the talent to be. She'd earlier painted the picture of Alice hanging above his fireplace – a work that was evidence enough of her ability – and had later met her future husband when he'd sat for a portrait of his own. Kingsley's wage largely supported the marital household, but Verity added to it with regular commissions.

Between them, they lived well, and both had been informed of Orchidea early on, following the swift progress of the relationship with genuine joy. Upon being introduced to her, they instantly recognised Orchidea as Jeremiah's saviour from the mourning for Alice that had defined him for far too long.

Verity told her brother she saw a side of him when he was with Orchidea that she had never seen before – a calm, confident, relaxed and serene side utterly at ease with the world; and she put this down to Orchidea's influence, an influence she regarded as utterly positive. The cleansing aura her brother radiated, the one Verity attributed to Orchidea, had been noticeable to his sister right from the beginning, even before Orchidea had made her first visit to see Meadowbrook; Verity had noticed it when he'd told her about meeting Orchidea at the reception following the play's opening night. Verity immediately saw something different in her brother that he continued to display whenever she and Kingsley called on him and Orchidea or vice-versa. It was unmistakable because it was such a dramatic change.

When the suggestion was first mooted to her, Orchidea was looking forward to meeting Jeremiah's sister, experiencing the familiar curiosity beforehand that is a prologue to being introduced to the sibling of one's beloved. When we fall in love, we tend to imagine the object of our affections emerged from a broken mould; the realisation they have a brother or sister presents this felicitous fantasy with an interesting challenge. Chances are we may recognise facial and personality similarities we thought were unique to one exclusive individual, and it can often be a strange sensation to see them reproduced, even if that sibling can sometimes resemble a waxwork or sculpture of our beloved that the sculptor didn't quite get right.

With Verity being Meadowbrook's sister rather than brother, Orchidea surmised that if she shared anything with Jeremiah it may well be his – to her – strikingly dramatic looks, which Orchidea felt reflected his artistic temperament; and she was right. Verity resembled an unsurprisingly more feminine version of her brother, taking those handsome features and softening them so they fitted the female visage. She also shared Meadowbrook's humour and warm, welcome personality; and her husband Kingsley was equally garrulous. Orchidea liked the pair of them as much as they liked her; and this mattered immensely to Meadowbrook himself. His sister was all-too aware what his previous romantic relationship had done to him.

If viewed solely as an exercise in exorcism (rather than convenient financial salvation), writing about Alice had been an unarguable failure; and that failure had maintained Meadowbrook's demons as omnipresent ticks. Although he had developed a way to hide these demons from the public and even his own circle of friends – acting out the caricature of a light-hearted literary aesthete as a successful distraction – it was different once he was alone behind his front door. That was when the absinthe was opened and Devlin flew down from his perch.

****

Ah, yes – Devlin. If Orchidea had given birth to Biba, Jeremiah Meadowbrook had fathered Devlin.

And who the hell was Devlin? Well, one thing that could be said in Devlin's favour was that at least he wasn't a lion. No, Devlin was in fact a raven, a brooding ebony parasite whose mission in Meadowbrook's life was to suck the colour out of it and repaint the scenery as black as his scraggy feathers – a shadowy, unhealthy grip on his master's existence that refused to let go.

And yet, the sacrifices Meadowbrook had made to compensate Devlin were comparable to the ones Orchidea had made for Biba, even if Devlin's presence was more secretive; for one thing, the feathered fiend was easier to hide out of the way whenever visitors called. Meadowbrook generally stuck him up in the attic and only ever let him out again when he was on his own. Otherwise, the bird would merely contradict the public script Meadowbrook had penned with such thorough dexterity.

Devlin had appeared the day Alice died, discovered as a strange unaccountable egg in the embers of the ruined house; retrieved by Meadowbrook as he sifted through the wreckage in a hallucinogenic trance, the egg was then housed in Meadowbrook's warm waistcoat until it hatched later that evening as he sat beside the fireplace of the one-roomed apartment loaned to him for free out of sympathy for his situation.

The helpless, ragged creature that forced its determined way through the shell was in need of a parent and Meadowbrook became its father the moment their eyes met. At that moment, Meadowbrook saw himself in the scrawny shape of that ugly little chick without a friend in the world, and he seized upon it as an instant gift dispatched to him from beyond the grave by Alice. An oddly inexplicable gift, yes, but one he had no choice but to accept.

Suddenly deprived of a passion, raising Devlin obsessively consumed Meadowbrook's time in the weeks following Alice's death and the bird quickly absorbed all the negative energy in the room, embarking upon a feeding frenzy that was hardly likely to be rationed in that dark, despondent climate. Brought up on a diet of despair and suicidal contemplation that it drew all its strength from, Devlin rapidly grew into a powerful and dangerous presence that reached its full size in less than a month, soon reflecting Meadowbrook's post-Alice depression back at him so that the negativity bounced back and forth between them in a morbid game of metaphysical tennis.

Even though Meadowbrook always hid Devlin whenever anyone called, the bird's distinctively earthy aroma was as instantly detectable as the odour left behind by a recently-emptied bowel, and that aroma was noticed by every caller until Meadowbrook became more skilled at disguising the traces. He couldn't fool Verity, though, with whom he was more open and honest than anyone else until Orchidea appeared.

Along with Meadowbrook's small domestic staff, Verity became accustomed to a sight that was the norm whenever Jeremiah was deprived of visiting company – that of Devlin settled on his perch in the corner of the room, with his black beady eyes permanently fixed on her brother in a way that she just couldn't interpret as the simple love of a child for a parent. It was deeper and more sinister than that, more like absolute possession and ownership of Meadowbrook's soul. It was a sight that never failed to unnerve her. After all, the only discernible words that ever left Devlin's mouth to be aimed at Meadowbrook always sounded to the human ear like 'You're useless.'

'Get rid of the bloody awful thing,' she said with a superstitious shiver as Devlin appeared to observe her advice with menacing contempt. 'Can't you just stuff it in a sack and dump it in the river – or maybe let it loose from your carriage window when you're travelling, and then keep on driving so that it loses track of you?'

'I couldn't just throw him out of the carriage window,' replied Meadowbrook. 'He'd only fly back home in the end. He knows where he's well-off and, anyway, he wouldn't know how to survive in the wild, what with him being hand-reared. And I couldn't drown him or kill him any other way either. That would be like infanticide to me. I was the first thing he laid his eyes on when he hatched and I'm his father. Those bonds feel unbreakable, whether I like it or not; there's an obligation there that I can't absolve myself of.'

Meadowbrook rightly or wrongly credited Devlin with inspiring some of his most successful works, so he couldn't claim the bird's presence was as entirely as negative as Verity felt. While it was true that these books had indeed been written with Devlin in the room, whether or not the bird's magical qualities could be viewed as having more than one effect on its father was open to question. Meadowbrook himself took the long view and pointed out that every best-seller he'd penned had appeared since Devlin came into his life. Publicly, he'd been happy to give credit to the patronage of Lady Sarah Stabinbach for the sudden change in his fortunes; but behind closed doors he remained convinced Devlin had played a part as well.

He had a strange relationship with the bird in that he undoubtedly held it in fearful fascination whilst simultaneously recognising its beneficial potential, wary of parting with it in case the muse followed it out of the window.

However, like Biba in relation to Orchidea, Devlin also had his frightening temper tantrums, which always began in the same way. Without warning, he would launch himself from his perch and land on Meadowbrook's shoulder as Meadowbrook attempted to continue writing. Meadowbrook knew what was coming, but on a couple of occasions had managed to postpone an explosion by gritting his teeth and ignoring the bird for as long as he could. It wasn't easy, though – Devlin would begin pecking his father's head, gradually building up the pace of the pecking and increasing the strength of the pecks until the excruciating pain was too much for Meadowbrook to handle. His threshold was passed and he pushed the bird off his shoulder. This was the cue for the clapping of thunder.

Flying and squawking around the house in a furious display of unprovoked, incandescent rage, Devlin's outburst prompted Meadowbrook to dive into the nearest cupboard and curl up in a terrified ball until the storm passed. Sometimes, these tantrums spanned mere minutes, whereas at their worst they could go on for hours. And then the dust would settle as if nothing had ever happened. Meadowbrook would take note of the silence and re-emerge from his seclusion, staggering into the light to see Devlin quietly waiting for him on his perch. The bird then remained there until the next outbreak, watching his father with a vigilant patience; there was nothing to indicate the chaos he had just presided over.

Orchidea had been told of Devlin just as Meadowbrook had been told of Biba, but she had never been introduced to the bird. Devlin preferred to be out of the way whenever Orchidea was present, finding the positive ambience she and Meadowbrook generated something that provoked nausea; and this suited Meadowbrook fine; he'd not been certain how much of a deterrent to romance the bird might have been. Besides, Devlin felt much more at home in the gloomier atmosphere that had prevailed before Orchidea had come along, an atmosphere that then always reasserted itself when she returned home.

With the problem of accommodating Biba dictating the days when Orchidea could be back in her man's arms, the visits tended to be every one or two weeks, often just overnight and occasionally extended to a couple of days. The pair made the most of every minute they could spend together, aware just how precious those moments were – even if this meant Meadowbrook still spent more time in the company of Devlin than Orchidea.

****

As Orchidea became more at home in Meadowbrook's home, her increasing confidence manifested itself in ways that appeared unusual to her man's close-knit domestic staff, though not unappreciated. They were regularly given the night-off when Orchidea visited, for the master didn't like to be bothered by servants in his beloved's company; their privacy was something he cherished ferociously.

Orchidea took advantage of their absence by reclaiming the kitchen and concocting all kinds of mouth-watering recipes that were newcomers to Meadowbrook's taste-buds. It amused him that a woman of her apparent fortune liked to be elbow-deep in ingredients as though she were a farmer's wife, but he had gradually become aware there had been times in her life when she had had little option but to steal to eat. Even when this dire situation had improved, she still wasn't always in a position to employ a cook – and she had never lost her fondness for doing the cooking herself.

A typical afternoon when he accompanied Orchidea around the local market so she could collect everything required for the dinner ahead was the first act in a lovely sequence of enchanting events that comprised the cooking of the meal, the eating of it, and the post-meal relaxation – all of which would be conducted in a relatively brief matter of hours. There'd also be some strenuous lovemaking as a warm-up for the food, of course; and Meadowbrook regularly provided entertainment in the shape of his favourite toy – a magic lantern. This was later accompanied by the marvel of three-dimensional images viewed through a stereoscope, which was a present from Orchidea.

Sometimes, Orchidea would play the pianoforte, bringing an instrument back to life that Meadowbrook rarely bothered with; on other occasions, Meadowbrook would recite poetry or read a ghost story beside the fire. These were truly magic moments that nobody else saw or shared – private, personal, perfect.

The purchase of the stereoscope was just one of many exchanges of gifts that characterised the adorably innocent springtime of Jeremiah and Orchidea's romance. Rings, bracelets, pendants, lockets, watches, clocks, candelabras, lamps, paintings, and sculptures – all were sought out, tracked down, and gift-wrapped. There were so many different ways in which they were able to express their love for each other, and they more or less employed them all.

For Meadowbrook, it was the only time in his life he'd felt truly loved. For Orchidea, it was the first time she'd felt loved for the right reasons.

Throughout this period, Orchidea escaped Biba and Meadowbrook banished Devlin, both creatures successfully prevented from preventing the two lovers living out an alternate existence they'd earned.

The First Picture of Summer

There's even a photograph of us together now, you know. How do you like that, eh? His sister has progressed from paint to photographic portraiture, capturing the reality of me and him together in a way that oil on canvas could only ever have romanticised it. I've seen the end result; he's already framed it, and it's probably the best image of me I've ever seen, perhaps because it portrays the truth – even if we're both dressed in togas, supposedly evoking the aesthetic glory of Ancient Greece! It's just one of those artistic fancies photographers indulge in.

I think we broke the rules of photography, actually. We're laughing. You're not supposed to do that. The whole process takes so bloody long that few sitters for portraits look anything other than utterly miserable – mind you, it's not as long as sitting for a pained portrait; photography is a process that takes minutes rather than days or weeks. But the trend seems to be that you're meant to echo the serious expressions of painted portraits, probably because the length of time from holding the pose to the camera exposure being achieved is so interminable. We couldn't help laughing, though; we were happy. And the final picture is evidence of how happy we were.

Remember that week?

It was my birthday week – yes, I know that means nothing to you; it normally means nothing to me either, usually because I have to spend it entombed with you just like every other bloody week of the year. But this time round it was different. There was a determined effort on Jeremiah's part to mark it in style. That's why you were left here for five days. I bet you didn't even notice, did you? What's five days to you? I bet you can't even tell if I've been gone for just one night or for five. Your concept of time is as distorted as my own, at least my own when I'm with Jeremiah.

While I was with Jeremiah that week – a week that seemed to span months – we heard Mafeking had been relieved and that one of those Suffragettes had been killed beneath the hooves of the king's horse at the Derby. It didn't matter to us if those two external events were separated by days or years; as he himself says, there are only ever really days anyway. When we're together, every day to us is a decade to everyone else. You surely must understand that.

You don't like me talking about Jeremiah, do you? I can see it in your eyes. You're a grumpy sod as it is, anyway, but informing you I have a life in which you have no involvement at all must be such a kick in the teeth. We even talked about getting married. How do you feel about that, then? I can't even remember if my first husband died or if he's still alive, but I don't see how it really matters. He's history. There is only the here and now, and those of us who are here and now have to live it. The sole reminiscing I indulge in looks back no further than the day before, when I had been wrapped around Jeremiah in the warm nest of his bed, and I get upset because I'm not still there with him.

It used to be the case that when I first visited Jeremiah I felt that my time with him was contained within a timeless bubble; now I feel like being back here is the timeless bubble; the time with him seems more real. *This* is the fantasy, even if it's the kind of fantasy nobody would fantasise about. Being with Jeremiah is real; being here with you is not. But I'm here with you more than I'm there with him, and that's not right.

He privately published a little book just for me as a birthday present – a one-off edition exclusively for me; it was a charming collection of pastiche nursery rhymes he'd written about me and him and people we know. Totally unique. And what did I get from you when I returned here, eh? A bite, a scratch and a cut – same as it ever was. We even talked about building an outdoor enclosure for you so that he could finally come and visit here and eventually move-in with me. The problem is I can't do that as things stand; there simply isn't enough land.

Don't worry – it won't happen unless I can extend the grounds. Our nearest neighbour has plenty of land; I must begin tentative enquiries to see if he'd be willing to sell. I'd make sure you had enough space to roam and run around, but I'd build fences so high and so strong that you'd never inflict any injury on anyone ever again, including me. Getting you out of the house would also mean I'd finally be able to decorate the interior of this place in a style that wouldn't have to account for the presence of a wild animal, just like other wealthy ladies of independent means manage to do. And my Jeremiah could come to me at last – with you well out of the way. My eternal hindrance to happiness, my perennial stumbling block to satisfaction – be prepared to wake-up to the overdue changes I've finally rung.

Hah! Your reaction is priceless.

My words haven't registered at all, for you merely give me the same response to every utterance, the same old look, the same selfish old look that says 'Me! Me! Me!' I know it so well, but it doesn't work in the way that it used to because the days when we were encased in here together without any indication this situation would ever change are gone now. I have seen an alternative to this imprisonment, and you can cut, bite, scratch and sulk all you like – it won't make any bloody difference. The hold you've had over me all your life has to be weakened – oh, not broken; it will never be broken. But no longer quite so strong and so impervious to any challenge. I suddenly feel strong enough to take control and wrestle some of that control from your grasp at last. My actions have proven a life apart from you is possible, and I intend to maintain that freedom now I have finally won it.

He and I have spoken of one day setting up a home somewhere between the geographical distance that currently divides us, a place we could share and accommodate both you and Devlin. You don't know Devlin, do you?

Devlin is the nearest thing Jeremiah has to you – a raven that hides in the attic whenever I visit. Jeremiah was present at Devlin's birth just as I was present at yours, and Devlin has a similarly dominant grip on Jeremiah's considerations. He holds Devlin responsible for the fact he hasn't travelled overseas or even exploited his national fame by visiting more corners of this country. He has felt housebound to an extent because of

Devlin's presence, and I know all-too well what he means.

If Jeremiah and I can establish a home whereby you and Devlin are taken care of, a home where neither of you can dominate me or him, we will have established some sort of Nirvana; we realise we can never entirely eradicate either of you from our lives, but as long as you're not dictating our lives, a blissful balance will have been achieved.

Of course, that's all in the future – and it's a vital plan for the future; not only do I need to loosen myself more from your grip, but Jeremiah needs to echo my intentions where Devlin is concerned. He drinks too much absinthe and smokes too many cigars for my liking; that bloody bird has instilled a self-destructive element in him that I won't have robbing me of my man. He's spent too long on his own with Devlin, feeling as if nobody cared if he lived or died, meaning he didn't care either. That has to change, and only I can do it. He *has* someone who cares now, so it's up to me to remind him of that fact.

At least when I am there I know Jeremiah tempers his habits; if I could be there permanently, he may well conquer them altogether. And I'm pretty sure he thinks the same of me. If he can get me to devote less of my time to you, I can spend more time as the person I am when I'm with him; and I *love* the person I am when I'm with him. I miss her when I have to pack her away and return here.

Why am I even bothering to say any of this out loud, eh? Your sole response is a roar and a ripping-up of a rug that's already been reduced to shreds by your claws. I guess I've become so accustomed to intelligent conversation with Jeremiah that I forget just how much talking to you is like talking to the bloody wall. Yes, go on – growl and snarl. It's all you can do, and it's all I could engage with for years. No wonder my head was dead.

Yet, sometimes I speak of my life with Jeremiah to you and I can see the helpless upset in your eyes. I swear I sight a tear, even if a zoologist would dismiss it as mere moisture expelled in a purely anatomical discharge with no emotional trigger. These are the moments when it breaks my heart that we cannot communicate verbally. I know there are things you want to say, feelings you want to express, but you are constrained by the limitations of your species, restricted to violent physical responses and clumsy, incoherent gestures to make a point because you can't articulate it any other way. I wonder who is in there, trapped for life and screaming with rage at the injustice of his sentence.

At such times, I become frustrated that I can't access the core of you as two-way speech would enable me to, that core locked away deep in the impenetrable animal hide that builds a permanent barrier between man and beast. Even in softer moments, when you rub your mane against me in what appears to be an affectionate expression, I know you do it because you want something from me – usually food or a run in the grounds. The ulterior motive is blatant. How I often wish it merely meant you love me.

Yes, I can read you far easier than some of the challenges I've relished in the library, but how I crave a better book of Biba, one that doesn't spell everything out with such primitive simplicity that even a child entranced by pictures and mystified by words would reject as too basic. But I'm imagining something utterly unrealisable. You will never be capable of speech or of expressing your wants in any way other than through aggressive actions; your emotional language is that of the untamed African landscape you have never known. Born into an environment entirely unsuitable to your savage instincts, you have had a chip on your shoulder from day one, and that chip will always be there.

No wonder you're so bloody angry all the time, you poor, imprisoned creature. I could easily let you break my heart if I spent too much time pondering on your own personal incarceration; but what would it achieve? There is no magic wand that can be waved to release you. Perhaps building an outdoor enclosure for you is the closest I can ever come to any sort of solace. It might at least ease the anger, the factor that has served to define both of us for so long.

And how that anger guided me; how your presence these last few years had become intrinsic to my own behaviour and outlook. How decisions had been taken and mistakes had been made solely to suit you. How a life without life had been constructed and barriers erected to keep others out for your sake. How winter had become a season that never ended, an interior climate that gripped my heart in an icy vice – until the moment when a miracle materialised like an unexpected spring bud and I summoned up the courage to say yes to Jasper Hampshire's kind offer, an offer that I anticipated politely declining, just as I have all others ever since you raised the drawbridge.

I remain ignorant as to where the word 'yes' came from, but come it did. Three little letters and suddenly I am somewhere beyond your reach at last. No wonder I was so anxious and scared when I was propelled into this unfamiliar world in which people's lives are not governed by consideration for an in-house wild animal.

Look where I am now, though. Yes, still here, still with you – but elsewhere too. I never had elsewhere before. The novelty of the spring has become the norm of the summer and I am in a better place, a place where I truly belong. I can deal with everything you throw at me now and none of it will drag me down in the way it used to. I accept who you are, *what* you are, but I will not let you define me anymore. Jeremiah defines me now, not you. When he experiences any physical sensation all those miles away from me, I feel it. We have become the twins I used to think me and you were. There is no future I can now conceive of in which he and I are not together. We cannot be apart. We are one.

But you will always be with me, even then. Just bear in mind that you will not dominate or control me, though. Tomorrow I shall make enquiries as to the availability of the land I require to build you a home separate from mine.

Home Time

Orchidea's home – or fortress, as she had become accustomed to referring to it as – was a rather dilapidated Jacobean mansion isolated and distanced from its nearest-neighbour; it was the archetypal rural residence for someone of money who didn't want to be disturbed and had nobody to impress. Jeremiah Meadowbrook's home, by contrast, was the more self-consciously upmarket Georgian townhouse model favoured by the metropolitan artistic, situated on the end of a lengthy terrace and within walking distance of all social amenities. There had been a time when Meadowbrook had sought to be amongst his fellow artists and relished being amongst them. Conan Blackcastle was just a block away, and all of the taverns, clubs, coffee houses and opium dens he had once enthusiastically embraced as places to be and to be seen were accessible on foot, near enough that his carriage wasn't really required to get to them.

The more Orchidea became familiar with Meadowbrook's home, the more she envied him being in the epicentre of a thriving urban environment where everything appeared to be on-tap if one wanted it; on the other hand, the more he heard of her own home, the more Meadowbrook envied her. The hustle and bustle of town life was something he'd initially enjoyed, but it now felt tiresome and intrusive to him. Granted, he had managed to write several novels and a play whilst resident at this house, but now it suddenly seemed ill-suited to solitude. He longed for country air and country quiet when attempting to pen his next best-seller, not the soundtrack of the city. As with Orchidea's reaction to his location, however, the grass was undeniably greener elsewhere.

Orchidea's suggestion that they find somewhere to share midway between their current addresses sounded like the ideal solution to his frustration with his surroundings. Not only would he be living with the love of his life, but he would also be one crucial step removed from where he was now, the claustrophobic cauldron of the urban. The environs that had fired and inspired him had gradually lost their appeal, perhaps thanks to Orchidea presenting him with a cleansing alternative to the somewhat superficial attractions he'd chased before.

His absence from many of those key hot-spots had been noted by those who continued to patronise them, though some blamed the character assassination conducted by Lady Sarah Stabinbach in her mad death-throes for his withdrawal from social life. That might have been true had Meadowbrook been confronted by a unified snub on the part of society; but support for Lady Sarah had disintegrated overnight when she'd turned on him, so that unpleasant episode couldn't really be held responsible.

The plain truth was that his previous pleasure-seeking felt false and irredeemably shallow next to his love for Orchidea. She was the one real feeling in his life that had the genuine ring of authenticity about it; everything else appeared transient and frivolous – cheap thrills for a cheap existence. The joy he now derived from buying gifts for Orchidea – and the anticipation of her reaction when the gift was presented to her – was something that gave him far greater satisfaction; the satisfaction he got from that lifted him higher than the satisfaction he got from entertaining a group of inebriated authors. He'd enjoyed being a celebrity, but that enjoyment didn't come close to what being the man in Orchidea's life gave him. Courting Alice was a memory that had drifted so far to the distant edges of his recollections that the experience of courting anew was an entirely fresh one to him, almost as though he'd never done it before; and he loved it.

The comic tone many of his works began to adopt following the Gothic melodrama of his fictitious retelling of life with Alice was ditched when he began writing his next novel. He wanted to reflect this new experience – both the romance of it and the traumatic reality of Orchidea's difficulties with Biba – in a book he hoped would represent a creative progression. The play had enjoyed a successful run and made a lot of money, but it didn't tempt him into shifting his energies permanently to the stage; he'd viewed the enterprise as an experiment, a challenge to see if he could master the theatre. The profits confirmed he'd done it, so he saw no need to try again.

One aspect of the life he'd led as the toast of literary society hadn't gone since he'd become more housebound, however, and that was the one that concerned Orchidea the most – his increasingly excessive and addictive reliance on absinthe and cigars. Laudanum had been very much usurped as his favourite mind-expanding beverage by the Gallic green liquid allegedly laced with poison, and chain-smoking had also become second nature. Not for Meadowbrook the ritual of reserving them as treats intended for post-dinner relaxation in the company of gentlemen, the acceptable side-order to discussions on cricket; he didn't view them as occasional social stimulants, but all-day accompaniments to his every waking action when alone.

Meadowbrook's problem was that being encouraged to overindulge as a literary sensation had created an appetite in him that made moderation in all vices impossible. Whenever something new provided pleasure, there were no half-measures. He could never see why he should have to restrict sources of enjoyment simply because overindulgence in them might prove detrimental to his health.

What Meadowbrook failed to appreciate was that he now had someone who cared for his long-term wellbeing, something he hadn't had since Alice's death. *He* sure as hell didn't care for his long-term wellbeing. He was quite content to pursue the Chatterton route of a doomed romantic exit via a selfish strain of narcissistic nihilism that didn't take Orchidea into account at all. But his professional success, and his wife's premature passing, had pushed him into a somewhat reckless disregard for his physical upkeep, and this recklessness had become a habit that seemed to suit his status as an artist – a status that demanded and expected excess. There are no ramifications with such recklessness other than for the person indulging when that person has no familial responsibilities and feels as though no one really cares what becomes of them, anyway; for Meadowbrook, this was a mindset he had yet to get out of, even though his circumstances had dramatically altered for the better; he was no longer in the same circumstances that had prompted such dependence on stimulants.

It was odd that, for all his recognition of Orchidea's game-changing significance in his life, he didn't understand that this habit needed to be curbed now that Orchidea was here. He couldn't see the connection.

If he had addressed the issue at all, he would probably have come to the conclusion that his continuing dependence on these twin evils was perhaps an ongoing one because he missed Orchidea so much when she returned home for a week or two between her visits. They induced temporary elation when there was no Orchidea present to provide it. Before Orchidea, they had been subconsciously used in an attempt to fill a void Meadowbrook hadn't even realised was there; now that Orchidea had entered his life and made him aware of that void by properly filling it in the best possible way, they shouldn't have been necessary anymore; yet he didn't even curb the habit when he and she were actually together, the time when they *really* weren't needed.

He had sold himself to her in the beginning as the strong one, the confident, self-assured partner who could take his anxious and nervous other half by the hand and give her the self-belief she had lacked; that's what she had responded to because that's what she needed in a man. But how secure was this strength or confidence if it required propping-up with absinthe? What did that say about Meadowbrook's long-term prospects?

Sure, everyone adopts a degree of manufactured perfection when becoming romantically involved with somebody new, wanting to make the best possible impression and persuading the other person they have so few faults that they're worth investing in. After a while, imperfections naturally begin to creep into the picture, but if love has been won, partners will generally overlook the failings of their other halves because they appreciate these are minor, initially unseen chinks in otherwise adorable armour. Meadowbrook's continuous reliance on substances to see him through the day suggested his confidence didn't exist without them.

Ironically, however, his confidence was genuine and uniquely substance-free where Orchidea was concerned. She had put him instantly at ease from the very beginning. There was just something about her that did this to him in a way that nobody else did. From the moment Meadowbrook had first spoken to Orchidea, the unplanned nature of how he had stumbled upon her meant none of his lines were scripted in advance.

With Alice, he had pursued her for months and during their courtship he had always meticulously mentally prepared everything that he intended to say to her before saying it. As a result, like any nervous actor forced to recite lines when all-too aware his future rested upon getting them right, Meadowbrook was rarely in Alice's company prior to their marriage without being on edge and anxious, terrified of buggering up the lines and buggering up his chances of capturing her hand in the process. He therefore associated being in love with being in a constant state of fretful agony, which was perhaps why the way in which he fell for Orchidea took him by surprise; it was utterly painless.

No, there was none of that anxiety with Orchidea. He may have required exhausting preparation to woo Alice and he may have required liquid stimulants to keep society entertained, but Orchidea's presence transformed him into the most confident, self-assured man on the planet. He had no need to bolster himself with anything around her, which said his addictions were no more than an idle habit to be addressed sooner rather than later.

For now, Orchidea was prepared to tolerate Meadowbrook's excesses and indulgences as tools in her man's artistic armoury – at least to an extent; but her concerns as to how addicted he was to them in her absence remained. She had seen with her own eyes that he seemed unable to function without them as a crutch even with her, the person who put him at ease more than anyone on the planet; how dependent must he be on them when she wasn't there? It was imperative to her that for him not to slowly kill the man she loved, he needed to temper his unnecessary reliance on such substances.

Of course, any cutting-down on such excesses and indulgences was going to be a hard task with Devlin a permanent fixture in the room during those plentiful moments when nobody else graced the residence with their presence. Meadowbrook's feathered friend gave him the same look whenever their eyes met between lighting a cigar or topping-up the glass; the look said 'Go on – do it; you know it always makes you feel better.' And Devlin had an immense influence on his behaviour when just the two of them were locked away together, dictating Meadowbrook's thoughts and actions without saying a word. The strength of Devlin's presence was enough.

Letters between Meadowbrook and Orchidea were rattled off on a regular basis, especially in the days following Orchidea's most recent departure, when the agony inflicted by their enforced separation tended to be at its most intense for both. There was talk of Meadowbrook installing a telephone in his home to ease the pain of parting, but Orchidea couldn't embrace the latest technological marvel of communication just yet on account of her home being too distanced from the nearest telephone exchange – for now, at least. The rapid spread of the new medium across the country would soon reach her neck of the woods, but the network hadn't done so yet. Therefore, at the moment, they were still reliant on the post and on the telegraph.

Whenever Orchidea's next visit edged close, the sending of a telegraph informing Meadowbrook of the date and time at which to expect her arrival at the railway station would serve as a considerable lifter of mood. It would also provoke a noticeable restlessness in Devlin as the raven sensed sunshine was imminent in the household, something to which he was naturally averse. Devlin preferred the long days and dark nights that divided Orchidea visits, days and nights when it was largely just him and Meadowbrook bar the occasional call by the likes of Meadowbrook's sister Verity (a designated enemy for Devlin) or Conan Blackcastle, who was unaware of Devlin's existence despite his durable friendship with Meadowbrook, one that had survived the severance of Lady Sarah Stabinbach's patronage of them both.

****

Jeremiah Meadowbrook had not one iota of doubt that his beloved was as devoted to him as he was to her. There had been no suggestions of wavering in her affections whatsoever; her letters had swelled into even more adoring expressions of love as their relationship progressed, and she seemed as smitten dozens of visits later as she had on that very first night. They were building something very special indeed and it was a joint enterprise. There was no trace of that somewhat desperate chase which had eventually worn down poor Alice when she'd sought an escape from a miserable family situation; Orchidea wasn't prompted into surrender after an interminably lengthy courtship and simply because she admired Meadowbrook's persistence.

No, she and he had fallen for each other simultaneously and had continued along the same path wholly in synch with one another. It was very much a partnership and had been from day one – which didn't bode too well for the two creatures who had always viewed themselves as the true partners of the respective pair.

Devlin needed to get the knife in as soon as he realised this relationship was putting down deeper and stronger roots. He had to at least try a little subtle sabotage. The raven aired his opinion through audible thoughts alone, being a tad more articulate than the lion, who made all his points via violent gestures. Meadowbrook heard every word as it travelled across the room in a relentlessly bilious stream of vile, vicious vomit that splashed, splattered and stained his eardrums – with every poisonous prediction intended to sour the kind of likely future that would be Devlin's worst nightmare where the union was concerned. Even if the bird began by praising Orchidea in the most complimentary of fashions, Meadowbrook knew he'd soon descend into the vulgar and the profane.

'Okay, I'll be nice and admit she's beautiful,' said (thought) Devlin. 'I cannot dispute what is evident to anyone with a fully-functioning pair of eyes. She's a bloody stunning-looking lady, actually – remarkably pretty; but she has that kind of oblivious prettiness which is enhanced by its diffidence, as though she's either unaware of or embarrassed by just how pretty she really is. And that's a really endearing quality in her. She lacks the smug, knowing arrogance that wears prettiness as a weapon, the sort that its owner has spent a little too long studying in the looking-glass. That sort comes with anticipatory recognition, an aggressive demand that the beholder must be seduced by it. No, that's as far removed from her prettiness as is possible to get.

'To be truthful, it's hard to think any man could meet her lovely face and not want to kiss her. There's an irresistible, magical magnetism in the structure of those features that makes it damn-near impossible to look at anything else once your eyes have settled on them. They really do draw the gaze in. And then when she speaks, there's the serene melody of that voice – that soft, seductive whisper of a voice that caresses the listener's ears like a warm, cleansing breeze detoxifying every unpleasant sound that has ever polluted them. It makes a vital contribution to the generating of the glow around her face that keeps the beholder under her spell for life. There. Is that nice enough for you?

'And, yes, the way she carries herself has a delicacy one associates with porcelain, like she could so easily shatter that the instinctive compulsion is to hold her close and not let go to prevent that breakage from ever happening. I get that. She's certainly in possession of every physical quality *you* ever wanted in a woman – that's for sure. She's elegant, graceful, sensual – she glides rather than walks, in the same way a ballet dancer moves across the stage; she seems almost out of place amongst the rest of you clumsy, stumbling, inarticulate apes, as though she belongs to some future strain of human evolution, where people can move without the effort of putting one foot in front of the other. No wonder her legs are so breathtaking.

'She's got legs that are not just long, but perfectly proportioned. Some women have potentially nice legs that fail to achieve this potential because they boast an overabundance of lazy flesh, and upon close inspection are found to resemble the pins of a chubby baby; then there are others with potentially nice legs that are just a bit too lean and lanky, a bit too reminiscent of a pubescent boy who's morphing into a man. *Her* legs are absolute faultless perfection, with every dimension of every individual segment, from toe to calf, knee to thigh, exactly as it should be. If an architect sat down to design the best legs imaginable for a woman's body, the chances are they'd end up with hers. And joined on to such a magnificent arse too!

'Ah, yes – that arse; buttocks as soft and succulent as a couple of delicious hard-boiled eggs begging to be nibbled! And those squeezy, supple, tender tits, designed with hands in mind that can act as permanent support without the need for a bodice. Good Lord, you're a lucky fellow, aren't you? You won't receive a slap on the cheek for exploring whenever she's near. You don't have to ask permission. Your hands have carte-blanche to wander. They have a free pass, a season-ticket. Not only can you look, but you can also touch. You have access all areas and none of those areas are ever out of bounds to you. That's an incredibly privileged position to be in where such a beautiful woman is concerned. Remember that. If you take the privilege for granted, it would be extremely foolish. This is your reward from her; what reward has she received from you?

'Alright, so you've introduced her to the spiritual, sacred side of making love, lifting her to a level of intense physical intimacy that transcends base lust and takes the union of man and woman to the highest of shared human planes. But she also loves a good, simple fuck – she bloody loves it. She loves it because she'd *forgotten* she loved it until she met you. You reminded her how much fun it can be – reminded her of the sexy, licentious side of lovemaking that sends the libido into overdrive whenever desire rears its horny head; and, let's face it, there's no greater turn-on than a graceful, elegant lady revealing herself to be a ravenous, primal beast between the sheets, as dirty, naughty, adventurous and unbridled as the most shameless of hussies.

'But admit it – go on; when you're wrapped around each other in bed and she gazes upon your face and tells you you're lovely, there's a part of you that can't quite believe it, isn't there. You look at her and see the most beautiful creature you've ever encountered right there in your bloody arms, and she's telling you *you're* lovely – *you!* When did anyone ever look at you and think that, eh? It sounds pretty implausible a compliment to me when it's being addressed at you. Think about it – how many times have you confronted your reflection and felt like smashing the mirror in disgust? Lovely – *you?* What the hell does she see in you, mate? It can't last, this momentary delusion of hers that you're lovely. She'll open her eyes soon enough and realise you only appear lovely because you noticed her when nobody else was looking. It's just a misguided manifestation of gratitude, that's all. Jesus, she's *way* too beautiful for you. Talk about punching above your bloody weight!

'Oh no, you won't be able to hold onto her for long, mark my words. You were just lucky you caught her at the right moment, when she was at an all-time personal low and had lost every shred of self-confidence and belief in herself. And yet you've gone and given it back to her when every other man she's ever been involved with has taken it away from her, you mug! You know what that means don't you? It means she's going to shine all that rediscovered self-confidence and belief in the direction of every available, good-looking titled bastard she attracts – and there'll be plenty of them for her to pick and choose from soon enough because you've switched the light back on inside her, you bloody idiot.

'In fact, she could be picking and choosing one right now. How would you even know, with her being so far away so much of the time? Women lie about these things without being remotely troubled by guilt or conscience; they think nothing of it, so she could have done it already, for all you know. You'll never find out if she doesn't want to confess it, because women can keep a straight face and give nothing away when they lie about things like that. It's a talent they have that men can never match. If she *had* slept with another man behind your back, you'd never be able to read the truth on her countenance any more than you'd be able to read War and Peace in the original Russian. She'll tell you what you want to hear, and if that's a lie you'll be none the wiser. You'll believe her.

'Really, why should she settle for you now she knows she can have any man she wants – any man who's a far safer long-term prospect than an unreliable, erratic loser like you? Just look at the facts: you're a middle-aged writer with a drink problem whose profession renders him an antisocial recluse whenever the creative muse strikes! Okay, so you're successful at what you do, but that doesn't necessarily make you the ideal husband – a good fling, a fun affair, perhaps; but long-term? Permanent? Forget it! Where's the appeal in you for a beautiful, intelligent woman, eh? What kind of future can you possibly give her? Dream on, mate!

'Stop imagining you can hold onto a woman like her for life and get real by admitting you were lucky to have her for just a short while; you shouldn't have ever got anywhere near her at all. It was nothing more than a fortunate fluke. You need to start finding your own suitable level and settle for it. Stick with desperate, ugly scrubbers nobody else would touch with a bargepole and be thankful for that. They're the best you could hope for because a gorgeous Goddess like Orchidea is way out of your lowly league, you hideous, grotesque gargoyle.'

'Fuck off!'

Devlin smiled a smile that married malevolence with smugness. He was Hymen, blessing the union of Orpheus and Eurydice by predicting their perfection wouldn't last. He'd got to his father and could now sit back on his perch and watch his words work away, seeping into Meadowbrook's as-yet untapped subconscious paranoia. For now, Meadowbrook could dismiss Devlin's poison and reject a bleak prophesy that had no relevance when Orchidea's devotion was so indisputable; but Devlin would repeat and recite this rancid catalogue of negativity, content the day wouldn't be long in coming before it would begin festering and fermenting in Meadowbrook's fevered head while his woman remained out of sight.

Perhaps the raven sensed he had to start planting seeds of doubt quickly, for events were progressing in a direction that didn't suit him at all. The biggest threat to Devlin's dominance was the same threat to Biba's dominance – the recently-hatched plan of Meadowbrook and Orchidea setting up a proper home together. At first, Meadowbrook would join his love in her current abode and then they would eventually find somewhere else that would be their own shared nest.

All of this depended upon Orchidea being able to purchase additional land neighbouring her own that would enable her to build an outdoor enclosure for Biba that would permanently exclude the lion from the house. Because of the isolation Biba's presence had thrust upon her, Orchidea had had little contact with anyone else in the vicinity, and she knew little about her nearest neighbour, whose house was considerably distanced from hers, even if his land bordered her land much closer.

It was like that with wealthy country folk; there was none of the cheek-by-jowl arrangements Meadowbrook was so accustomed to in the town environment, at least not in terms of residences. The respective rural homes of so-called neighbours could be a mile apart, but the outer rims of their estates would angrily brush against each other like rival whores fighting for the same patch on a street corner.

Whilst Orchidea and Meadowbrook may have talked politics, they were essentially cosseted from events beyond their bubble; oddly enough, however, what worked in Orchidea's favour when it came to purchasing the desired land was one of those outside events.

It occurred one afternoon when she was taking the train to town for a visit to Meadowbrook: news broke that Archduke Franz Ferdinand, heir presumptive to the throne of the Austro-Hungarian Empire, had been assassinated in Sarajevo. The events that unfolded in the following days and weeks, leading to the eventual declaration that Britain was at war with the Kaiser's Germany, created a degree of minor panic amongst some of the gentry.

Fears over a potential German invasion prompted a few members of the landed class to contemplate the long-term value of their estates, so somebody suddenly making enquiries about available land was bound to get an easier ride than had been the case during peacetime. It was still no overnight sale in Orchidea's case, however, though every setback on the Western Front played into Orchidea's hands.

Before the negotiations even got underway, never mind reached their completion, however, there was the smooth, effortless establishment of a double act as the norm.

The concept wasn't a novelty; it was now the way things were; Meadowbrook and Orchidea came as a pair. Biba may have hated it; Devlin may have hated it. But it was fact. And there were so many moments when this union was highlighted as something truly touching – like when Meadowbrook's new novel rolled-off the presses and he dispatched the first copy to his beloved. She telegraphed him upon receipt of it, confessing she was in tears when turning the page and seeing it dedicated to her.

Oh, joy it was to be alive in the high summer of Jeremiah and Orchidea. They again went riding together out of town some afternoons, then strolling for a good few hours in the countryside and studying residences they stumbled upon as potential homes for their planned abode together. They again talked of marriage during these enchanting excursions, hand-in-hand and eye-to-eye, solidly sealed in the intoxicating wrapping that binds lovers as one like the coating of a chrysalis.

They'd return to Meadowbrook's place and make wondrous, passionate love before Orchidea again took over the kitchen and concocted one more delicious recipe that would be followed by further entertaining activities based around music, literature or novelty toys like the magic lantern, stereoscope or – the latest addition – the gramophone. The evening would climax with the pair bathing together before retiring to the bedchamber and sealing their ecstatic union for eternity by connecting in a way neither had ever (or *would* ever) connect with anyone else.

The gradual revelation of the realities of Biba didn't strike Meadowbrook as especially odd or unique; he had his own animal burden and was relieved he wasn't alone; as far as he was concerned, it was simply another distinctive bond that bound him to his beloved. He accepted it and didn't allow it to get in the way. Devlin, on the other hand, would grumpily groom his feathers in the attic whilst all this was taking place, praying his poison would work, even if the likelihood seemed unlikely at such moments of unprecedented, ecstatic happiness.

Generic Domestics

Mr Wooldridge, the valet-cum-coach-driver – a self-trained, 'posh' Scot with the kind of elevated accent that does its best to hide its Scottish roots with linguistic pretension, even though no one would ever mistake him for an Englishman. Ironically, the curious combination actually made for a marvellously rich and musical speaking voice, redolent of warm wood, mulled wine and a roaring fireplace.

Mrs Maggs, the housekeeper-cum-cook – proud of her cockney ancestry, but equally intent to highlight her rise up the social ladder by emphasising her 'aitches' whenever addressing the master.

She was solid and plump whereas the valet was tall and thin. He had a head like a skull with a thin smattering of half-remembered red follicle netting swept across its crown; she had a heavy head resembling the tough exterior of a medicine ball topped-off by a dense wire-wool mane tightly pulled away from a face that betrayed backyard origins. Somehow, they went well together, however, and their running of the household worked. They shared seniority, and had a couple of younger maids and a stable-boy under them. That was the extent of Jeremiah Meadowbrook's domestic staff. It suited him and it suited them. And when Orchidea came, they all got the night-off.

On such evenings, they sometimes went their separate ways and on other occasions they all went on a jolly outing to the local picture-house together. Widow-woman Mrs Maggs and the maids liked a good comedy, especially the Keystone Cops, whereas confirmed bachelor Wooldridge often enjoyed the occasional heavyweight epic by the likes of DW Griffith – something the maids in particular found hard-going. But they might decide on the nature of their cinematic night-out via the toss of a coin. Either way, it was better than working.

This wasn't one of those evenings; it was instead one of those in which the master had shut himself away with a request not to be disturbed, for Orchidea had departed that morning and he generally reacted in the same way, usually for several days afterwards. The maids were already in their beds at the top of the house, leaving Mr Wooldridge (Maurice) and Mrs Maggs (Millie) to wind-down by the fireplace in the kitchen. Maurice supped soporifically on a glass of brandy and languidly perused the London Illustrated News through the spectacles perched on the tip of his nose whilst Millie indulged in some therapeutic sewing with her own spectacles occupying a complementary position to Maurice's.

They were always ready to be summoned to the master's quarters if need be, but they relished the tranquillity of such nights, when the bell was silenced by their master's need for solitude and the only sound accompanying their repose came via the plodding, mechanical monotony of the ticking clock on the kitchen wall.

There were certainly worse ways of making a living.

'Well, I can't understand why he don't just marry her, Maurice,' said Millie without looking up from her needlework.

'Aye, well; chances are she might already be wed, Millie,' replied Maurice without looking up from the magazine.

'You really think so?'

'You doubt it?'

'Well...'

'Think about it,' said Maurice as he rested his Illustrated News on the kitchen table they both sat at and removed his spectacles. 'She only ever comes here for a day or two at a time every couple of weeks; and he never visits her as far as we know. She just comes here. Does it not strike you she and the master are simply having an extramarital affair rather than a courtship?'

'Well, yes, I agree it's a strange arrangement.'

'And we both know she doesn't sleep in one of the spare bedchambers, so it's not as if she's saving herself for her wedding night.'

'Neither of 'em's spring chickens, though; I don't see why they should have to wait. The master's a widower, after all. She could be a widow.'

'Aye – and she could be another man's wife. If she's a widow and she and the master love each other, what would there be to stop them getting wed – unless there's already a *Mister* Orchidea, eh?'

'I ain't never noticed a ring.'

'Aye, but she's not likely to keep it on when she's playing away, is she?'

'Maybe not – but if the master knows, I can't see why she'd bother, anyway. And if she *is* a married woman, he *must* know. Oh, I dunno. I just wish they could marry. He seems so happy when she's around, and so bleedin' miserable when she ain't.'

'At least when she's here, we get a night-off and that bloody bird is out of the way.'

'Oh! That bird! I don't know why he puts up with it in the house. Gives me the willies.'

'He told me he raised it from a chick. I think he feels obliged. I'd strangle the damned thing given half a chance myself, mind.'

'You and me both, Maurice!'

'Aye, well – let's just be thankful he keeps it with him and doesn't let it have the run of the house, eh?'

'It's bad enough when it has a tantrum – what a bleedin' racket!'

'Not tonight, though, thank the Lord. It's quiet as a graveyard up there. The master doesn't need that bloody bird kicking up a fuss when his lady's gone home. He must feel wretched enough as it is. I just wish Miss Orchidea could see what she does to the household when she's gone – how this gloom descends and we all have to walk around on tiptoe for days as if he's fallen into a deep sleep. The fact he doesn't visit her and she only comes here – and just for a few days at a time – tells me there's no reason other than a Mr Orchidea back at home. And that's why they'll never be man and wife, alas – in my opinion, anyhow.'

'She don't seem the type to me, though.'

'What?'

'Well, y'know – a *scarlet woman*. She seems so quiet and gentle, not the sort who would have two men on the go at the same time. She don't come across as a hussy at all; she always looks to me like the thought of it would appal her. And whenever I see her and the master together, they seem so suited and so at ease, you'd think they were married already; such a good match.'

'Aye, but...'

'And a woman can usually tell when another woman is that sort – the sort who'd cheat on her husband; it's in the way they carry themselves, a certain cockiness about 'em when they walk in a room, like they believe they can have any man they want, like no man could resist 'em. They may as well have "Slut" stamped on their cleavage it's so bleedin' obvious. But I can't see that in her at all. She's so lovely.'

'Aye, but we barely know her, Millie. Sometimes I drive them in the carriage together and sometimes you serve them something to eat; but we're basing all our character observations on seeing her when she's being the lady in front of the servants. We're never going to see the real woman behind all that. Then again, perhaps the master never even sees the real woman himself, just sees the version she becomes when she's with him, the married woman engaged in an extramarital affair. And if the master can turn a blind eye to it, who are we to judge?'

'Oh, I ain't judging, Maurice. What with the master being an artistic sort and all that, you have to cut him a bit of moral slack.'

'Takes all sorts to make a world, so they say.'

'Just a shame they can't be together properly.'

'They can only really do that if they marry, and – as I've said – I don't think that's going to happen.'

There was a cessation in the conversation as Millie mused on the frustration arising from the absence of a happy ending. Maurice was poised to place his spectacles back on his nose and pick up where he'd left off with the London Illustrated News when Millie then returned to airing her train of thought out loud.

'I wondered if he was doomed to be a lonely widower for good,' she said, 'and then when he brought Miss Orchidea here for the first time I thought he had the chance to be happy at last.'

'He *is* happy, though, when he's with her,' replied Maurice.

'For a day or two, I know; but it's not the same, though, is it? He must want to be with her longer than that.'

'I don't know, Millie. I've seen plenty of marriages in my time where there's no happiness at all. The household I was raised in wasn't exactly a place of joy – far from it – and my parents were married for the best part of forty years, detesting one another and glowering across the kitchen table every day with us bairns manning the barricade. Maybe we should just be thankful the master's grabbing whatever happiness he can, even if it is in small doses and might only have a short life-span.'

'I suppose so. I was lucky to grab the few years of happiness I had with my Eddie, God-rest-his-soul. I wish we'd had longer together, but I wouldn't swap what we did have for the world.'

'Aye, well – there you go, then. We none of us know how long we've got on this earth, so best to take what you can when you can, eh? If the master and Miss Orchidea have to settle for this arrangement, at least they've got that. It's better than nothing, even though I'm pretty certain the master wants more.'

Mrs Maggs yawned, removed her spectacles and placed her sewing on the small wooden table dividing her from Mr Wooldridge. She glanced at the clock on the wall and saw it was coming up to 10pm.

'Well, Maurice,' she said as she rose to her feet and stretched rather theatrically. 'I'm away to my bed. You be much longer yourself?'

'No,' replied Wooldridge. 'I'll be off up shortly. I don't think the master will be wanting anything else tonight. I'll give it till a quarter-past and then I'll turn in.'

'Okay. G'night then, Maurice.'

'Aye, g'night, Millie.'

Wooldridge and Mrs Maggs may have known about Devlin, but neither knew about Biba – nor were they aware the 'mystery' of the arrangement between their master and Orchidea might shortly become more conventional after all.

At least that was the plan.

The Nights are Drawing-in

Ebenezer Chapel, my neighbour.

Never seen him, never met him; but that's his name, apparently. He's a Jew, a businessman who made his fortune from something-or-other in the City and then reckoned his fortune entitled him to play the gentry game in the country. In a weird way, we share something in that we're both outsiders; but there the similarities end. He has made a conscious decision to woo rural society, whereas I have deliberately shunned it. I have had no option but to do so, what with certain *Panthera* issues; but it seems Mr Chapel has done his best to engrain himself with the wealthy residents of the vicinity and has attempted to add to my woes by turning them all against me.

That's what I've been told, anyway.

I suppose my unconventional lifestyle threatened his clichéd concept of English country life, one which he was eager to be absorbed into. Perhaps he surmised the locals whose support he sought to cultivate might already view me with suspicion, and adopting an antagonistic stance towards me was one way of ingratiating himself with them. But his gamble backfired.

As long as you don't encroach upon their little corner of the world, the English couldn't give a shit what you get up to behind closed doors. And if there's one thing they dislike, it's a bully. Yes, Biba attacked one or two intruders early on, but then the intruders' status as poachers made them detested bogeymen amongst the county set, anyway; I even heard that a few prominent members of the community aired their approval by wishing they too had a lion on the premises to ward off trespassers.

Of course, there's also the undeniable fact that the method of Ebenezer Chapel's social elevation has awakened in those wealthy residents of the vicinity certain prejudices that even the colour of money cannot win over. I may be an eccentric outsider, but I was bequeathed a fortune; I didn't have to do something as vulgar as building one up. And that will always count for more when it comes to the gentry; an heiress trumps a self-made man every time. So, having tried (and failed) to besmirch me as a dangerous undesirable in circles I don't even frequent, Mr Ebenezer Chapel has hardly endeared himself to me. Not the best starting point from which to approach him on the tricky topic of buying that section of his estate that borders mine.

When I purchased this property many moons ago, I was in a desperate state, and the seller knew it, upping the price ridiculously to capitalise on my desperation. I paid the asking price in the end, but only because I had no choice. Ironically, I now find myself in the position of having no choice again. If Jeremiah and I are to spend more time together, he has to be able to visit me as well as me him; and the only way that can come about is for Biba to be safely distanced from the house in an outdoor enclosure more befitting the fact he's an animal. I simply don't have enough space in the grounds as they are to build the kind of thing I'm thinking of, so I have to turn to my nearest neighbour, who happens to be Mr

Ebenezer Chapel, a man of business poised to receive a test of his acumen.

****

Old Sam being (along with numerous other job titles) the manager of my estate, I dispatched him 'next-door' to put my proposal to Mr Chapel. I received a reply in writing around a week later, telling me the land wasn't for sale and certainly not at the price I considered a fair one. I expected something along those lines, so I wrote back with a second proposal within a fortnight. The response was similarly rigid. No sale and, again, not at the price I was proposing. I relayed this news somewhat despairingly to Jeremiah. He encouraged me to be persistent, to wear my tight-arsed nasty neighbour down until a deal was on the table.

Perhaps to raise my spirits – and to surprise Jeremiah – I compensated for my frustration by spending some money on a novel new purchase: a motorcar.

It was a Rolls Royce 20hp painted in blood-red and had only had one previous owner, who convinced me it was worth investing in, despite the paint-job he'd inflicted upon it. I bought a driving licence, as is legally required, merely to identify my vehicle and me as the owner-driver, and then I took it for a 'spin' (as they say) round the neighbourhood, doing my best to remember the 20mph speed limit, even though I did get a little carried away. I'd been given an instruction in the rudiments of driving a motorcar by the man I bought it from, who seemed to find it humorous that a woman should want to drive such a vehicle; but it didn't seem too great a challenge, certainly easier than steering a horse-drawn carriage, anyway.

To begin with, the motorcar was as much an occasional toy for me as the old hot air balloon had been; but I thought it might be worth trying to drive it to town rather than taking the train at some future date when I visited Jeremiah. This seemed a tad ambitious when I had only driven it around quiet country lanes to begin with; I wasn't sure how I'd cope behind the wheel in busy old town, so I didn't announce its purchase to Jeremiah straight away. I wanted to arrive at his doorstep in it without him knowing beforehand, but I'd still need to become more familiar with it as a means of travel. I was so accustomed to being driven – whether by coach or train – that actually being in control of the novelty transport I was taking, and realising every decision en route was solely in my hands, felt like a large responsibility I wasn't certain I was entirely qualified to have.

Yes, the motorcar was a distraction, of course it was – and the building of an airfield a couple of miles away whetted my appetite for another form of transport too as visitors began flying over the estate with regularity; but I hadn't given up on buying the land. I made a third offer and though it too was rejected, I had a feeling my persistence was indeed beginning to wear Mr Chapel down. His written rejection betrayed a tone of detectable exasperation with my constant proposals. I think he had belatedly realised I wasn't going to take no for an answer, even if the dragging out of the process was incredibly wearisome. I suppose that's why I developed an interest in motorcars and aeroplanes – they seemed to be technology's solution to my frustration with not being able to take my relationship with Jeremiah onto the next level.

Rumours of a potential German invasion when Mr Asquith announced we were at war with the Kaiser came to my rescue with regards to buying the land. Ebenezer Chapel appeared to believe the value of his estate might not be as great as he'd imagined once he'd presumably consulted with some of the other landowners in the neighbourhood, and my fourth offer was received slightly differently. Although he still refused to sell, this time it was solely down to the amount I offered as opposed to an absolute refusal to even consider losing a dozen acres. I knew if I kept pressing, he'd waver sooner rather than later.

Not that any optimistic belief of my neighbour edging closer to a sale helped when Biba began to exhibit behaviour that made an outdoor enclosure more imperative than ever.

Yes, the whole concept had been hatched as a means of enabling me to receive Jeremiah as a guest (and as a possible dry-run for our future home together), but it suddenly seemed imminent separation between Biba and myself was necessary purely on health grounds. His temper tantrums now spanned hours rather than minutes, and they grew ever more aggressive. One of my handmaidens – who had looked-after Biba for years – was almost killed in an unprovoked attack that required three of us to pull Biba off her; a surgeon was summoned to the house and the girl in question was dispatched to a nearby hospital where it took her the best part of a month to recover from her injuries. I myself was more fortunate, but I was still subjected to a series of unprecedented assaults from Biba that left deep flesh wounds taking weeks to heal. At the time, I couldn't understand what was happening.

In retrospect, perhaps Biba sensed something in the air, something that suggested his dominance of me and of the household was slowly coming to an end. As he couldn't communicate verbally, he reacted in the only way he knew how, by utilising his immense physical strength to lash out at those within his daily radius. I had learnt to anticipate Biba's movements and responses to situations throughout the years he had been my shadow, and I had developed ways and means of dealing with them to minimise the potential for trouble. Outsiders who only saw the strangeness of the scenario were ignorant to the fact that even a lion could be controlled by methods most would apply to unruly children or domesticated pets such as dogs, and the fact I had successfully used them since Biba was a cub proved they worked.

However, when Biba entered this new phase of violent outbursts, none of these coping mechanisms appeared to work anymore. I'd always known in advance when Biba was going to explode, yet I could no longer predict an eruption; they were happening without warning now.

The combination of Biba's erratic and unpredictable violence, uncertainty over sale of Ebenezer Chapel's land, and separation from Jeremiah drove me into a dark netherworld of despair I hadn't seen since Jeremiah and I had established our beautiful parallel universe. With him, I felt alive; when alone, I was dead – and I was only alive for such a short space of time per month that it was hard not to feel I was essentially a reanimated corpse in Jeremiah's company. No wonder motorcars and biplanes appealed; they were tools of escape from the Hell my home life had descended into. I had intended to keep all this from Jeremiah, wary of involving him in something he was powerless to resolve, but it was unavoidable that my unhappiness began to infect my letters to him and inevitably proved to be a source of worry.

When I visited Jeremiah during this difficult period, it was impossible to hide the injuries inflicted by Biba. My hands looked like I'd been washing them in a sink full of broken glass, whilst some of the bruises made my legs resemble the skin of an apple that had fallen from the top branch of the tree and had then rolled down the side of a mountain. It wasn't a pleasant sight, but the scars of Biba's temper were internal as well as external. I felt exhausted, utterly drained of the lust for life Jeremiah had helped revitalise in me.

That bloody Jew next-door was dragging out the sale of the land and imbuing me with a genuine distaste for the way in which Jews conducted their professional affairs. No wonder they seemed to control all the businesses and international organisations that kept the world spinning; their tactics appeared to be to grind the rest of us down until we were so weary that we eventually surrendered, leaving the Jews to laugh all the way to the bank – which they already owned.

Unfortunately – and this is the saddest aspect of the whole sorry saga – it even began to affect my relationship with Jeremiah. A couple of occasions in which I visited during this testing spell saw me suffering from symptoms of fatigue that left me unable to embrace our precious time together in the usual enthusiastic manner. And perhaps picking up on this, Jeremiah overindulged on the absinthe far worse than he ever had before. It felt as though my own distress was being viewed as incompatible with the escapist womb we had always inhabited and he didn't know how to deal with it, maybe he simply sensed his own helplessness and how he couldn't deal with it when we spent so much time apart.

Yes, I had always done my best to keep my life with Biba and my life with Jeremiah as distinctly separate entities, so I suppose it might sound contradictory to now express disappointment that Jeremiah failed to be there for me when I was in a bad way as a result of something I'd done my utmost to spare him from. But I couldn't help but feel he had let me down right when I needed him more than ever.

Perhaps his behaviour – which, to be fair, provoked immense remorse in him that he later did his best to make amends for – placed the first embryonic seeds of doubt in my mind as to the long-term prospects for our relationship. These were only tiny seeds, I must stress, little more than miniscule grains in the soil that could well fail to take root at all; but the strength and certainty he'd radiated with such irresistible force in the beginning now seemed to be faltering. Maybe I'd absorbed all he had, or maybe we were now just catching each other on especially bad days. He was midway through working on a collection of poetry and admitted he was never at his sociable best when in the thick of the creative process, and I was being battered by all the factors I've already mentioned.

I guess we both required something from one another at that moment that neither of us was capable of giving. Still, that didn't mean we wouldn't be able to again; and maybe I was just so rundown I had read something into it that wasn't necessarily there. I continued to put pressure on Ebenezer Chapel to sell, and the aim remained the same.

The motorcar was something I still viewed as a frivolous plaything, but its appeal undoubtedly grew as everything else in my life seemed to be struggling. I started going for drives taking me nowhere in particular with increasing regularity, just an hour or so on an afternoon as a means of getting out of the house; and I became more confident behind the wheel as a consequence. Motorists were something of a rare breed back then, and one got to recognise fellow drivers in the neighbourhood, acknowledging each other on the road with a beep of the horn and a wave. It was a fairly exclusive club we belonged to.

Biplanes were by now becoming vital military weapons as valid as battleships or cannons, though I sensed once conflict came to an end – as it always eventually does – their use would be as pleasure vehicles in the same way the motorcar already was. I wasn't unaccustomed to flying high, having made a good few journeys in the balloon, and the thought of being back in the sky, only this time piloting myself, was one that became something of a favourite fantasy during this period. And, boy, I needed my fantasies right then.

Before the War turned in the Allies' favour, the climate for some landowners remained tense and the future still uncertain. Therefore, after what felt like decades of delay, Mr Ebenezer Chapel finally agreed to sell me twelve acres of his precious bloody land, upon which I could build Biba's outdoor enclosure. I could almost see the blood dripping from that hard Jewish stone as I wrenched the land out of his grasp, even if it came at an inevitable price. I was genuinely starting to doubt it would ever happen, and that doubt had seeped into so many other areas of my mind that madness felt just one step away.

The euphoria that overcame me as this deal was sealed seemed to put so much into perspective, and I felt the purpose of buying the land in the first place could help restore some of the magic to my life that recent strains had severely threatened. Jeremiah sounded as euphoric himself when I broke the news over the telephone – yes, the network had stretched to my part of the country at last – and the weight lifted from me infused everything with colour again. Jeremiah told me his poetry collection was to be of love poems dedicated to me and said I should regard it as his reward to me for all I had endured of late. And, as effective icing on the cake, the day the land came into my possession, the guns fell silent on the Western Front.

The one real worrying legacy of this abysmal period, however, came during my last trip to see Jeremiah on the eve of the deal being sealed. I wasn't as ill as I'd felt on the previous two visits, perhaps because I sensed success was imminent, though he himself was a tad too wild for my liking again. When we lay on the bed following lovemaking, languishing in that hazy interlude between sex and slumber, my lazy eyes glanced across the bedchamber and settled on a silhouette situated on the far side of the room, distanced from the bed. As I tried to focus upon it while slumber demanded I surrender, I swore the shape was that of Biba.

I had never seen Biba when in Jeremiah's company. This was not a good sign at all. Separate lives, that's what I had practiced and preached all along. Yet there was my curse, now even ominously casting the ugly shadow of stress that characterised home across the one corner of the world that had always been immune to it. This had been my escape, and now Biba had even invaded that.

****

I was a selfish, self-centred prick bombarding my body with vices it didn't require in the company of the woman I loved. I don't know why I did it, and then something happened that perhaps offered an explanation as to my unnecessary nihilism, a reason for my reliance on substances that were not needed when Orchidea had always negated their usage by virtue of the calming effect she had on me.

As we were wrapped around each other on the bed in the exquisite aftermath of making love, I assumed Orchidea had fallen asleep and I opened my eyes one last time before joining her. This was when I saw his sinister silhouette on top of the wardrobe – that feathered fiend who had exclusively restricted his torment of me to all those days and nights when

Orchidea was absent. He should have been in the attic, but now he had unforgivably gate-crashed our private tranquillity for the first time.

All of his gleeful prophesies of how Orchidea would quickly tire of me and shortly cast her net wider as my limited appeal began to wane re-entered my thoughts. It occurred to me that this was Devlin's doing; he may as well have been holding the bottle of absinthe to my mouth or lighting the cigar hanging from my lips. I was behaving precisely the way that would bring about Orchidea's departure and right at the very moment when instabilities in her home life required a solid shoulder for her to escape to and lean on here.

I was proving how useless I was, turning a blind eye to her problems and being no support for her at all. Devlin was right.

And now he was watching over us, piercing mine and Orchidea's bubble with his beak, observing his work with malicious relish. And I'd let him in without even knowing it.

'I simply want the world to stop where it is...and go back a bit.'

Dennis Potter, 'Brimstone and Treacle'

What Passes for Passion after a Fashion

She's still at the painted stage. She's still cladding her limbs in things that register with the desired area. She's still working at ensnaring, so is forced back into everything she packed away when she called time last time. Wiping the black from her eyes, loosening the nylon from her thighs, she unzips the boots that say 'fuck me' on their heels and slips into the bed that retains the hot and cold divide – but not for long. Her work is nearly done.

Someday soon, she will stand in that room and say what needs to be said with both lips and eyes. She will make that sacrifice. She will giggle. She will sigh. She will whisper. She will lie. She will surrender. She will erase the loving fingerprints from her skin and hire out the hallowed ground again. She will do what was once so hard because it had been so long, and she will do it because she now knows it's easy. She will give the signal and invite the assault. She will speak the lines that seal the crime. She will howl at the moon and summon the demon. And when the demon enters, she will not protest. She will acquiesce.

Come, demon. Come, slither and soil. Come, deface and defecate. Come, slide and glide over that sacred surface so recently tended by the tender and vacated by the designated dated. Come, all heaving and breathing and puffing and panting and dribbling and drooling and slavering and snivelling. Come, creep and crawl. Come, scratch and sniff. Come, lick and kiss. Come, smack and slap. Come, grip and grab. Come, from tongue to toe, from hole to hole. Come, liquid and lather. Come, swallow and shower.

She will still air the request for the demon not to stop. She has yet to get to where she asks him to slow down, a plea inspired by fear he will release what risks mixing and mingling with the last tenant's leftovers. She will recycle the illusion of a rule with an exception and recite the script that convinces with conviction. It doesn't matter. It's not important. It's no big deal. Many have been here before and many have signed their names on the door. It's just another signature to add to the list, nothing more and nothing less when feathers are needed for the nest.

The demon strips the ceremony of all meaning, but with her blessing. Why give meaning to a means to an end? There *is* no Special One. There is just settling for the best of a bad bunch because she has what he wants and if she gives in and gives up she might secure security. Wrench it from the stars and drag it down to earth – boring, businesslike earth. Drain away the magic and reduce it to the mechanics. Once, she skimmed the ceiling of Heaven, but now she is satisfied with the lie of the land.

Part II
...falling out

Separate Lives

Clocks stop and gather dust in the home of Jeremiah Meadowbrook, whereas beyond its doors time speeds-up, passing by at a phenomenal pace. Well, it does pass faster the older you get, doesn't it? Women vote, Irishman kills Irishman, hemlines rise, stock-markets fall, silent stars acquire the power of speech, and jazz spins from every turntable – all in the blink of a raven's beady black eye.

Conan Blackcastle is once more a man-about-town, only now the town has changed. All of the playboys drive motorcars, escorting flappers to subterranean dives pumping out the sound of New Orleans, melting pots in which faces are black as well as white and nobody cares what school you attended. Blackcastle is having the time of his life as the senior ladies man of the racy new set, revered and replicated by his younger devotees to whom he is a hero, guru and inspiration.

Absinthe is yesterday's escapist substance; cocaine is the drug of choice for the hip and the happening, reflecting the new speed of life.

Ironically, Blackcastle in a way has become the society successor to the kind of figure Lady Sarah Stabinbach had been in his youth – drawing bright young things around him as high-priest and mentor to the mores that again govern designs for life now arms have been laid down. He hosts parties, though nobody would have referred to his hedonistic gatherings as 'salons'; that is such an antiquated term, and besides, these events have no pretensions to political discourse; everyone is there to dance, snort, fuck and forget. Blackcastle has survived and prospered from the turbulent turning of a world no longer at war yet not quite sure which of the myriad options available it will opt for.

Conan Blackcastle sees little of Jeremiah Meadowbrook nowadays. Not only is Blackcastle busy as the uncrowned king of the social scene, but Meadowbrook is too preoccupied with deeper emotional matters to devote time to what he regards as the transient frivolities of society. Blackcastle has undergone his own dark explorations of the soul and has emerged back into the sunlight with a renewed appetite for life, a refreshed recognition that yesterday and tomorrow are beyond our control whereas today is all we can dictate – and he is determined to maximise the pleasure today can offer.

Meadowbrook, on the other hand, has consciously expanded the withdrawal from the superficial that began with entombing himself at home with Orchidea. The disadvantage of this tactic is that there is no break from the introspective isolation, for Orchidea's absence has been extended by circumstances he cannot affect. He has been a helpless witness to Orchidea's struggles, dispirited by separation and neutered by an awareness of his own powerlessness.

Meadowbrook is a hedonist exclusively in private now – the saddest, most destructive form of hedonism imaginable; the days when he would entertain a crowd at a society event are long gone. He has little interest in jazz, let alone cocaine, and has no desire to own a motorcar. The news that Orchidea now owns one and promised to drive to town in it intrigues him considerably, but it doesn't persuade him to also invest in the internal combustion engine. There'd only be one place he'd want to drive to if he owned a car, and that destination remains out of bounds.

Orchidea may have finally bought a dozen acres from her neighbour, but the planning and construction of the outdoor enclosure for Biba is one more time-consuming task. And this task is occupying her to the extent that she doesn't even appear to have the time to visit him.

****

Note to Self – My girlfriend has just taken up flying lessons, inspired by Amy Johnston and Amelia Earhart. She's already purchased her very own biplane and tells me she's been up in the air several times with her instructor, a former fighter pilot who apparently flew a Sopwith Camel across the Western Front with the RFC. While I'm excited for her to have such an extravagant hobby, I worry that the amateur aviators (virtually all men) it will bring her into contact with might prove a more dashing and attractive bunch to her than me. Am I just being paranoid?

Self to Note – It certainly is an extravagant hobby, without a doubt, and you seem to suggest it's a passion of your girlfriend that you yourself are excluded from. If you feel you'd like to be a part of this newfound fad, perhaps it might be opportune to ask her if you could accompany her on a flight if/when she acquires a pilot's licence. As with motorcars, aeroplanes appear to have become another luxury toy for the affluent that attract a certain kind of man – rich playboy types always looking for the latest thrill-seeking craze. One could view them as a self-indulgent frivolous lot; but, if they're old enough, they may well have played their part in the War and have earned the right to enjoy themselves in their own privileged way.

At the same time, it's understandable that you're bound to feel a little left-out and that your girlfriend mixing with such men might mean she is tempted to spend more hours in their company than you're entirely comfortable with. Despite the fame of Amy Johnston and Amelia Earhart, women in such circles remain comparatively rare, and the novelty of your girlfriend's sudden arrival into their world could well spark some pissing contests between the men, leading to more than one of them plotting to get into her knickers.

It depends how much trust you place in your girlfriend's faithfulness and whether or not she loves you so emphatically that her eye is incapable of wandering and she cannot be so easily swayed by a flash posh-boy pilot. As you're clearly not married, I surmise you don't live together; this implies she has a life outside of your relationship, and unless she's a teacher at an all-girl's boarding school she must therefore inevitably come into contact with other men on as regular a basis as you yourself must come into contact with other women. If you love each other with equal devotion, infidelity should not be an issue on either side.

Alas, you know how men's minds work. Perhaps that's half the problem for you when she's put herself into an environment abundant in the bastards.

When confirmation came that Orchidea had successfully purchased the land she'd earmarked for Biba's outdoor enclosure, work on the ambitious project could finally begin and Jeremiah Meadowbrook felt that this was the key development which would take the relationship onto the next level. With the lion no longer a resident of Orchidea's actual house, he should be able to visit her at last, free from all the safety concerns that had served as a block to him reversing the routine that had defined them as a couple from day one.

Orchidea had kept him updated on developments as the land purchase edged closer, with the urgency of the news relayed to him via the most immediate medium, the telephone. They still wrote letters on a virtually daily basis, but the days when Orchidea would confirm the time and date of her visits by sending a telegraph were all-but gone now. Nothing conveyed a message as quickly as the telephone. They had already established a fixed time when they'd speak on the invaluable appliance every evening, but Orchidea started calling Meadowbrook randomly whenever it appeared she was close to sealing the deal. It was clearly as important for both of them that this land purchase went through and the time they spent together could be extended way beyond anything they'd known so far.

When the news was broken to Meadowbrook that it was at last a done deal, he was ecstatic for Orchidea not merely in relation to their relationship. He had seen for himself the physical damage done to her recently when Biba's violent outbursts had been getting worse. The cuts, scratches, bruises and bites were so bad that he'd advised her to see a surgeon; but she was convinced having enough additional land attached to her home so that Biba could live entirely separately without inflicting any further harm to her and her servants was the only solution. None of that would have been possible without persuading her obstinate neighbour to part with his property, but she had finally done it.

Although the completion of this task would be something Meadowbrook would feel the benefits of, the actual work itself was one of Orchidea's exclusive preoccupations from which he would remain excluded. During the planning and construction of Biba's enclosure, Biba would continue to be Orchidea's ill-tempered housemate – with all the same old problems that situation had always entailed proving to be as exhausting as ever. Pleasingly, as work began to gather pace on the actual building (apparently assisted by Orchidea's loyal handyman, old Sam), Orchidea's enthusiasm was writ large with every letter and telephone-call that updated Meadowbrook on events. He was as desperate for her plans to succeed as she was – and it now seemed as though that might actually be poised to come about.

Rather worryingly, however, Meadowbrook began to detect a hitherto-unseen tone of obsessive fanaticism in Orchidea's daily missives on the subject. Orchidea was overseeing the work in the manner of a building-site foreman, but it soon became evident that the project being given the go-ahead had exposed a hyperactive strain of overenthusiastic neurosis in her that appeared to be dictating her day-to-day existence at the expense of everything else. He'd never known her be quite like this before, and it unnerved him.

Yes, Meadowbrook could understand her desire to ensure the work was done right – after all, it was the long-awaited fruition of something for which she'd endured years of unimaginable anguish; but it was apparent the operation to create an outdoor home for Biba seemed to have taken possession of her to the point where it was the only thing in life that mattered.

Naturally, he cut her some slack. Having still to experience Biba in the flesh, he could only envisage the strange scenario from all that had been relayed to him by Orchidea; the shocking scars on Orchidea's hands, arms and legs were proof enough that this was a unique problem to which any potential solution deserved the greatest amount of dedication and concentration on her part. It was bound to loom larger in her consciousness than the few precious moments she was able to grab with Meadowbrook.

Yet, he couldn't help but become concerned that she was throwing herself into the project with such all-consuming gusto that it both demanded and exhausted her fulltime attention, forcing other interests to be put on ice until it was completed and draining her ability to devote any time to them at all. It was as though she was incapable of spreading her commitments and could only focus on one thing, with that one thing being something she gave her all to while it consumed her.

Perhaps this was the first real sighting of an aspect to Orchidea's personality that Jeremiah Meadowbrook had previously been blind to – the fact she embraced a new obsession with such exuberant verve that it put every other concern very much in the shade before the shade then slowly erased it from her list of priorities for good.

As he observed events from the distant sidelines, denied any hands-on participation, it was difficult for him to regard the project as a shared passion; he did his best to be involved by following its progress on the outside and repeatedly giving her words of encouragement, but it wasn't the same as being there beside her to watch the enclosure taking shape; and his presence could at least have presented her with a break from the obsession that might have been advisable.

He hated himself for doing so, but it was undeniable that he began to wonder (with some considerable anxiety) if this was the way Orchidea operated when a fresh passion took possession of her.

Did she always stumble upon something new that fired her imagination at a moment when there appeared to be no other comparable stimulation, and then abruptly clear the decks of everything that had preoccupied her prior to that discovery, regardless of whether or not something amongst that everything was worth preserving? Did she recklessly dive into the new and immerse herself in it until her attention span expired and the new then took on all the jaded qualities of the old? If there was that kind of permanent restlessness in her, one that was constantly on the look-out for the next source of stimulation, what would happen once Biba's enclosure was completed? Did this restlessness mean when that next source of stimulation came along, she'd simply bail out of whatever she had committed herself to before as if it had never happened?

If this was indeed the case, such a butterfly-like, ephemeral attitude to life essentially meant Orchidea would never fully enjoy the long-term benefits of any passion that captured her imagination and controlled it with the kind of manic vigour this one did. She'd never be settled or satisfied because she appeared to lack the emotional maturity to appreciate the eternal value of something good when she had it in front of her. It was almost a juvenile sense of deriving a thrill from a here today-gone tomorrow fad that would rapidly become boring until shortly superseded by another here today-gone tomorrow fad.

Such an approach was fine for an artist whose reluctance to remain trapped within a successful formula infused their art with a constant freshness and prevented stagnation and repetition; but if applied to a non-artistic life it had the potential to be disastrous – not just for Orchidea herself, but for anyone else she had drawn into her orbit. The damage to others could be severe, but would Orchidea's recklessness even take note of that?

As this unsettling theory occurred to Jeremiah Meadowbrook – and that's all it was, a theory – the frightening thought that the swift progress of his romantic involvement with Orchidea could possibly be bracketed along with all of her other short-term obsessions was a cause of intense concern.

What if the speed of their coupling had actually been an example of the way in which Orchidea threw her lot in with everything that moved her to act? What if Meadowbrook was merely the latest in a long line of temporary obsessions that had characterised her life before she had even met him? And, if so, what did that say about the prospects for their future life together? But as he could feel the distant rumblings of that possibility while he tuned in to the ongoing saga of Biba's enclosure, Meadowbrook did his best to banish such unpleasant thoughts from his head. And then she announced she was going to start taking flying lessons.

Again, this was something he encouraged her to go for as he felt it might help distract her from the draining subject of Biba whilst she lived the life separate from his own; he wanted her to be doing something in his absence that could provide her with some sort of enjoyment. Yet, he was equally paranoid that embarking upon such an adventurous hobby would distance her even further.

As much as he detested such thoughts, he began to visualise the pilots she'd encounter when taking her flying lessons; he inevitably saw them as handsome, charming, confident playboys who may well appear exciting alternatives to him in Orchidea's eyes. His imagination began to concoct silly scenarios in which one pilot in particular would befriend her, a friendship which once established would then create a conducive climate for said pilot to invite her on a platonic picnic or perhaps a punt down the river or a meal at his favourite restaurant or a drink at his country club or eventually...yes...a fuck in his bed.

Utterly groundless imaginative speculation, of course, but Meadowbrook was fired by frustration at being left out of Orchidea's latest pastime, something matched by his sense of helplessness at not being able to contribute to the cause that bordered on obsession.

The building of Biba's enclosure was one more project from which he was excluded, one more that he merely experienced vicariously because he was shut out from the practical reality of it. Biba's enclosure was something he had recognised as the first step onto the next stage of their relationship, but the time Orchidea devoted to it ironically postponed that next stage for what felt like indefinitely; the actual planning and construction seemed to take longer than the interminable time it took for her to buy the bloody land to build it upon.

Throughout this painful period, his sole contact with Orchidea came via the letter or the telephone; being starved of physical contact with her was unbearable, so he hoped the collection of love poems he'd written for her would serve as a reminder as to the place of their union in the scheme of things. He'd shelved the novel he was midway through in order to switch to verse because he felt the need to again make Orchidea aware of how much she was loved overrode commercial concerns.

She was well aware of the book's contents. He even recited a couple of the poems over the telephone to her. She expressed excitement over its publication and her pre-publication prediction was 'It'll be lovely.' He had no cause to doubt the sincerity in her prophesy; after all, ever since they'd first got together, showering each other in gifts, especially of the unique, one-off personalised variety, had become a hallmark of their relationship. Dedicating his last novel to her had moved her to tears; being delivered her telegraphed reaction upon receiving it was one of the most cherished moments of his life. Why should he have anticipated anything other than an identical response when he had slaved over verse composed in her honour?

Yet, smack bang in the middle of Orchidea's new obsession, the latest product of a union that had transformed her for the better was greeted like the unwanted inherited artefacts of an unloved deceased relative.

I Am Not Worthy

At times, I'm almost convinced it didn't really happen and that it was all in my imagination. Then I go over events in my head and I tell myself it *did* happen. To receive a collection of poetry dedicated to me that sings my praises in the style of previous praises from my beloved has actually shaken me the day after I proved myself unworthy of such praise. I cannot confess my crime and break Jeremiah's heart, but I have to stress that I am overwhelmed to the point of shame by such an intense, loving tribute. I do not deserve it. I have soiled the purity of what we had, yet to tell him is too hard. *How* to tell him is hard enough.

How the hell do I explain that a man came to me in the night, materialised out of thin air, and ravished me in a way that confirmed I yearned to be ravished? After all, I willed him to come. I wanted him. But I don't know why. He means nothing to me. This spectre of imaginary masculinity morphed into a woman midway through ravishing me and I wanted her even more. I woke myself up furiously masturbating, and both the man and the woman were gone. But they had been there, of that I was certain.

They had befriended me earlier on the day they appeared in my bedchamber. I wasn't sure if they were a married couple or brother and sister, but the moment I met them I saw in them exactly what they wanted to do to me. I didn't raise any objections because I now knew I was capable of giving them what they wanted – what *I* wanted.

Oh, Christ. Am I at that familiar stage again? Have I reached that damnable point I always seem to reach whenever life is good, that point when I press the eject button and jettison myself from what has revived me for fear it cannot last, when the desire to end it before the magic dissipates and dissolves dictates my actions? I supposedly do this to appease Biba and to avoid getting hurt, but I do so without once considering how much hurt I may be inflicting on others who have invested heavily in what I co-founded. It is self-preservation manifested as profound selfishness.

Am I now back where I've been before, when temptation that carries the seeds of destruction appears before me and I surrender to it, despite knowing all-too well that it will lay waste to everything I hold dear? Jeremiah doesn't deserve this, but I can never help myself from doing it; I do it every bloody time. Yet, this was the one time I thought I'd escape the habit. And as I torture myself with the whole business, I look across at Biba and swear he's smiling.

****

There had been a change in me without my initially knowing it, a change that altered the face I showed to the world and altered how the world reacted to it. I became aware of this change gradually. When I first met Jeremiah, there had been no change, which I suppose makes it all the more remarkable he noticed me. Yet, he saw something no man had seen in a very long time, and I was bowled over by the astonishing fact that someone I had been attracted to first in print and then in the flesh actually wanted me. I hadn't even released my old sidekick from her dungeon at this point, but Jeremiah somehow detected her faint, distant traces on me.

Yet when his interest finally encouraged me to release her, being back in her skin wasn't necessarily an instant fit; like a new pair of shoes, I had to get used to wearing her before I felt entirely comfortable. Once I did, not only was I able to enter into the most electrifying physical relationship of my life with Jeremiah; I also discovered the impact of this relationship on me was radiating something to others I was coming into contact with.

Okay, I know she had warned me.

'I suppose the problem now is that if you keep me free and don't stick me back in that bleedin' cell, I may well start attracting other fellers on your behalf.'

Those were her very words, but I seriously doubted her prediction when she made it. Jeremiah noticing me was such an aberration from what had become the norm for me, such a freak occurrence, that I had no reason to assume it was going to keep happening once we got together. Besides, I was so consumed by falling head-over-heels in love, I wasn't aware any other man existed on the planet. I *had* my man. I didn't want anyone else's.

But love leaves strange fingerprints. It switches the light back on in your soul so that the illumination streams through the windows and shines on everybody you encounter. Some of those you encounter react to it in ways you hadn't anticipated when you were still ignorant of the subliminal signals you were sending out. My long-standing reputation as that odd widow-woman with the lion had provoked fear and suspicion both *of* me and *in* me, minimising face-to-face contact with the outside world.

Yet suddenly I seemed to be meeting a lot of people, and not only had the confidence I'd gained from my relationship with Jeremiah made me genial towards these people; they now appeared to respond in kind. Some – needless to say, *men* – responded in ways that took me by surprise. I had forgotten what it was like, but I enjoyed it. It was harmless and it was nice having my improved mood reflected back at me and people being pleasant to me. I wasn't used to that.

Because of Jeremiah, I was smiling a lot more. I was happy, and nothing transmits happiness to other people quite like a smile. Strangers were taken aback when they met this bright, breezy beam of sunshine after expecting to encounter a morose, moody recluse. Granted, I had indeed *been* a morose, moody recluse for several years before Jeremiah, locked away with Biba and as much of an exile from polite society as Biba himself. But the world and everyone in it looked very different from the moment I began absorbing Jeremiah's belief in me; my perception of the world went from monochrome to colour overnight as he imbued me with the self-confidence that had been absent for so long that I could hold its absence being as responsible for my exile as Biba.

The day after Jeremiah and I wrapped ourselves around one another on his bed, I felt that everybody I saw on the way home could read upon my face the story of the night before. I especially felt it when we stopped at the coaching inn for the horses to be changed; I couldn't have undergone the sensation of being naked and exposed during that hour's pause in the journey any more than if I'd stripped down to my birthday suit and danced my way through the inn itself. I also sensed the same sensation of being an open book in the way my handmaidens looked at me when I strolled into the house.

Right there and then, I was embarrassed, feeling awkward and uncomfortable with such a response, probably because I was so unaccustomed to having something positive to radiate that these reactions unsettled me. Also, it had felt like a clandestine coming-together that was to be shared with no one else, so believing the truth was blatantly obvious in a mere cursory glance at my countenance was akin to an unwelcome invasion of my purest privacy. By the time it came to the day after Jeremiah and I had first slept together, however, I had a definite spring in my step and felt as though I wanted to clamber up to the roof of the house and declare my love to the whole world. I had something to celebrate at last, and it would seem the whole world knew about it simply by looking at me.

Surely – and not so slowly – I accepted there had been a change in the way I presented myself to the outside world, however unconsciously I did so; but I didn't mind. I wasn't ashamed of my new love, and if it left its evident mark on me, so be it. I had nothing to hide. I just hadn't anticipated that these traces would manifest themselves as luminous transmissions to all who came into contact with me during the high summer of my romance with Jeremiah. Several offers were laid before me on several occasions, but I dismissed them with amused flattery; I was committed to Jeremiah, though attracting attention from other men was undeniably something of a morale-boost. It didn't matter if these offers came from decrepit old rakes in the nearest village or naive, testosterone-filled builders beginning work on constructing Biba's outdoor enclosure; the fact they noticed me at all confirmed to me that Jeremiah noticing I existed wasn't some misguided compliment on his part.

It told me I was present and correct as a living, breathing woman who still had the ability to catch the male eye – and that was something I'd failed to acknowledge for years.

I suppose this factor, one that continued throughout my relationship with Jeremiah and began to gradually affect me the more it seeped into my consciousness, was responsible for putting the idea in my head that maximising my reborn sensuality for the sake of pure pleasure wasn't such a terribly immoral notion as long as it didn't make its way back to Jeremiah. Just days before I even contemplated such a notion, it would have been utterly unthinkable, but this only really occurred to me as a possibility when he was at his most selfishly wretched as future husband material. I had expressed my concern that his indulgences implied he would end up killing himself and he had flippantly replied 'That's the plan', sending a chill down my spine. It made me feel I was merely an obstacle to his intended suicide.

I was ill that day as it was, and being married to a temperamental artist suddenly seemed like a far-from desirable prospect for the first time. Was I prepared for everything it entailed if this had been a premonition of what might lay in wait for me? His behaviour angered and depressed me so much that it seemed to snap me out of the lovesick daze I'd been in for a long time around him; it more or less persuaded me to look farther afield when there were still plenty of offers on the table, almost as though doing so was an act of petulant revenge.

Why not take advantage of these offers, eh? Well, I was only taking advantage of them in my imagination, to be honest; and the more outrageously wicked the fantasy was, the greater the arousal; I even went to the shameful extent of imagining I was being fucked by someone else when having sex with Jeremiah. But actually doing it for real? I wasn't certain about that. Could I really do it and have a clear conscience afterwards? I could lie, I suppose. A woman can do that.

Jeremiah need never know, I told myself at moments when the internal debate raged, and chances are any encounters would probably amount to nothing of any substance, anyway. It would be an utterly loveless exercise, merely giving me further confidence in my newfound physical persona as a desirable, sexual animal; it wouldn't involve love and therefore wouldn't impinge on my relationship with him. That was the way I approached it; that was the mindset I had slipped into, convincing myself it was okay. *Was* it okay to think that way? I thought so.

Yes, at the back of mind I knew it was bad; but that was what excited me, I guess – the thrill of the forbidden. The consequences of enticing the forbidden into my bedchamber didn't enter my head, of course; they rarely do. But it was still a big, brave step from thinking it to doing it.

It was only later – when it was far too late – that it occurred to me that enacting such a fantasy was terribly wrong. It was an awful abuse of trust and a careless discarding of a deep, meaningful vow I had made in a moment I should have regarded as sacred. So, what if I had been prompted into reservations by some worrying signs? They could have been attended to and resolved. I had certainly endured far worse headaches at the hands of men who were way beyond helping.

But considering 'cheating' on Jeremiah was ironically the debut stepping stone of a slippery slope leading all the way back towards the kind of men who *weren't* Jeremiah Meadowbrook, and they knew they could deceive me because they wore the guise of the familiar and not the dangerously different. It was me reverting to a long-discarded type, behaving like a young, gay and carefree maiden simply because I was suddenly being treated like one. Yes, it was a nice, flattering feeling, but I wasn't what those men assumed I was. It was a lie. I was spoken for and I loved the man who spoke for me. I knew he wouldn't dream of doing behind my back what I was contemplating doing behind his.

I had oh-so quickly forgotten where all this bloody confidence had come from – the loving, beautiful union that had transformed my life for the better.

Anyway, having persuaded myself infidelity was not a crime (in thought, if not in deed) I still didn't go looking for it. I just figured that if it found me, I wouldn't object as long as I was attracted to the man making the approach. And with me being distanced from Jeremiah for so many days between visits, I wondered where the harm would be in simply accepting an offer to have dinner at the house of a man interested in me. I'd received plenty and turned them all down because it felt wrong. But *would* it be wrong – just a meal, I mean? It wouldn't have to develop beyond platonic friendship, would it?

I was awfully lonely so many evenings and Jeremiah was so far away, so why couldn't I do something like that? I had acquired an outgoing urge that craved company; and if the opportunity for something else presented itself to me at a moment when I was in the mood, would it really be so terrible? This thought kept my mind open to the idea.

And so to the couple in question...

Ah, yes – that strange, mysterious couple who gifted me a moral conundrum. They materialised before me one morning when I was overseeing the foundations of Biba's enclosure. They wandered into my field of vision and introduced themselves in a casual manner that implied they were passing through the neighbourhood, expressing curiosity as to what was going on. Ordinarily, I avoided contact with wandering strangers for fear that Biba might appear and take it upon himself to maul them; but I had deliberately locked Biba indoors whilst I supervised the work on his intended new home, and I was caught unawares when this couple enquired as to events playing out before them.

I did my best to explain what was happening without alarming them to the possibility of a dangerous wild animal suddenly gate-crashing the scenario. I was pleasant towards them as I was now pleasant towards everybody, and their response to my subconscious sunbeams exposed the dangerous consequences of this new approach to the public.

They had a wildly sensuous, gypsy-like charisma to them, but free of Romany grubbiness. The woman spoke with an indefinable European accent. Dark-haired, dark-eyed and in possession of fulsome red lips that had a glistening gloss implying she had just drunk something warm and wet, she undressed me with a look that curiously didn't provoke a blush or embarrassment on my part.

The man bore a striking facial resemblance to her, albeit wearing a thick black beard as a brooding concession to testosterone, and he groped me with his eyes, squeezing every erogenous area with such intense hunger that I came close to fainting. It was obvious they both wanted me; I believed it wholly, and that belief was something I had never really had before. They wanted me; I wanted them. Why not? I glanced across at the house and saw Biba staring through the window at me. If his eyes could speak, they were telling me to invite the couple indoors there and then.

But the couple went on their way a few minutes later and I was left alone, damp and trembling from the effects of an erotic assault in which not a hand was laid upon me. They never left my thoughts for the rest of the day; fantasies flashed through my head and tormented me with an added ingredient of guilt, especially when I spoke to Jeremiah via the telephone before retiring for the evening. But even then, when I was belatedly reminded why what I was thinking was unforgivably sinful, I still couldn't get them out of my head. And once I was in bed, I willed them into the room.

The man was alone when he appeared. I remained rigid beneath the bedcovers, watching him disrobe as though I was some sort of Peeping Tom and he was unaware he was being observed. He didn't say a word. He was built from the same bricks used to construct the proverbial shithouse, in possession of an incredible physique, the kind that suggested he regularly engaged in the most strenuous strain of masculine labour – probably carrying heavy weights on his shoulders. I had never seen a naked man with such a body. And you know that expression, 'hung-like-a-horse'? I think it was first said with him in mind. He was standing proud and he was *huge.* I wondered how on earth I would fit it in me, but I was willing to try.

He looked me in the eye for the first time and smiled, approaching the bed with a cocksure arrogance that implied I had drawn the winning ticket in the lottery of life. I had a feeling foreplay was out of the question. He whipped off the sheets, pushed opened my legs and pierced my fidelity as though lancing a boil with a harpoon. I don't know how long it lasted, but it was hard, pounding and exhausting fucking utterly devoid of love, like being pumped by a freshly-oiled machine. And I enjoyed every second of it, coming half-a-dozen times as he failed to pause once. His energy seemed inhumanly insatiable.

When he finally pulled out and showered me in the steaming, creamy fruits of his labour, I paused for breath, wiped the discharge from the target and saw he had become his female double, licking those fulsome lips in anticipation of a feast. The body before me now was hairless and curvaceous, albeit as well-toned as it had been in its male form. I was too shattered to react and declare this was unfamiliar territory to me. I was laid on a plate for her, utterly helpless and incapable of resistance; she was free to do whatever she wished to do to me, so she did it.

The moment our eyes had met earlier in the day, I knew she wanted me, and she certainly knew what she was doing once she got her hands on me. The mirror image of my own body brushing up against me was an unusual, strange sensation; I was accustomed the way the bodies of the opposite sex slotted together perfectly. But she had the same appetite for my quivering, perspiring frame as he had, and her hunger for satisfying that appetite was no less relentless in its execution.

He had the hard, tough, hairy hide of a bear; she felt soft, smooth and silky; it was arousing in a completely different way, but she received an identical response from me as the one her male incarnation had received. I eventually became so tired whilst she was pleasuring the pair of us that I believe I fell asleep with her head buried between my legs and the serpent in her mouth still exploring the landscape deep inside me. That's the last thing I can remember of the encounter before waking-up wanking, anyway.

And then the first edition of Jeremiah's love poems was delivered to the door – an entire collection of praise for a woman who had just proven herself unworthy of it. No wonder I felt so overwhelmed by (and undeserving of) the gesture. It was too much. I was not the person I had been or the person he thought I was.

Oh, Christ. Why did we have to be separated all the time? None of this would have happened if we could have been together permanently and the ache of separation hadn't left me so susceptible to temptation. No wonder Biba seemed uncharacteristically happy that day, so devoid of temper tantrums. He hated it when I left him to visit Jeremiah and he must have been hoping I wouldn't be leaving him to do it again. He'd probably heard me screaming in the throes of sexual frenzy the night before and figured that sealed it. God, I'd never felt guilt like this before.

****

Jeremiah broke with tradition and called me on the telephone that afternoon to ask if the book had been delivered. A handmaiden answered it and I asked her to tell him I wasn't available. I just couldn't face it. He rang again later and this time I decided I had better speak to him; I didn't want him to think I was avoiding him, not when he was so keen to gauge my response. Alas, he didn't receive the response he was clearly expecting.

I actually found it hard to speak, to articulate what I was feeling. There so were many unfamiliar silences at both ends of the line it was agonising. He was shocked into speechlessness by my reaction, whereas I struggled to express myself without confessing what had happened the night before. It was awful. He couldn't understand the feelings it had provoked in me and rightly pointed out that the sentiment behind the book was no different from all the other personalised presents he had produced throughout our relationship; but it was the most extravagant of them all and it had arrived at the worst possible time.

'You sound as though you want to end it,' he said. *'Do you want to end it?'*

No, I replied – and I didn't. But I was scared. I was just such a bloody mess at that moment. Everything that had dragged me down of late – Biba, the land sale, Jeremiah's own recent lapses into self-indulgent nihilism, and (of course) guilt over what had happened in my bedchamber less than twenty-four hours earlier – swarmed around my dizzy head like a thousand chattering voices I couldn't shut my ears to.

Flashbacks of being ravished by the husband & wife (or brother & sister) wouldn't leave me be, and the memory sickened me. I had committed myself to something big that I suddenly felt unworthy of delivering, and as my courage deserted me I was overcome by the urge to withdraw back to my isolated little hole with just Biba for company. I couldn't handle a book proclaiming how wonderful I was right now, even if the small handful of poems I'd managed to read in it were lovely and moving. If they'd been written by Shelley to Mary, I would have hailed them as masterpieces; but they were written by Jeremiah to me, and none of his sentiments rang true at that moment.

I wasn't a Goddess and I wasn't a Saint, but it seemed Jeremiah was painting me as one in every poem. There was a voice telling me the person I was with him wasn't really the real me after all, that she was a charlatan who I had allowed to get out of control; yes, she'd warned me it might happen when I released her, but now I was wondering if it was time to escort her back to that dungeon. Regardless of what Jeremiah had rhapsodised about in verse, the reality away from the printed page was that I no longer wanted to be kissed or touched or fucked by anyone. I was disgusted with myself.

By the end of the telephone conversation, we appeared to have reached an uneasy understanding, but it felt like something had changed. A wall had appeared between us that had never been there before, and the ramifications of that telephone conversation would sadly dictate our discourse forevermore. Jesus, how could we have got to this point – *us?* When I put down the receiver, I cried my eyes out for hours. I was as if I had built a bonfire of every affectionate trinket representing our relationship, with that book sitting on the top – and although I hadn't lit it, I had a match permanently glued to the palm of my hand.

****

Focusing on beginning the building of Biba's enclosure was one way of coping with the emotional fallout of events, as was seeking pleasure in pastimes that didn't involve being ravished by strangers. When it came to the former, old Sam was entrusted with the task of recruiting the labour force, which turned out to be led by his nephew. I had already devised the layout of the enclosure, which was along the lines of the kind of thing London Zoo would have recognised. I wanted Biba to have room to run and to have plenty shelter from the elements, but in order to ensure the safety of oblivious visitors, the fencing surrounding the enclosure had to be tall, strong and secure.

Endlessly modifying the design of the enclosure had occupied a good deal of my time whilst waiting for my tight-fisted Jew of a neighbour to sell me the bloody land, but whilst the delay may have driven me to despair it at least enabled me to get the enclosure exactly how I wanted it – on paper at least. Now I just had to rely on the builders, carpenters and landscape gardeners to bring those plans to life.

As for pleasure, the motorcar grew as a source of brief escape from home-life. Visiting Jeremiah was always something that took up a hell of a lot of time and kept me away from Biba for at least twenty-four hours, whereas I could nip out for a drive for just an hour or so and feel utterly refreshed. And, naturally, the more time I spent behind the wheel the more confident I became as a motorist; I even came to believe driving to Jeremiah's wouldn't be such a far-fetched test of my nerve after all, even if the prospect of a visit filled me with uneasiness in the light of what had happened.

And then there was the biplane!

I bit the bullet and revisited my fondness for air travel that I'd once expressed via the hot air balloon, inspired by the nearby airfield. When I purchased an aeroplane of my very own, I housed it in one of the hangars there and secured the services of a pilot who'd flown in the War as an instructor. My previous experience as a passenger in the balloon helped, as it showed I had a head for heights, but nothing could have prepared me for that first flight in a biplane!

The rush and the excitement that overwhelmed me was such a tonic after everything I'd been through of late, and I began having weekly lessons, determined to relive the thrill as regular as was possible. There really was nothing like it. Even if my presence there was something of a novelty, I could point to the likes of Amelia Earhart and Amy Johnston as proof women could fly just as well as men. This to me was a far more important indication of progress than winning the right to vote.

Building the enclosure, which covered around ten of the twelve acres I'd bought from Ebenezer Chapel, was no easy task. Some might have said I'd been a little too elaborate in my design, but I had to bear in mind that this would now be Biba's home after spending his entire life living indoors with me. Yes, he loved nothing more than being outdoors, but he had never actually *lived* outdoors before. The aim was to eventually bar him from the house completely, so I had to make sure his new home contained every amenity a wild animal of his stature required in order to live as content and fulfilled a life as he could ever receive in captivity.

I was stuck with Biba for good, but there had to be some sort of rebalancing of our living arrangements if I was to achieve any sort of sustained life that he didn't dominate completely.

I admit I was fastidious about it, but I felt I owed Biba this. I couldn't abandon him; that would have been inconceivable. He was part of me; he had *come* from me. We had an unbreakable bond, and however much he had asserted his natural instincts in the most ferocious manner recently, I knew he couldn't help it. My relationship with Jeremiah and the absences from home that relationship required had unsettled him considerably, perhaps leading to the increased violence of his temper tantrums of late. He believed he owned me, and wouldn't tolerate any competition, even competition that had yet to enter his own personal orbit.

We had a symbiotic understanding that meant not only could I anticipate his movements, but he could anticipate mine as well; he picked-up on my mood and seemed to sense when I was troubled – which kept him quiet – and when I was happy – which provoked further aggression. If I was happy, he interpreted this as me being distracted from him, and he was right. But I believed if he saw I was being distracted by something that was for his benefit, he might calm down a little.

The time needed to ensure the builders, carpenters and landscape gardeners did the job properly by supervising them and tolerating no lapses in the standard of the work did take possession of me to an extent. With relations between Jeremiah and me still delicate, I needed a substitute passion for a distraction, and the enclosure became it. Perhaps obsession might be a more opportune word than passion, for it did dictate my every waking day for a while. Driving out for an hour in the motorcar was a temporary release from the stress; taking a weekly flying lesson was another.

But for the rest of my time, building that bloody enclosure was all I was concerned about. After a faltering start that necessitated me laying down the law to the builders and making it clear I would be as severe as any site foreman if unhappy with the progress, they realised I was serious and got their act together. I then began to start spending more hours out in the car buying furniture for the house, planning for how it would look when Biba no longer lived there. And this also put me back into a far more confident state of mind where neglected aspects of my life were concerned – like Jeremiah.

Song of the Swan

'Can I come and see you next week?'

That was the question Orchidea put to Jeremiah out-of-the-blue on the telephone. Work on Biba's enclosure was not yet near enough to completion for the lion to be safely left to roam alone, so Orchidea would have to rely on her trusty staff once more, despite Biba's erratic behaviour of late. But it had been a long separation, the longest they had ever endured in-person, and Orchidea reckoned they needed to remind each other of who they were together before they both forgot. If anything could do that, reuniting could. Needless to say, Jeremiah struggled to contain his enthusiasm regarding the request, but the minute he put down the receiver, he was struck by a panic that was new to him.

Orchidea's seemingly confident attitude contrasted with Meadowbrook's nervousness. Their roles now appeared to have been reversed from the position they had taken in the beginning. Aware he had made a bit of an idiot of himself during Orchidea's previous couple of visits, Meadowbrook had taken her lengthy absence from his home as a kind of unspoken (and deserved) punishment. Yearning to hold her again was superseded by gratitude that she had decided to come back, and this gratitude shaped his approach to the reunion. He fretted over her visit in a way he never had before, conscious he had to be on his best behaviour and curb the self-indulgences that had increased throughout the period he had been left with no option but to settle for Devlin as company.

Since the disaster of the poetry collection, they had maintained contact via the telephone and the written word, though the book was something neither of them mentioned again; it was so associated with unhappiness for them both that they avoided it completely, as though it had never happened. But it *had* happened, and it was because of that error of judgement that Jeremiah Meadowbrook anticipated Orchidea's visit with an anxiety that had always been alien to him where she was concerned.

Even though they hadn't been together in a while, they were still officially a couple, and Meadowbrook imagined the scenario as though he was in the army, stationed in India or some other distant outpost of the Empire; long separations would be feasible were that the case, and reuniting with his beloved was bound to be fraught with potential difficulties as a consequence.

Although Orchidea had always displayed an endearing, blushing coyness on the subject of their sexual relationship if it were ever mentioned out of context, she had shown no such inhibitions in the bedchamber, even though affectionate groping on his part was never objected to, wherever it took place. For the first time, however, he was worried how she might respond after their time apart should he attempt to pick up where they left off. Would she react to a squeeze of her posterior as though he were some stranger copping a feel on a crowded station platform?

Even thinking such a thing almost erased the entire nature of their relationship in his head. He had never thought that way about Orchidea previously, never having to anticipate a variety of responses to his every gesture in her vicinity beforehand; there had never been any of that pre-match tension. That kind of shit was what had consumed his courtship with Alice; it hadn't been how he and Orchidea had conducted themselves as a couple. There had been no real courtship at all; they had come together in an instant because they had instantly clicked. Perhaps the lack of a lengthy pursuit was why Meadowbrook had undeniably taken Orchidea and her devotion to him for granted; he hadn't had to work at it. And now he did.

In the days running up to the reunion, Meadowbrook became convinced Orchidea was going to change her mind at the last moment and ring to say she couldn't come after all. He would have taken such a message as confirmation they were over, a situation inconceivable before the misfire of the poetry collection. It had been an extremely testing period for Meadowbrook, this separation; but he had bided his time, feeling Orchidea would come back eventually. His patience appeared to be paying off at last, though anticipation of her arrival was riddled with nerves.

Orchidea had decided to drive to Meadowbrook's. Increasing confidence behind the wheel had gradually pushed her farther afield than quiet country lanes and she had driven into several neighbouring market-towns in her search for furniture and artefacts for her Biba-free home. She figured she was now good enough as a motorist to brave a big, bustling metropolis. She knew she had to do so eventually, and this seemed like a good test of her motorist mettle.

When she announced her intended mode of transport to Meadowbrook, he saw the changing vehicles she had used to bridge the geographical divide through the tenure of the relationship as a portrait of progress – hot air balloon, coach-and-horses, train and now motorcar. How far the world outside their window had travelled whilst they'd been otherwise engaged!

Considering the time that had elapsed since she had last made this journey, Orchidea surprised herself by how easily she slipped into the old routine. She packed a hamper – as she always had done – and she assembled her handmaidens to issue detailed instructions for Biba's care in her absence. She also advised old Sam to be as strict as she'd been in supervising the work on the enclosure while she was away; this would be the first time she'd travelled to see Jeremiah without Sam joining her as far as the station. She could now stick all her luggage in the boot of the motorcar, so didn't need him this time.

Meadowbrook's rusty routine on the eve of Orchidea's return also kicked into a familiar pattern, albeit one soundtracked by his latest sonic distraction, the wireless. Although he liked some of the BBC's output, he found it a little too austere at times and often enjoyed exploring the dial for hours, picking up endless foreign stations and feeling as though he was eavesdropping on a wider world he'd never had the opportunity to explore in person. Hearing voices in his drawing-room that were being beamed across the Channel from the European mainland had a magic to it that entranced him and strangely diluted his loneliness. Whenever the wireless was on, it felt as if someone else was always in the room.

Devlin was understandably unsettled as he observed his father overseeing preparations for Orchidea's visit. The two maidservants were busy washing and replacing soiled sheets, whilst Meadowbrook's valet Wooldridge was dispatched to make the old stables round the back a convenient storage space for Orchidea's motorcar; Meadowbrook had pensioned-off the horse-and-carriage a while back and the space that used to house them had stood empty ever since. It seemed as good a place as any for Orchidea to park her precious vehicle. Also, a bath was run so Meadowbrook could ensure he would be at his most sweetly-scented for his beloved's return. He had gone to seed somewhat lately, feeling as though he had no reason to make himself presentable because there was nobody to impress anymore. And now there was.

The raven had relished having Meadowbrook all to himself during the separation and the prospect of a little sunshine flooding through the dismal environs of the Meadowbrook residence via the return of someone guaranteed to lift his master's mood was not one that provoked pleasure in Devlin. He listened intently to the telephone conversation Meadowbrook had with Orchidea the night before she set off and sneered at what he saw as his master's weak neediness.

Meadowbrook, anxious for his beloved not to be afflicted by the nerves that were now afflicting him (but nerves he anticipated she herself might experience a revival of considering the gap since her previous visit), was falling over himself to put her at ease, emphasising how she just had to 'take it easy' and how there was no rush for her to get there. Unaware of just how proficient she now was as a driver, Meadowbrook didn't want her to be zooming along the King's Highway in a recklessly breathless fashion because nerves had got the better of her.

Devlin actually took some solace from seeing Meadowbrook so apprehensive in a way he never had been before in the run-up to Orchidea coming to see him; it suggested to Devlin that there was a lot riding on this visit that could so easily see the whole relationship crumble if it went wrong. He couldn't see how Orchidea could possibly respect the desperately eager-to-please weakling he now saw Meadowbrook being in his attitude towards her. There was still hope.

The drive to town was Orchidea's strongest test to date, but she kept her composure when confronted by heavy traffic, reminding herself that she was currently training to be a pilot – even if the skies were less crowded than earthbound roads. To be fair, congestion only began to slow her down when she was no more than a mile or so away from Meadowbrook's home, and by then she was already well-prepared for the potential emotion of the reunion.

She pondered on all the activity that had kept her busy during the separation – Biba's enclosure, driving, flying – and wondered what Meadowbrook had been doing to occupy his own time; her distractions had served a valuable purpose that had helped lift her out of her private mire and had put her in a strong enough frame of mind to return to her beloved's arms. She wasn't to know her beloved's lack of distractions had weakened his frame of mind to the point whereby he was now closer to what she had been when they first met – no longer the strong rock of the relationship she could absorb the confidence of.

****

Jeremiah had told me I could park the car in the old stables round the back of his home, and that he'd be there to guide me in at the time I said I'd be there. I'd given myself plenty of leeway in anticipation of traffic, but actually arrived a little earlier than intended, pulling into the hidden cul-de-sac designed with the horse-and-carriage in mind. There was no sign of Jeremiah as I bumped along the cobbles, so I brought the car to a halt outside where I remembered his stables being. I wasn't as nervous as I thought I might be once I was back, so there was no real need to gather my thoughts or take any deep breaths. I exited the car and opened the boot to retrieve the hamper.

I made my way round the back of the house to the stables a good five minutes or so before the time Orchidea said she'd be there, so it was a pleasant surprise when I saw an unfamiliar vehicle with a very familiar figure pulling a hamper from it. The nerves that had afflicted me beforehand were born of a desire not to fuck this up, but also of a conviction she wouldn't actually come. Now that I'd seen she had, it was just a case of not fucking it up.

She didn't hear my footsteps until I was just a few feet away and when she turned to see me I thought she was going to burst into tears. Her eyes glistened with saltwater, enhancing the sapphire sparkle in a way that told me my very appearance before her was all she needed to melt into my arms. Reading my thoughts on paper or hearing them spoken on the telephone helped keep the reality of our love an abstract concept she could distance herself from; when I was there in person, right in front of her and not a disembodied hand or voice, she remembered the truth of the magical connection we had made and she knew once again why it mattered. Only I did this to her – *me,* no one else. She was mine and she couldn't deny it.

Yes, I melted. I couldn't help it. The minute I saw him I was overwhelmed by his presence all over again. Not seeing him for so long had enabled me to put the power of his physical presence and the impact it had always had on me out of my mind, and that had made it easy to contemplate all the shameful fantasies that I'd regretfully made reality on one uncharacteristic occasion; but as soon as he was there before me, I was his woman once more. Why had I pretended otherwise when nobody else could do this to me? It was as though I needed to see him again to prove this was real, and it was. My eyes watered, my legs began to tremble and I gripped him with such intensity it was as though I was willing myself to be absorbed by his secure interior.

Here he was, my Jeremiah, all living and breathing and lovely and warm, just as he'd been before. Yes, I had done my best to forget, but now I remembered and I surrendered to the emotional pull of something I'd consciously turned away from because I knew what it did to me. It served as confirmation that whenever I was in Jeremiah's company I would never be able to resist him.

I felt strong again at that moment we embraced, but perhaps it was a more equal exchange of strength now, for I remained uncertain as to what happened next. When we slowly stepped apart, the business of steering the motorcar (which was an impressive little set of wheels) into the stables was attended to, and then I escorted Orchidea indoors as if she'd only been away for a couple of days. Even the servants seemed pleased to see her, greeting her like she was the missing mistress of the house come home from a long overseas sojourn; and their pleasure looked genuine to me.

When we were left alone, I couldn't resist showing off the wireless, which was a handsome piece of furniture in its own right; its presence complemented the mixing and mingling of centuries that characterised my interior decor, and then Orchidea added to it by pulling out a gorgeous vintage oil-lamp that was in the hamper along with her usual snacks and ingredients; she said she'd picked it up during her recent search for her own interior decor and thought it would be more at home in my residence than hers. She was right. As ever, Orchidea knew my taste better than anyone else.

We held hands on the chez-longue, just as we had on that very first night. There was no excessive caressing of my body on his part. I sensed he was hesitant for the first time, as if he wasn't sure of how to react to my being there and whether or not we would be resuming our former intimacy from the start; but I respected that, for I had a feeling he was remorseful of his behaviour before and wanted to assure me he'd changed for the better and there'd be no repeat of it. There were no cigars and there was no absinthe; he said his wine cellar was now completely empty of the latter, which came as a pleasant surprise. He said he'd given up both, and I had no reason to disbelieve him. I could smell his Eau de Cologne far stronger than I ever had before because the scent wasn't overpowered by tobacco for once. It was touching how hard he was trying, though his efforts weren't robbing him of his personality; he was still Jeremiah, just a better Jeremiah than the one who had given me such cause for concern on the last few occasions I'd been with him.

Even when we followed the old routine by giving the servants the night-off, thus enabling me to take-over the kitchen, he didn't once hug, kiss or grope me during the preparation of the meal. This actually struck me as quite sad, so whilst the oven could be left to do its business for an hour or so, I suggested we pop up to the bedchamber as a means of filling the time.

I retained my reserved expressions of affection with Orchidea right up until she hinted we should make use of the hour or more it would take the food to be ready. This was my cue to return to where she and I had always been at our most comfortable with one another, where I could feel free to roam across the much-missed curves and contours of her beautiful body and know she had no objections at all. It was the biggest relief of the day after her actually turning up in the first place. The tensions I'd harboured ever since her arrival were mercifully gone, and the lifting of them enabled me to speak from the heart once we slid effortlessly into the afterglow. It's a man's job to say sorry.

Unfortunately, to begin with I basically went through the motions, giving him what he wanted without necessarily seeking pleasure from it myself, and that was something I'd never done before in bed with Jeremiah. It had always been a two-way pleasure. Naturally, it was nothing to do with nerves like the first time; it was because I still felt a tad uncomfortable with the thought of lovemaking after my encounter with that couple at home. What gradually sank in, however, was the belated realisation that sex with Jeremiah genuinely WAS lovemaking, not simply fucking. I'd forgotten.

He had lost a little weight since we'd last shared a bed, and exposure to a raw brute of a man had almost erased the fond familiarity I had with Jeremiah's more refined flesh. It was like the difference between a flagon of ale and a glass of claret. Jeremiah's was the skin of a man whose self-indulgent abuses had yet to leave a real mark on it; the only contrast his body had with that of a younger man was in a small scattering of lines indicating mere wear-and-tear. But compared to the flaccid neglect I suspected to be writ large on the naked frames of most men his age, he wasn't in bad shape at all. By the end, I had lost my initial reservations and enjoyed it. Then, as I lay with Jeremiah behind me, he made his heartfelt apology.

I told her how sorry I was for the way I'd behaved, how selfish and stupidly self-destructive I'd been in the face of her own suffering, and how much I regretted that badly-timed book of love poems, the motivation of which had been genuine, if naive. I also confessed how terrified I was when I feared I might have lost her because of all these things, and explained how this fear had governed my hesitation in being my regular hands-on self in her presence before getting into bed. It was the most passionate I'd ever spoken about our relationship to her in person; I usually saved all that for the written word. But it was utterly necessary to both emphasise my remorse and express my joy at her return whilst she was there lying with me.

I bared body *and* soul to her in that moment, more so than I ever had to anyone; she saw me completely stripped to the core of who I was, and when you expose yourself to somebody so honestly, devoid of any artifice whatsoever, you do so because they have won your absolute trust and you know this is a trust they will never betray.

Because of the position we were in as I spoke, I couldn't see her face, but with each point I made she squeezed my hand in the most loving, tender and understanding fashion; she didn't have to reply verbally; that gesture said so much more, enough to make me fall in love with her all over again. I knew then we were back on track. We had overcome the first major stumbling block of our relationship and we had emerged stronger and more together than ever before. We made love a second time immediately thereafter and as we held each other once it was over, this time looking directly into each other's eyes, I swore I'd never make the same mistake twice and I'd never let her slip from my grip again. I meant it.

I was immensely moved by his apology and the way he spoke about us; he did so without any poetic flourishes, but still possessing a delicate eloquence that was unmistakably him. Perhaps his words and the moving manner of their delivery had an added poignancy that affected me deeply because I harboured an apology of my own that I could never say out loud. The guilt hit me anew at that moment, but I had ways and means of dealing with past events that sat uncomfortably on the shoulders of the present: I simply behaved as if they'd never happened. And that was the tactic I employed to get through what was one of the sweetest, most touching episodes of my whole life without breaking down and destroying it in the process. That incident with the man and the woman in my bedchamber – it never happened. It never happened. It never happened.

When we finally sat down to eat another of Orchidea's mouth-watering specialities, she commented on the fact that when she first saw me naked she thought my body had all the classic proportions of an underfed bachelor. Her maternal instincts had told her to fatten me up a little, and she noticed all her hard work appeared to have gone astray since she'd been absent. I told her there was only one way to solve that, and we appeared to have made a good start. We retired to the drawing-room after dinner and made the most of contemporary technology for relaxing entertainment via the gramophone and the wireless.

She talked of Biba's outdoor enclosure and how she'd insisted it be somewhat sunken beneath the level of the ground surrounding it. She wanted to recreate the landscape of a lion's natural habitat as best she could in the space of just ten acres, doing away with the manicured land as it had been when she bought it. She said it was proving to be a challenge for the builders and landscape gardeners she'd brought in, but she was pushing them hard; the whole project had to be done right if it was to be done at all. She also spoke with great excitement of her flying lessons and how she reckoned it wouldn't be too long before she acquired a pilot's licence; she insisted as soon as she had I would be joining her for a flight. I replied I couldn't wait, and I couldn't. To actually be involved in one of Orchidea's passions that existed outside of our personal bubble would be wonderful.

Perhaps because there had been such a gap between seeing each other, some of the routines we revisited had an almost nostalgic glow for me. We went riding together for the first time in quite a while; it was actually the first time I'd ridden at all since I'd last done so with Jeremiah. At one time, riding would be the same kind of temporary escape from Biba as driving now was, but I'd slipped out of the habit and so had Jeremiah. He no longer owned any horses, but we hired a couple from the stables where we'd always gone (just outside town) and crossed the familiar fringes of the rural landscape with the wind in our hair like we'd never been out of the saddle. It was exhilarating. I had driven us to the stables, giving Jeremiah his first exposure to my driving skills! I told him he should invest in a motorcar himself, but he seemed uncertain of its benefits as a tool of freedom. I suspect he still missed his old horse-drawn carriage.

Some of the twentieth century's inventions had caught his imagination, but these tended to be ones for the housebound, such as the gramophone and the wireless; the ones that were outdoor innovations appeared to leave him cold. He could see the convenience of a car, but he bemoaned the increase in street traffic the internal combustion engine had brought with it – as well as the petrol fumes it pumped into the atmosphere. I reminded him the streets weren't so nice-smelling when they were piled high with horseshit and ran with the effluence of open sewers, but he pointed out men were employed to clear all that away on a regular basis; you couldn't rid urban environments of the shit that came from a car engine. It inhabited the air permanently. I didn't notice it so much in the country, where motorcars were less commonplace.

The thought of travelling in the air with Orchidea may have had a novel ring to it, but travelling with her when she was behind the wheel of a motorcar was just as unusual an experience for me. We were both so used to being driven – either by drivers of coaches or trains – that for Orchidea to be in control of a vehicle was strange albeit exciting. I wondered how she was able to divide her attention between concentrating on driving and continuing a conversation with me at the same time. It was a skill I instantly admired, though one I doubted I could acquire myself. She was very much at ease driving, however; I could tell she'd been getting plenty of practice in, and I could see no reason why this wouldn't be her permanent mode of transport from now on.

Although I'd travelled in a motorcar before (mainly taxicabs), I wasn't as accustomed to it as she clearly was, and I have to admit that witnessing Orchidea's dedication to it as a superior replacement for a horse-drawn vehicle still didn't persuade me as to the merits of investing in my own. But at least it did present one advantage to us in terms of our relationship, and that was the fact that travelling to see me was now far less of a logistical challenge for her; no longer having to rely on train timetables meant all she had to do was put her foot down on the pedal and she was away at any time of the day she wished. The power of getting from A to B had been wrestled out of the hands of the railway companies and was now down to Orchidea – and how she relished the liberation!

We spent a couple of lovely days together, and I enjoyed the experience enough to suggest perhaps it was time Jeremiah came to see me at home at last. Although Biba's enclosure was in no way completed, I figured we could work our way around it, and maybe it wasn't such a bad idea that Jeremiah finally got to see Biba with his own eyes. The reunion had imbued me with such renewed confidence in our relationship that I felt we could do anything. I had utterly banished unpleasant memories of recent mistakes, and I had been given a wondrous reminder of what really mattered. It had been a necessary lesson I badly needed, but it highlighted yet again the contrast between the grim realities of home life and the blissful parallel universe life I lived with Jeremiah.

Perhaps bridging the gap might help end the schizophrenic divide that separated the two in my head and would ultimately lead to the oft-discussed marriage we again discussed. Jeremiah coming to visit me would be a good start.

Orchidea raising the subject of reversing the traditional pattern of our relationship by me visiting her instead of the other way round was for me the final seal on overcoming our recent difficulties. Yes, she was taking the lead in a way I had in the beginning, but to me that said all the wavering I suspected on her part prior to her visit was more a product of my own internal anxiety. She even insisted I should be introduced to Biba, something that I regarded as an interesting challenge considering the fact Biba was a fully-grown lion; but I surmised if Orchidea had spent years sharing a home with Biba as though he were a particularly large domesticated dog, I shouldn't baulk at a mere introduction. Biba had been such a central figure in our relationship that for me not to meet him seemed silly, especially if we were to move our relationship onto the next level at last. I agreed this was a good idea and we began to plot the order of events.

It was provisionally arranged that Orchidea would drive up to see me again in a couple of weeks and when the time came for her to depart I would accompany her back to her own home, where I would stay for a couple of days before returning alone on the train. Needless to say, I was ecstatic. This was further evidence of the success of our reunion, and all the doubts and paranoid fears that had gripped me in the run-up to the reunion completely evaporated. The leaves may have slipped into golden slumber and dropped from branch to pavement, but that crispy carpet was certainly no signifier to an autumnal swansong for our love; this felt more like spring again – a new chapter ready and waiting to be written.

Parting didn't feel as hard this time round. I wasn't as down as I'd been on the last few occasions, for I had seen for myself the improvements Jeremiah had consciously made in his lifestyle. He had belatedly recognised the factors that had caused so much concern for me and had done his best to remove them from his day-to-day life. He had expressed genuine, heartfelt remorse over the way he'd been behaving and this to me proved his commitment to what we had. How could I not respond by proving my own? Even though I knew it would be a tricky proposition, bringing him back home with me in a couple of weeks would be a step forward. Besides, it shouldn't be too long now before Biba could become a permanent outdoor resident and once that happened Jeremiah visiting me as much as me visiting him would be the long-overdue norm. After that, who knew?

Many possibilities presented themselves to us and we were now in a strong enough position to make the most of them. We'd got through the worst and it had only taken a reunion that reminded us both of the special connection we had to get us to this stage. When we were together, nothing seemed beyond us. The future looked very bright indeed at the moment when Jeremiah kissed me goodbye. The taste of his lips on mine was a cherished flavour that was my very own Madeleine Moment – as soon as he'd kissed me upon arrival, I was back home, and I remained there until I returned to the actual house I knew as home. But home with Jeremiah existed on a higher plane altogether.

I was used to bidding Orchidea farewell on the station platform; doing so by kissing her through her open car window was a different experience, but one imbued with so much promise. Next time I kissed her goodbye I'd be back on another station platform, albeit her own local station. Just a couple of days earlier, I'd been convinced Orchidea would call to say she couldn't come and see me after all, and yet here I was, kissing her goodbye following a reunion that had revitalised us completely. I waved her farewell as she drove away and turned to return to the house. I thought I'd caught sight of Devlin peering through the attic window out of the corner of my eye, but it must have been a trick of the light.

The Heavens Opened

Are you happy now I feel so bloody awful? You were appalling when I returned from Jeremiah's – worse than you'd been in a long time.

You'd done some real damage in the house whilst I was away and then bit me on the arm the moment I walked through the door. But I seemed to sense what I'd be walking back into. I left Jeremiah's feeling so uplifted, yet almost as some sort of premonition, I was overcome by a terrifying feeling of dread when I was about a mile away from home. I almost crashed the car and had to stop it for ten minutes or so to try and regain my composure. I couldn't understand what the hell was wrong with me. It had been a lovely clear sunny day all the way up to that point, and then the moment I put the brakes on and pulled over it was as if the Gods had dimmed the lights to complement my panic. The sky was suddenly grey and the heavens opened.

It hadn't rained like that for ages – spring and summer had been gloriously dry – yet as soon as I got in you wanted to go out. You tried to drag me into the grounds with such force that you dug your teeth in my arm and drew blood; I hadn't even put my luggage down when my reappearance said to you I'd only come back for the sole purpose of walking you around for hours – in the pissing rain. I was already shaken from what had happened to me in the motorcar and just wanted to sit down and gather myself together; but no, not when Biba wants to walk. So, I had no choice. I grabbed a thick coat and an umbrella and out we went – just for you. I was soaked to the bone.

That set the pattern, didn't it? All of the lovely warmth that flowed into me from Jeremiah when I'd kissed him goodbye, warmth that stayed in me for most of the journey home, had gone. In its place was this, a seesaw of emotions day after bloody day. I go for a flying lesson and I feel exultant for its duration; then I come back and I'm down again. If things are going well on the enclosure work, I feel good; if they're not, I feel bad. This constant swinging backwards and forwards is exhausting. And you are demanding of me so bloody much. I thought I'd had the worst of it with you, yet your impatience and the way that impatience spontaneously explodes into fury if you don't get your way in an instant is getting worse; and it's draining the life out of me.

No wonder my alternate life with Jeremiah feels like pure fantasy once more. How on earth can he come here? It would be like expecting a character from fiction to step off the page and walk into the house. Oh, Tom Jones is at the door again and he's brought Mr Pickwick and Jane Eyre with him! I must have been kidding myself. The two lives are completely incompatible.

But anything seems possible with Jeremiah, you see, when we're cocooned in our little bubble that nobody can pierce or penetrate; when he's deep inside me and we're one person, it's like a womb we're ensconced in together, and every time he withdraws and I leave the womb it's like I go through the nightmare of being born all over again, and it's killing me. I'm not certain how many more times I can endure the crisscrossing between the two lives. Yes, I'm somebody else, somebody I really like, when I'm with him, but it's not enough time to become her for good. I wish it was. But I'm destined to be the person I am with you for much longer, and I don't know if I can keep being both people.

And, anyway, would he be the man he is with me if he came here? The change of scenery might change everything. His physical pull still affects me like no one else when we're together, but how can that be transplanted to my life here? The moment I return here from him, I feel like there's no future in our relationship at all – the opposite of how I feel when I'm there at his home.

Some days I get so weary with it all that I almost wish you could escape the grounds and run wild in the locality so someone shoots you down. On other days I feel like going out on the roof and throwing myself off – or maybe deliberately crashing the car and hoping I go flying through the windscreen. I hate thinking this way, but it's what my mind does when I'm running on empty. I hallucinate and imagine all kinds of insane scenarios because I often believe I *am* insane.

That's why I've practically moved into my bedchamber as if I'm some aged invalid, leaving the rest of the house to gather dust. That's why I'm in bed now, at this very moment, in the middle of the afternoon, reading every bloody column inch of a newspaper that doesn't help my mood at all; it just makes me angry because the world is being infiltrated and overrun by idiots and Jews and Communists. Or maybe it just looks that way from the perspective of an all-day bedchamber with the curtains drawn.

And here you are, laid across the end of my bed, watching over me like my own personal demon, forever watching over me, watching over me. But you were a gift from a demon, after all, so that makes sense. Being your mother is comparable to an eternal penance at times like this. Yes, at times like this. At times like this I am your mother and you are my keeper, and whoever I am when I'm with Jeremiah is utterly dead in the water; yes, that's me floating in the lake, face down – drowned. When they drag my body out they'll say 'My, I used to think she was actually quite pretty; she had a lovely smile, and now look at her – hairy-legged and haggard; she didn't even bother to make herself beautiful for the Grim Reaper, even though she arranged the appointment with him in advance.' Christ Almighty – what a way to go, eh?

Jeremiah is now my source of long-distance emotional support; I feel he's the only one who really cares, yet by being that person he's fulfilling a function he was never supposed to fulfil. That wasn't meant to be his role at all. I did my best to keep him from all this in the beginning. I didn't want it impinging on the special thing I had with him; he was my escape from it. But now he's been dragged into it and I feel like I'm his project, his mission, his poor soul in desperate need of sympathy and salvation. Where's the escape from it all now?

The last thing I ever wanted was his pity. Being pitied by the man I love would be the worst thing in the world. That would totally alter the nature of the relationship, yet it feels as though that's precisely what's happening, like I'm inducing his pity when every letter or telephone conversation revolves around you and how shit I feel. And ironically, after Jeremiah cleaned-up his act, I am now the one who is drinking too much.

Hah! I speak of Jeremiah when I'm lost in this despondent fog and your look changes. Your eyes offer advice to him, don't they? They say that he should be out there, joining Conan Blackcastle and all the playboys in the jazz clubs, and he should snort cocaine and fuck all the flappers and do all the wild hedonistic things he can't do when he's saddled with a basket case like me. Yes, they say he should return to what he used to be, the man-about-town, feted and celebrated as a society wit.

That's who he still was when I met and fell in love with him; but now I've allowed you and all the baggage that comes with you to seep into his life, and me and him are no longer bound by romance but by misery – a misery that should always be restricted to me and you. It's *our* misery, no one else's. Why would I want to saddle anyone else with it – certainly not the man I love?

Perhaps I should never even have told Jeremiah about you to begin with. I should have worn a wedding ring and made out I wanted him solely to be my clandestine extramarital lover; our relationship would be an affair, and I could just be his bit-on-the-side rather than his imaginary intended. That would have been more convincing than the truth, wouldn't it? It would certainly offer a plausible explanation as to why he could never visit me at home and why I could only visit him no more than two or three times a month and for just one or two nights at a time.

Yes, I should have said I was still a married woman and that my husband was an extremely jealous and suspicious man. I could have said he rifles through all my personal possessions and private correspondence and intercepts all my mail, which is why none of my gifts from Jeremiah could be proudly displayed in a conventional fashion, but would have to be hidden in a locked closet; it would be as though I was a shameful scarlet woman forced to hide my most treasured artefacts from prying eyes for fear of exposure and scandal.

I could have said when my husband is supposed to be working away from home, i.e. the days when I'm with Jeremiah, he actually hides somewhere on the estate so I only *think* he's working away when he isn't. I could have said that this enables him to spy on me and monitor my movements, and that he's often secretly followed me all the way to town when I visit Jeremiah. I could have said he's got a close friend who's a senior police officer at Scotland Yard, one who he's asked to dig for dirt on Jeremiah to use against him as some form of blackmail, as in 'Leave my wife alone – or else.'

Yes, that would have worked. If I'd gone down that road, this current depression could have easily been explained away. I would've said my husband was no longer absent from home so much anymore, which restricts the opportunities I have to visit Jeremiah. I could say that I don't share a bed with my husband, so there are no sexual relations between us, but he sleeps in the room above mine and lies on the floor to try and overhear my telephone conversations with Jeremiah through the bedchamber floorboards. I could have made out as if I was completely submissive to my husband's terrible temper, and that I was complicit in him throwing tantrums like a spoiled child because my dread of them led me to always comply with his wishes. I'd tolerate it because of my low self-esteem brought on by successive men putting me down throughout my life.

Yes, that's a believable scenario. It would have given Jeremiah a series of explanations as to why we couldn't spend more time in each other's company, why we could never live together and why we could never become man and wife. *I'd* believe that story, and I'm sure he would too. It's just a pity he knows about you, for I can never use it now.

So, what am I to do, eh? Yes, when that damned enclosure is completed, you will have your very own outdoor home at last; and you'll love it. You're always itching to be out as it is, so it'll be what you've always wanted. But what about me? Where does that leave me? If I'm no longer required to be at your beck and call all day long, what am I supposed to do?

****

Let me in, that's all I ask. Don't shut me out. I hate hearing you so low, so hopeless, so despondent. Yet, you alter like the weather. I cannot accurately gauge your state of mind because it changes every time we speak.

One day you sound suicidal, the next the fire is in your belly. One day you're exhilarated by a flying lesson, the next you're bedbound and just want to remain beneath the blankets, convinced an international Jewish conspiracy is poised to push us into global Armageddon because of some scaremongering horror story you've read in the Daily Mail, as if every Jew is your nasty neighbour.

I remind you of how much better you always are – we both are – when we're together, but the grand plans we made when you were last here have fizzled out. You appear to have slipped back into that paranoid, neurotic mindset you were in during that dark period when you stopped coming to visit me. You continue to write and you continue to speak to me on the telephone; but I cannot hold you, and that is something that would energise us both. You know so, but you resist.

And sometimes your correspondence seems designed to alienate or anger me. And I cannot understand why. I know I upset you before, and the thought that I could have caused you any distress is something that cuts me deeply. I have tried so hard to make amends. Some days I despair for you so much that I feel like throwing caution to the wind and simply turning up at your door unannounced. But what will I find there if I do?

Autumnal Hate Mail

Dearest

Just a brief missive to inform you it has been a hectic day here – Biba's enclosure is nearing completion, which has improved my mood no end since we spoke on the telephone yesterday. It is in the main thanks old Sam's nephew, who has bucked-up his ideas and has gradually proved to be something of a landscape gardening genius, I have to say. His labourers were quite an obstinate obstacle to my plans in the beginning, but they have slowly taken my advice on board and the end results are pretty impressive. For the first time, I can actually see the plans on my drawing-board coming to life, which just shows a woman can create something of aesthetic value as much as a man. Who would have thought that, eh?

As an amusing aside, Sam also saw fit to inform me that his nephew young Samuel (named after his uncle) harbours unrequited lustful thoughts for me! Hahah! Silly boy! He is quite good-looking, but there's something about him that doesn't appeal to me – something not quite to my taste. Maybe he's a tad too 'rustic' for me – none too bright other than with his hands. Sam never fails to remind me of his nephew's desires whenever the young man shows up for a day's work, however. One would imagine Sam sees himself as Jane Austen's Emma, the master matchmaker trying to set up some sort of ill-fated marriage!

I thought that would make you chuckle. Ludicrous, isn't it – especially when I'm the least vain person I know, barely even snatching a glance of myself in the looking-glass most days! He must be accustomed to rough, uncouth farm-girls who don't bother either. I simply don't have the time to indulge in such fripperies when so many more important things need attending to.

We shall speak on the telephone tomorrow.

Love you,
Orchidea

What the hell am I supposed to say in response to that? Oh, yes, I have just soiled my long-johns at the hilarious and utterly ridiculous notion of a brawny bumpkin being turned-on by a beautiful wealthy woman who's never seen in the company of the man who is actually meant to be her beloved. Not quite to her taste, eh? Has she forgotten who is *supposed* to be to her taste – or am I just a pen-pal now that she cannot be bothered to come and see me anymore?

How do I know she hasn't fantasised about rolling in the hay with this muscle-bound, bucolic brute, unable to resist his no-doubt huge country cock? Perhaps it wasn't even a fantasy. I can see him hard at work on constructing Biba's enclosure, topless to accommodate the heat, biceps rippling in the sunshine, stirring salacious scenarios in her reactivated quim.

Perhaps he was covered in dirt and she offered her bath to him at the end of the working day, intending to provide him with a towel that she forgot to leave in the bathroom. She collects it when he's already begun to wash himself and she's about to deposit it through a crack in the door when she can't help herself from peering through it. This is when she catches sight of his awesome member and she hurries away to slip into something more conducive to seduction. Five minutes later, out he strolls, droplets streaming down his wide expanse of chest with naught but a slender towel wrapped round his waist.

By then, she has already donned a skimpy silk dressing-gown with a hemline high enough to expose stocking-tops when she reaches up to retrieve the tea from the top shelf. As she stands beside the hob, waiting for the kettle to whistle, he approaches her from behind, kisses the back of her neck and presses his hard throbbing prick between the cheeks of her soft, tender backside. His hands squeeze her breasts and when she turns round to face him, the towel has already fallen to the floor. She sinks to her knees to swallow his cock and then he carries her into the bedchamber to give her a rough rural seeing-to. And I bet she loved it - if it happened. Who's to say it didn't? I'd never know, after all.

I only know what she tells me.

Dearest

I sincerely hope you are well. I have been overwhelmed by activity, something to which I am hardly accustomed! Now that Biba is very much at home in his new enclosure, expense spent on furniture he would have undoubtedly destroyed when he lived indoors has increased tenfold. One such item was purchased today – an actual four-poster bed which I decided to pay for in person on account of the seller being a near-neighbour of mine, the Marquess of somewhere-or-other. I forget. There are so many titled toffs in this neck of the woods that it's easy to mix them up.

The item will be delivered later in the week, but the payment has now been made, even if the Marquess himself was something of a saucy old creep. There was something incurably lecherous about him; I knew that the moment I met him; I could see it in the way he looked me up and down, as if he was picturing me in my undergarments. And then, once money had changed hands, he invited me back to his home that evening for dinner! I saw no sign of a Marchioness, so he may well be on the hunt for a wife – or perhaps a mistress. I diplomatically declined his offer and made my way off the premises with haste. I don't know what it is lately; must be something in the air where gentlemen of a certain age are concerned.

For example, I was accosted not once, but twice by randy old rakes last week, when I was simply searching for further items of furniture in the nearest village. Perhaps my social seclusion in recent years has bestowed an aura of mystique upon me – the reclusive lady with the lion. Men suddenly seem to be drawn to me as though I was invisible before – even if they're always the sort to make my flesh crawl! One of those fruity relics even claimed to be a descendant of Alfred the Great, as though that would persuade me to let him fuck me! Amusing how deluded these archaic relics are, isn't it?

Will speak again soon!

*Love you,
Orchidea*

PS I shall be popping over to see my friend and neighbour Marianne again tomorrow evening – I know I've told you about her before – so I shall telephone you when I return, a little later than usual.

Oh, how side-splitting, my dear. What the hell does she imagine such stories do to my fragile confidence in our relationship eh? I don't really want to hear about how many men have been propositioning her! She tells me these things as though I am nothing more than some generic female friend who pops over for tea once or twice a week and loves a good gossip hinting at naughtiness. I thought I was her bloody fiancée! Has she already forgotten who I am and our relation to each other just because I haven't held her in a while?

And I noticed she didn't say she 'diplomatically declined' the Marquess of somewhere-or-other's offer of 'dinner' by informing him she was already spoken for, which she is supposed to bloody be. Perhaps she relishes the attention and the sudden possession of power over men, power she never imagined herself capable of owning when we first met, eh? Remember her as she was then – when she was so timid and anxious with regards to her own desirability that I had no cause to doubt her commitment to the only man who saw her as a criminally neglected beauty?

What have I created by giving her the confidence she previously lacked? Now it seems she cannot come into contact with any member of the opposite sex without inspiring an erection – and being very aware of it. Congratulations – she is a normal woman again. And how do I know she found the men she aroused to be as repulsive as she claims? How do I know she didn't take them up on their offers? I don't know anything anymore.

The geographical distance between us was there from day one; it remains the same barrier to our seeing more of each other as it was in the beginning. It hasn't magically appeared in recent months as some sort of gesture of permission on my part for her to sleep with other men behind my back just because she's too far away for me to find out. It is not a convenient cloak of distance that gives her free rein to pursue philandering merely because I cannot see her. Or is it?

Dearest

I shall keep this brief, as I intend to speak to you later via the wonders of modern technology! Anyway, I had an unexpected visit today from Viscount Lucre. I have no idea how he tracked me down, for I have not made his acquaintance in decades.

I realise I may never have mentioned him before, but I confess I had all-but forgotten his connection to me. He was a close friend of my former patron, you see – the dear old one whose fortune was bequeathed to me following my stint as housekeeper – and he was a regular visitor to the household back in those extremely distant days. It was certainly a shock when Lucre turned-up without warning on my doorstep I have to say, although I have followed his progress via the press over the years. You may or may not be aware that Viscount Lucre has recently divorced his wife, a somewhat scandalous affair that apparently excited Fleet Street, though he appeared unflustered by the fuss, happy to be rid of her.

The divorce hasn't affected his standing in diplomatic circles either. He is shortly to take up the post of Governor of the Bahamas and told me I would be welcome there anytime I wished. He will be sailing there in a couple of weeks and even said I could join him on the journey! He certainly painted an alluring portrait of Paradise and I have to admit I was tempted.

I appreciate how it must sound to some, but I can't seriously imagine Lucre harbours any sexual desires towards me. I never saw him that way and could never now. The thought is so silly. Besides, there is Biba. There is ALWAYS Biba – the ultimate passion-killer!

Love you,
Orchidea

Just as well Biba is the ultimate passion-killer, eh? Yes, if it wasn't for inconvenient old Biba, she'd probably have taken up the gay divorcee on his kind offer and fucked him all the way to the bloody Bahamas! Christ! Is she just stupidly naive or is she simply incredibly insensitive? Can she not see this man may have carried a torch for her for years? Finally, he's free from his wife and he looks at Orchidea, seeing a woman seemingly unattached and living alone – two free agents in the same boat as far as he's concerned. What's to stop him imagining she's available? It doesn't appear from what she's said that she was poised to correct his understandable assumption either.

She was *tempted,* was she? Fucking wonderful! That makes me feel fucking fantastic. This coming from someone who can't even be bothered to set aside a couple of days to come and see me, yet she's tempted by a two-week journey by ship to the Bahamas just because a rich and single toff puts the offer to her. Fuck me. When did she become so bloody cavalier with regards to my feelings – or is this all part of some subconscious campaign to turn me off and provoke me into ending our relationship because she cannot face the stress of doing it herself? Where the hell has my Orchidea gone?

I wish I knew what was going on in her head right now, but I know what is going on in *mine.* She is driving me to the brink of insanity with her careless disregard of my emotions, forever filling my fevered head with thoughts of her opening her legs for strangers simply because I am out of sight and evidently out of mind. What did I do to push her into this uncharacteristic neglect of my love and everything we have ever stood for?

I tried my best to convince her I had changed for the better last time she came here, bending over backwards to prove how regretful I was of my previous misbehaviour, and I assumed she'd got the message. There was nothing in her reaction then to suggest otherwise. And yet now she imparts information of her home life to me with such casual carelessness that implies she never once considered it likely I'd be assaulted by the kind of paranoid images that have tormented me for weeks.

I don't know what the hell has happened here, but somehow she imagines none of this would hurt or upset me by saying it out loud or she simply no longer cares what I feel. What scares me the most is that were the shoe on the other foot and my letters to her were packed with stories of women who had propositioned me and invited me on holidays with them, I suspect she wouldn't actually be hurt or upset at all. The fact is no women have propositioned me or invited me on holidays with them because I am not sending out signals to members of the opposite sex that I am available for dalliances. I am not remotely interested because she is supposed to be my beloved!

From the way she talks, it is as though we are nothing more than friends of the platonic persuasion. Perhaps that is all we are to her now, with so much time having passed since we last lay together. Was I just her stepping stone to someone else, a mere facilitator of her erotic recovery?

Can my lovely Orchidea really be so bloody mercenary?

Dearest

You are confronted by competition! I presume elaboration is unnecessary, for you are well-versed in my political persuasions and how they have been hardened more and more by despair over so much of this insanely depressing climate we have been subjected to in recent years. I speak, of course, of that prophet whose intervention is so welcome. Thanks to Marianne, I have received a first-hand introduction to this most amazing of men.

How I wish you could have been with me yesterday. I was present at a speech by Sir Oswald Mosley and can honestly say I have never heard my own dissatisfactions with the political stagnation of this nation voiced with such eloquence and intelligence. He is as gifted and stirring an orator as he has often been painted in the press, not only having the nerve to say out loud what so many think, but articulating it in a persuasive fashion that will win converts to the cause for years to come. Of that, I have no doubt.

I always felt he was unjustly dealt with by both the Tories and Labour, but if he has been forced to form his own party out of desperation in order to break their redundant duopoly, so be it. I cannot blame him. It says so much about the state of politics in this country that someone of Mosley's calibre should be allowed to languish on the fringes when his true place is at the heart of British Government. I cannot think of any other individual more qualified to deal with the pressing problems that face so many than him.

He is one of the few people in whose private presence I'd struggle to contain myself. I mean it. I'd become a gibbering wreck, falling at his feet and declaring my undying love for him. I'd give myself to him without a second's thought. He is my hero and I am his dedicated devotee. He could have me however he wanted me – servant, friend, mistress or plain simple whore! Hahah! Even thinking about him makes me quiver. There are so few great men left and he's one of them. He has the potential to drag this nation from the gutter which a coalition of Zionist banking institutions and politicians subservient to those institutions have plunged it into by telling the truth and offering the only remedy; this is unarguable to anyone fortunate enough to hear him speak in person, something that makes his rise all the more inevitable – and gives one hope again. I never thought that would be possible.

I come alive every time I read one of his speeches, and hearing one in person was electrifying. He touches something deep in me because he is able to articulate my viewpoint far more eloquently than I ever could – and I'm clearly not the only person he has this effect upon. Look at the Daily Mail! At least one paper recognises that having the nerve to actually tell the bloody truth and deal with that truth by formulating unsentimental and constructive policies is the only way out now. And some of the old Suffragettes you used to admire so much are on board too – the likes of Mary Sophia Allen and Mary Richardson.

We were ALL so sick of being lied to for so long, being lectured to by those whose entire philosophy was based upon being in thrall to a wealthy elite to which they themselves were slaves, handing over their democracies to unelected plutocracies just because the price was right. They regarded us with nothing short of complete contempt and any dissenting voice was silenced until a man like him finally emerged and refused to be silenced. We needed someone to come along and speak for us, and he has done that.

I have observed from a distance over the last few years just how this spineless ruling class has allowed the country and Europe as a whole to submit to the enemy's will so that not only has the enemy taken control of all our international institutions, but it has also quietly taken control of so many of the institutions of our major cities. It has been an invasion by stealth conducted over decades. As Mosley himself has said, 'I openly and publicly challenge the Jewish interests of this country, commanding commerce, commanding the Press, commanding the cinema, dominating the City of London, killing industry with their sweat-shops.' Everyone knows all the significant businesses and establishments are in their hands, but so few are prepared to air concerns over one group of people wielding so much power for fear of being labelled Anti-Semitic, the default insult of those whose interests must be fiercely guarded at the expense of those who aren't shareholders in their elitist enterprise. And we the people have had no say in this project. It has been imposed upon us by those who hate everything we stand for. This has been their way of destroying that, and they have all-but succeeded.

The information we have no access to is limitless, for they control it all. What we see in the newspapers or on the cinema newsreels or hear on the wireless is what they want us to see or hear – and they sell it as the truth when it is nothing of the sort. It is their propaganda. They simply put it out there and hope there are enough stupid people in the world to buy it as fact. Some of us ask awkward questions and aren't so gullible, but our numbers are small because we have so few platforms to make our voices heard. If we had the BBC or Fleet Street in our hands, we would have the power to wake up this country from its inertia and open its blind eyes. We have to act now, before the takeover is complete. And we have to place our trust in HIM. He alone understands what we are going through.

Most people do not make the effort to find the truth, to locate the books and magazines that speak it. You know better than anyone as to what a voracious reader I am. You know that if I sought to locate the correct reading material I am uniquely positioned to locate it. And I did locate it. Therefore, I researched my subject before committing myself to it. I feel I have the sufficient knowledge to make that judgement. I only wish more would do as I have done rather than believing the lies that the press barons other than Rothermere have told to pursue their dishonest agenda. If only more could see that HE is the kind of man we need to save us. Can you imagine what a force we would again be if Mosley were to take power? We could drag ourselves out of the mire that Hoover failed to drag America out of and in the process take on the sinister international powers that are doing their utmost to destroy all we hold dear, and are doing so in collusion with those we have elected to represent our interests. I dream of such a rebirth.

This is why so many of us have been rejuvenated by HIS arrival, someone who has the guts to speak out against the madness of this cultural genocide and say enough is enough. We all need to take back control, and he alone could do just that. He can stop the rot with the kind of force that is so desperately needed. He is an example to us all. How can one not admire him? He has shown up his contemporaries as the wretched losers they are. He alone is a shining light of hope in the Dark Ages we've let ourselves be sucked into through our unforgivable apathy. Of course, there are those who have done their utmost to blacken his character ever since dared to take a stand, but they will rue the day they doubted him. History will remember him as its saviour and his doubters will be the ones recalled as the causes of the chaos he rescued us from. And he is detested by all the right people – everyone I myself detest.

I joined the New Party last week. I am now a member and I say that with pride. Years from now I want to be able to say I was there, that I was on the side of the winners even before the war. Seeing him speak was final confirmation for me that I am heading in a direction that events and those responsible for them have been pushing me in for a long time. My patience has been worn so thin for so many years that I just couldn't deny it any longer. I have to commit myself to this now because the other parties no longer speak my language. They have let me down too many times. They have sold this country down the river and lost my support forever in the process. Well, this has gone far enough now and I am not ashamed to declare I have nailed my colours to the mast. I am standing up to be counted!

I care not how others may react to my conversion – and to think at one time I would have ideologically allied myself with the Bolsheviks because I read of how corrupt and cruel the regime of the Tsar was! No, I had to make a stand, however miniscule and irrelevant to the wider world. Many dark days and nights in which Biba has occupied so much of my time were made tolerable through reading because it was the one thing in my power I could do alone. You know that, my love. And now reading has brought me back to sanity, to a place where I once again have hope that the world is not beyond saving. I fear opposition will provoke bloodshed. They are not going to lie back and surrender their ill-gotten gains, so we should be prepared for the fight before the battle commences. Let us pray the right side emerges as victor and perhaps all will not be lost.

Yours lovingly
Orchidea

Oh, my love. So, she has finally and completely taken leave of her senses at last! Sad to say I could see it coming as her disgruntled attitude towards our elected representatives has grown and grown, something that was understandable, perhaps; but she appeared to take it personally. Throughout our relationship, my own interest in the political landscape has been energised by talking politics with Orchidea; though I have always tried to avoid being claimed by either side, it seems Orchidea herself has thrown her lot in with one side at the absolute expense of the other.

The draining experience of buying that land from her neighbour appears to have been interpreted as symptomatic of an entire international conspiracy that has been capitalised upon by bloody Mosley, that posh, preening prick with an ego so huge it couldn't be contained by either the Tories or the Labour Party.

Now she finally has a focus for her unshakable conviction that an upcoming global conflict is imminent. Does she seriously believe the leaders of the free world will allow that to happen all over again? We two may have been spared participation in the War, but we saw it played out enough times on the cinema newsreels; and wasn't it supposed to be the war to end all wars? But naturally, the threat of the Jews – with Ebenezer Chapel leading the procession from the synagogue, of course – will drag us towards Armageddon regardless, so better to sign-up to the side she thinks is going to win before it all kicks-off, eh?

I remember when we first met she confessed to being a secret admirer of Bonaparte; how long ago and innocent that all seems now! I don't think she has any real idea of the morons she will be attaching herself to if she commits herself any further to this current cause, though. It doesn't matter if some of their superficial show of strength strikes a chord in our admittedly complacent culture, the one that facilitated the Crash; you embrace it all or nothing – you can't just cherry-pick what suits your sensibilities, like *they* do with Nietzsche. It doesn't work like that.

Christ, woman – Mosley isn't a million miles from that deluded wop *Il Duce*, or the kraut fuckers that lit a bonfire of books for writers they deemed to be decadent and degenerate, as if they had been appointed literary censors for the whole of Europe. She really wants to ally herself with them?

She'd drop her knickers at a moment's notice if Sir Oswald strolled into the room, then. Yes, he's such a bloody gent, isn't he? He screwed his wife's sister and her bloody stepmother. What a catch! She is the perfect angry, alienated individual without a voice that Mosley and his cronies seize upon and exploit – just like religion used to. They know how many millions are dissatisfied with the way of the world, sick of how the old left and the old right have run everything into the ground; they know how much desperate people in desperate need of hope are susceptible to wild conspiracy theories they can make plausible by nominating the same old scapegoat.

And they – the Italian fascists, German Nazis or Mosley's lot – formulate an overly simple solution they can sell to anyone vulnerable enough and politically stateless enough to buy it. And, lo and behold, she has!

I have picked up on her increasingly angry exasperation with the ruling elite for many months now, though I generally tend to regard it as one more manifestation of her slide into despair with which the wider world of politics has no association at all – a slide she appears unwilling to allow me to try and assist her to arrest. Either that or she somehow imagines if she can pull one more poisonous rabbit out of her hat, it will put an even wider gap between us than the miles that separate us.

I don't even know if she's doing this consciously or unconsciously, but she seems to be trying to alienate me on a daily basis, as if expressing deliberately contentious viewpoints will somehow provoke such disgust in me that I will be left with little choice but to wash my hands of her forever. She appears to be determined to demonstrate she is no longer the same woman I fell in love with, having undergone a strange metamorphosis. But I still love her.

Yes, even this latest announcement will not prompt me into issuing the ultimatum she seems to be wilfully pushing me towards making. If she wants that, she will have to do it herself, for I still love her with all my heart. I always will. Her lurch rightwards does not serve as a deterrent to something that is much deeper and far more meaningful than the latest tedious ideological fad adopted by both the powerful and the powerless. Hell, if there's another bloody war, so what? How many have there been since we met? No, I don't blame her for falling for the hyperbole.

These are strange days for all of us, my love.

Marianne

Marianne – that was the name of Orchidea's near-neighbour and new best friend. She was the vicinity's other notable female motoring enthusiast and another wealthy widow to boot. Orchidea needed a female friend within short driving distance, something Meadowbrook recognised; and now she saw a hell of a lot of her. In fact, if Meadowbrook had counted the number of times her name was mentioned by Orchidea during their nightly telephone conversations, he'd have come to the conclusion that Marianne appeared singularly responsible for dragging Orchidea out of the depression that had taken hold of her in the weeks following her most recent visit to see him, those weeks when she spent most of her days hiding beneath the blankets in her bedchamber.

Marianne had been one of Orchidea's nodding acquaintances on her drives around the locality, and the two women had received a more hands-on introduction when Orchidea pulled over one afternoon upon finding Marianne by the side of the road with an overheated radiator. Unlike many motorists – especially the female breed – Orchidea knew her way around a car engine and was more than capable of solving a small problem; reading was something she'd had years to dedicate time to, after all, and as soon as she'd made her mind up to purchase a motorcar, she first decided to know the workings of the machine inside out.

Such knowledge came in handy where these temperamental vehicles were concerned. She'd done the same thing when it came to the aeroplane. Perhaps these skills were a legacy of all the years she'd had to fend for herself; after all, if there's no man to call upon, one needs to be able to solve a problem without being able to call upon one.

Marianne was something of a local archetype. There were a lot of ladies like Marianne haunting the draughty old mansions of the Shires – wives or widows of a certain age who had children either away at boarding-school or university or already married with families of their own. They had a lot of time on their hands and they sought solace in gossipy female company (females as bored as they were) or in the arms of younger men (or other women's husbands) or in the faddish playthings of the idle rich. Marianne seemed to cover all bases.

Marianne had apparently had a more contended marriage than Orchidea's brief misery with matrimony; even though the betrothal had been a dynastical business arrangement characteristic of her youth, Marianne had been fortunate that the older man she married was a kindly sort and largely allowed her to lead her own life, only requiring her to do her duty on official occasions and give birth to an heir and a spare. She did these duties and enjoyed her life.

As a widow, there had been no slowing down in this enjoyment, and the motorcar was merely the latest purchase in Marianne's pursuit of pleasure. She was impressed with Orchidea's knowledge of that subject, and even more so when she found out about the flying lessons. She insisted Orchidea must take her up as a passenger on the first flight after she acquired her pilot's licence.

The two women rapidly became firm friends at the point when Biba had just moved into his enclosure, so Marianne was able to visit Orchidea at home in a way that was entirely new to Orchidea. She had longed to play hostess for years and she finally had her opportunity with a woman who shared her widowhood as well as her appetite for adventure. Orchidea's appetite had suffered something of a blow of late, but Marianne's presence pulled her out of the bedchamber hideaway and provided her with something approaching a home social life, which was a novel experience. Orchidea would drive over to visit Marianne too, whose residence was about a mile away; and sometimes they'd enjoy outings together – to museums, galleries, antique shops and the cinema.

Marianne was also a lapsed Tory who had become a devotee of Sir Oswald Mosley and his New Party, something that caught Orchidea's attention when she was so politically rootless despite being so politically engaged. She did her usual thorough research beforehand and then accompanied Marianne to a public meeting at which the man himself spoke in order to see what all the fuss was about. This exposure to Mosley's renowned explosive oratory provided Orchidea with another new passion, one she embraced with the characteristic vigour she always reserved for the new.

Orchidea excitedly imparted these new passions to Meadowbrook via the written word and the telephone; she and he were in constant touch with each other, yet it felt more like platonic friendship when they were reduced to contact that didn't involve being in the same room. He was happy to see she seemed to have been lifted out of the dismal depths she'd dropped into following her most recent visit, but whenever the subject of another visit was raised by him, there was always some convenient excuse as to why it couldn't happen.

However, perhaps the most convenient excuse of all was the one Jeremiah Meadowbrook was in denial of, i.e. the fact that he was in love with a woman who was an untrustworthy narrator of her autobiography.

Lest we forget, this is the legend of the lady with the lion, whose life had spanned a century and who shared that life with a big cat she had given birth to following ravishment by a demon. The story she told of Marianne sounded entirely plausible to Meadowbrook because next to everything else that fitted the logic of the landscape they both inhabited, it *was*.

But there is another version of this story concerning Orchidea's new best friend, one in which Marianne was an utterly fictitious construct ingeniously devised to cover Orchidea's back.

****

Something changed when the project that had consumed so much of Orchidea's imagination and time crawled over the finishing line after the marathon to end all marathons. Her reaction to the news when relayed to Meadowbrook over the telephone was an audible mixture of relief and disbelief, but he prayed it would serve to retrieve her from the worrying depths she had sunk into lately. At this point, the name of Marianne had yet to infiltrate their long-distance discourse, so he wasn't to know an unlikely angel was imminent.

Yes, the day Biba's enclosure was finally completed Orchidea almost couldn't believe it had arrived. The whole exercise had been fraught with difficulties from the moment Orchidea had hatched the plan as a solution to the increasing strain of sharing a house with a lion; buying the land to build it upon was a stressful drawn-out nightmare in its own right, but the team of builders, carpenters, landscape gardeners and general labourers who carried out the work exhibited their inexperience with such an ambitious operation on enough occasions to push Orchidea to the brink of despair.

Throughout the project, progress moved at the pace of the proverbial snail, but gradually Orchidea began to see her plan taking shape before her eyes. Biba's violent outbursts seemed to intensify as the work eventually neared its completion, almost as if he shared Orchidea's frustration with the endless delays, so when the time actually came for Orchidea to escort him into his new home, both appeared a little bewildered and shell-shocked as they strolled into the space Orchidea had designed for him.

Once on the other side of the wrought-iron fencing securely surrounding the enclosure, Orchidea was surprised at how large Biba's new home seemed.

There were specially planted trees and bushes and intentionally positioned logs and boulders; there was a wooden hut-cum giant kennel Biba could shelter in whenever the elements took a turn for the worst and there was even a large pond he could bathe in. The sunken effect worked wonderfully, elevating the land around it so that one could look down on Biba when one stood on the other side of the fence, thus minimising the unnerving impact for visitors of being face-to-face with the lion. It also gave Biba an interesting landscape he could run through but also climb up and down, something that a totally flat surface wouldn't have made possible. The effect of the whole enclosure was breathtaking for Orchidea, causing her to momentarily drift into a trance.

It was due to this that she failed to notice a stranger whose own admiration for the stunning addition to the local landscape was noticed by Biba, who began to charge towards the visitor as soon as he caught sight of him. Orchidea turned too late and saw Biba making for the open gate and the unfamiliar figure on the other side of it. She called out Biba's name, but Biba took no notice.

Biba had quite a start on his mother, but she nonetheless ran in the same direction, stumbling over the deliberately bumpy ground and envisaging some innocent wanderer onto her land being gripped in Biba's awesome jaw before being shaken as though he were little more than a helpless rag doll. This was always her worst nightmare whenever someone inadvertently strolled into Biba's territory, and how tragically ironic that it should happen just as she was poised to move Biba into a home that would prevent such an incident from ever taking place.

Foreseeing the outcome ahead of it, Orchidea screamed to the man to stand perfectly still. By the time her eyes could see in the present tense rather than an imagined future one, she realised the man was doing just that. In fact, he was as inanimate and static as a statue, but what was most remarkable was that Biba was too.

With Orchidea expecting Biba to pounce and bring the man down, the lion instead stopped once he reached the man's feet and Orchidea saw he was sat looking up at him like a dutiful dog waiting to be given an edible treat. And then – astonishingly – the man held out his hand and Biba did as a dog does by giving him his paw, which the man then shook before using his other hand to pat Biba's mane.

Orchidea observed this amazing spectacle as if witnessing a bit of cinema trickery on the silver screen. She couldn't believe it was happening right in front of her eyes. As she approached the pair of them, she found Biba rubbing up against the legs of the stranger and nudging him in the manner of a small domestic cat; Biba was rarely this affectionate towards Orchidea, let alone a stranger. What the hell was going on?

The man lifted his hat to Orchidea and laughed. 'I think I have made a friend,' he said with a chuckle.

'But I don't understand,' gasped Orchidea. 'He's never been like that with anyone before, ever. What did you do to make him so submissive? He hasn't ever even been like that with *me* – not since he was a cub, anyway.'

The man attempted to offer Orchidea an explanation, but she was too mesmerised by the incredible sight of Biba behaving like an utterly passive pet to pay attention. It was so bloody strange that she couldn't help laughing out loud. 'I don't know how you did it,' she said. 'But you have just saved your own life.'

Orchidea waited to catch her breath completely and then introduced herself; the man returned the compliment. He looked a little older than her, but not much. His manners were the charming inheritance of a long line of gentlemen, and he was fittingly handsome in a very old-fashioned way. His jaw was still recognisably square, but the edges remained strong enough to suggest it had been chiselled by a professional craftsman in his youth; his thick hair was greying, but retained flashes of jet; his eyes were dark but glimmered with kindness; his build was broad without being bulky; and his voice was warmly baritone, putting Orchidea at ease with every utterance. He had a similarly soothing effect on her as he appeared to be having on Biba.

And then, in what seemed to her to be an inexplicable response, she abruptly burst into tears.

'Oh, my dear lady,' said the man, placing his hand upon Orchidea's shoulder. 'I do hope I have not caused you any upset with my unannounced appearance. That was not my intention, I do assure you.'

Orchidea tried to reply, but the strain of recent weeks conspired with the events of this day as well as the shock of what had just happened – and the combination broke her. She struggled towards the house and the stranger supported her on the short walk. Biba followed them without a murmur, evidently in love with the man who had suddenly gate-crashed the normal, established dynamic.

Orchidea fainted as they reached the door, and the man was assisted by a couple of handmaidens as he helped Orchidea indoors and then stood awkwardly as though uncertain of what he should do next while he watched

255

the handmaidens lay their mistress on a sofa in the drawing-room. After a pause, he reached in his coat pocket and produced a small vial, tentatively approaching Orchidea with it.

'Smelling salts,' he said reassuringly to the concerned handmaidens. 'They may help.'

He knelt down beside Orchidea and gently wafted the vial beneath her nose. She stirred instantly and wiped her eyes. 'Oh, I'm sorry,' she said. 'It's just been a very emotional day, and I thought Biba was going to kill you out there and...and...'

'No explanation required, ma'am,' he replied, placing the vial back in his pocket and rising to his feet. 'I shall intrude no further and leave you to rest. Your distress suggests you have experienced difficulties of late and I would not wish to pry or impose upon your hospitality when you are not at your best. I shall...'

'No!' said Orchidea with an intensity that surprised her as she grabbed his wrist. 'Please do not leave just yet. I...I shall offer you an explanation, but I require a few moments to compose myself. Please take a seat and bear with me.'

'If it pleases you; as I said, I would not wish to...'

'I'm okay now, thank you,' replied Orchidea as a handmaiden passed her a handkerchief that she wiped her face with before dismissing both handmaidens from the room. Biba, meanwhile, settled at her feet and purred.

'There,' said Orchidea with an uneasy smile bordering on the embarrassed as she raised her gaze to the stranger now sat in an easy-chair. 'I must apologise for what just happened. I...'

'My lady, there is no need,' interjected the man. 'You are not obliged to explain anything to me.'

'I know that,' replied Orchidea. 'But I want to.'

****

Fifteen minutes later, the stranger had received the whole story – or at least the version Orchidea chose to recount to him. Different audiences required different interpretations, lest we forget. He hadn't interrupted or interjected throughout a tale Orchidea told at a furious, frenetic pace, as though she'd been impatiently waiting for the man to come along in order that she could tell it. He sat with his elbows resting on his knees and his hands resting on his chin; a pensive, intelligent expression rented his countenance and he nodded slowly, digesting the information he'd received and clearly needing a moment before issuing any verbal response.

'I am much moved,' he eventually said softly, 'moved that you have been trusting enough to impart such an intensely personal story to a stranger who was not obliged to be in receipt of it. Alas, I cannot produce a solution to the plethora of problems that plague you – indeed, I doubt anyone could claim to be in possession of a solution; but I am your humble servant, ma'am, and I gratefully offer you my services if they may be of any use to you.'

'But you will stay for dinner?' asked Orchidea.

'Well, I...'

'Oh, but you must. Please – I would consider it an honour; and you could consider it my way of saying thank you for your kindness and patience – and for weaving such a wondrous spell upon Biba.'

Both looked down at the lion, settled at Orchidea's feet and purring away with his eyes closed and his colossal head resting on his paws. 'What did you do?' asked Orchidea. 'It was remarkable.'

'I am not entirely sure,' he replied. 'I have always had a particular gift with animals, though I have not had much call to utilise that gift with ones most would consider wild. *I* would not consider your lion especially wild, however. He seems a most contented beast, does he not?'

'He does now, yes; this is not his ordinary temper, though. He has become increasingly violent of late, hence the building of the outdoor enclosure for him to permanently live in.'

'And he has always resided indoors with you up until now?'

'Oh, yes; but it couldn't go on for much longer.'

'Ah, well. Perhaps it is for the best. After all, I cannot be here to sooth his temper on a daily basis.'

Orchidea smiled strangely and then begged to be excused in order that she could ask the cook to whip something up in as short a time as possible. Dinner was served within the hour, which was long enough for Orchidea to escort the man around the house, even though there wasn't much that could be called exceptional apart from the library, the room that was for so long her refuge. Biba remained barred from it and he impatiently waited outside as Orchidea closed the door and showed off her impressive collection. She curtailed the guided tour in order to dress for dinner, a task she attended to in a hurry with the assistance of a handmaiden.

It was notable that she donned an especially glamorous dress she had never worn before – one she had been fitted for with Meadowbrook in mind months earlier and had never been in the right mood to wear due to the unique circumstances of those months; she also painted her face for the first time in a long time. In fact, she made more of a concerted effort to highlight her natural beauty for the benefit of a stranger than she had for her most recent visits to Meadowbrook; but she no longer had need to impress Jeremiah, had she? He was won long ago.

Dinner was followed by a moonlit stroll with Biba and the stranger around the entire perimeter of the enclosure. Orchidea found his presence uniquely calming; considering she had never laid eyes on him until just a few hours before, the impact of this effect on her was particularly potent; and that's not even mentioning the even greater effect the man had on Biba. Now, that *was* incredible. Nobody had ever possessed the ability to subdue Biba with a simple gesture or look in the eye or soothing speaking voice; but this man had. Orchidea had always been the only person who could control Biba, but even years of experience of knowing and anticipating the range of outbursts Biba was prone to hadn't prevented Orchidea from often being powerless in the face of his aggressive rages. And yet, along comes a stranger and Biba is putty in his hands. It was bizarre.

But perhaps both Biba and Orchidea were affected so deeply by this man's timely intervention because they were both in a heightened state of susceptible vulnerability. Orchidea's distressed and depressed emotional condition had naturally been transmitted to Biba – who was rarely far from her side – and it had turned Biba tetchy, angry and short-tempered; this was then bounced back to Orchidea, whose own mood worsened as a consequence.

Orchidea had been feeling as though she were on the cusp of redundancy with the completion of a project that would in many respects liberate her from the daily drain of attending to Biba's needs; her role in her own life suddenly felt undefined, hence her somewhat desperate search for fresh stimulation, whether via the motorcar, the biplane, or simply revelling in being a magnet for male attention again. But all of these distractions had failed to fulfil her for more than a brief moment, and then she had slipped back into despondency.

Lost, lonely and lacking direction, Orchidea was weary, defenceless and classic easy prey for any passing politician, religion or kind stranger who caught her eye and offered something that revived her from the coma she had succumbed to. This man had unknowingly appeared with timing that was immaculate, to say the least.

She wasn't even thinking about him in a romantic or sexual sense that evening; that didn't enter her head at all. She just needed a friend there and then – someone to talk to, someone to unload her troubles onto, someone to share a few hours with and to feel better for having done so. He was undoubtedly charming, but Orchidea could see there was no artifice to his charm; it was natural, not studied; it came to him as easy as the breaking of wind in public comes to the uncouth. Many men who exhibit charm do so because it moves them onto somewhere they want to be; they have learned how to use it as a tool for an ulterior motive. This was not the case with him, and Orchidea could tell by the fact he listened to and absorbed what she had to say; his expression when she spoke and his reply to what she said proved it. He was exactly what she needed there and then.

When the moment came for the man to make his way home – which he claimed to be not too far away – he kissed her hand and acceded to her request (or demand) that he must come and see her and Biba again sometime soon. When he strolled into the mist already swirling around the estate and vanished from view, Biba audibly sighed. Orchidea decided the lion could sleep in the house for one more night and then the pair of them retreated indoors.

This was the moment at which the depression lifted, along with a tremendous weight from Orchidea's mind. This was the end of something old, borrowed and blue and the start of something new.

This was Marianne.

Generic Domestics Revisited

'Same again?' asked Wooldridge solemnly as Mrs Maggs entered the kitchen that the valet was sat in, doing his best to get a grip on Joyce (without much luck). He put down his copy of 'Ulysses' with palpable relief.

'Afraid so,' replied the visibly flustered housekeeper. 'He wants two places laid at the table and two portions of Miss Orchidea's recipe served-up.'

'Ah; I hoped he'd be a little more accepting of the obvious by now.'

'What – that she ain't coming back?'

'Aye – it must be three months gone since she was last here. Keeping up the pretence that she'll turn up after so long can't be good for him. This weekly ritual of cooking and serving a meal she used to make for him when he's eating it alone – well, it's a sign he hasn't accepted what we both know to be true. It's like the old Queen having Prince Albert's shaving equipment laid out every morning, isn't it? He keeps up the pretence in the face of the facts.'

'He clearly misses her, Maurice.'

'I don't dispute that, Millie, but how does going through this routine help? He sits down to eat and she's not there facing him across the table, just an empty chair and a plate of uneaten food staring back at him. It's like all those framed photographs of the two of them that Miss Verity took dotted around the drawing-room and his study – as though he thinks having them on display will somehow magically conjure her up again when we both know it's not going to happen. All that *has* happened is that Miss Orchidea has replaced the late mistress Alice as the absent spirit of the household. She may as well be dearly-departed, for I can't see her gracing this residence again. I reckon the affair is well and truly over. He's seen her once in the last six months – how is that a proper relationship, eh?'

'I know; but what can we do but attend to his requests? That's our job. Yes, I wish I could see the pair of them at the table, gazing into each other's eyes with matching smiles when I serve up the meal like in the old days, of course I do; but if she ain't here, she ain't here. Yet the master acts like she just popped out and she'll be back any minute, I know – like the other week when it was their anniversary and he had me cooking a special meal with it being a big occasion; you'd have thought she was due to arrive any second. But, of course, she never came.

'It was like a birthday party being held for someone who'd just died. He used to be bad enough in the times between her visits, drinking too much and locking himself away with that bloody bird and everything; but this is worse, really – all this pretending. It breaks your heart, to be honest.'

'Aye,' said Maurice with a solemn Scottish shake of the head, 'and it's not as if he's taking advantage of the situation by seeing other...er...*ladies,* is it?'

'Well, I dunno if that would help either,' replied Millie with a scowl.

'Probably not. But it seems Miss Orchidea gets to have the best of both worlds, happily picking and choosing which man she wants whenever the mood takes her while the master is left alone, sat waiting for something

– or some*one* – that's never going to come, like Greyfriars bloody Bobby. It seems to me he's saving himself for nothing, honouring the memory of somebody unworthy of being honoured in such a way.'

'You reckon she been carrying on with some other gentleman, then?'

'Well, I always said I reckoned she had a husband at home, and I suppose it's possible she might have just used the master as a stepping stone to someone else as well, trying him out as a dry run for the real thing. I can't say for sure – of course not; all either of us can do is speculate. But if one of them has been playing the field, it's not the master. That's one thing we do know for sure. I mean, when did he last leave the house, eh?'

'Maybe she fancied dipping her toes in the water, and after a bit of fun she decided against risking everything with the master and chose to stay with the safety of her husband – if there *is* one. It's a damn shame, though. I thought the master had finally found the right one after all these years of being alone.'

'I can't argue they seemed happy together, but if her commitment was as great as his, she'd be living here by now. I know he's been busying himself doing other things, but this weekly meal thing...I don't know. He may as well ask the two of us to join him at the table. We're here for him; she's not.'

'We're being paid to be here, Maurice. It's our job.'

'Aye, but isn't it a woman's job to stand by her man? That's if she ever *was* his woman, of course. I think she was hedging her bets all along, never prepared to plunge into the whole commitment just in case something better came along. She's been playing the master from the start

264

and now she's just dropped him like a stone. You can't toy with people's feelings like that and expect to walk away without leaving a trail of destruction behind you. The master may be the one who suffers in the short-term, but she'll be the real long-term loser, mark my words. She'll be the one sat alone in her old age because she threw away the one good thing she had in her youth, always thinking the grass was greener elsewhere. You pay the price for such selfishness in the end.'

'I reckon they'll both lose out in their old age – both be left alone when they could and should be together. There ain't no winners in this game, Maurice.'

'Maybe not; but whereas it takes two to make a relationship work, it only takes one to screw it up.'

'But *we* don't really know which of them did screw it up, do we, Maurice?' exclaimed Minnie with a sigh as she momentarily took the weight off her feet and rested in the rocking chair on the opposite side of the table to Maurice. 'We take the master's side because he's our master; but *he* could have been the one who screwed it up, for all we know. He can't have helped matters, drinking too much and all that. You see, Maurice, some women judge a potential husband like they might judge an expensive household appliance before investing in it; if it's pricey, they want a guarantee it's gonna last them a good few years and they'll get long service out of it; they don't want to have to buy another in a couple of years if they shell out a good few quid. You ain't never been married, with all due respect, so maybe you don't appreciate that.

'A woman studies a man as a long-term prospect; and even if she's not thinking about babies and all that, she

265

still tries to look ahead, to try and picture her man and the life he can give her ten or twenty years from now. It's not just about what he does for her today; it's also about what he might do for her tomorrow. If she can't see him being the secure rock she needs in the future, sometimes she'll cut her losses prematurely. I reckon that's what Miss Orchidea might have done. I think it's unfair if she has, because the master was prepared to change his bad ways for her; he proved that when he stopped drinking absinthe and dumped them foul-smelling cigars, after all. But perhaps it was too late for her.

'The thing is, Maurice, there's plenty of talk about the aristocracy marrying for money and their marriages just being these loveless contracts between wealthy families that need to keep the line going; but everyone does it to an extent, especially women; they size everything up as if they're starting a business when they enter into a union. I know men like to paint women as the ones with their heads in the romantic clouds when they get involved with a man, but it's the men that are more like that, in truth. They're the ones that write all the poems about it, aren't they? Women don't. Women are the hard-headed realists; men are the romantics. That could be why so many men move from woman to woman and struggle to settle with just the one for life; they always crave that intoxicating feeling that comes from the beginning of a relationship; that's what they get the most pleasure from, falling in love rather than learning to love someone.'

'You sound as if you're on her side, Millie,' said Maurice with a stern expression.

'No, not really,' replied Millie. 'I think she's made a mistake. But if it's down to her that this is over, part of me can see why she did it. She's obviously one of those women who think that way.'

'Maybe so; but you still think she'll end up as lonely and alone as the master?'

'It's possible, yes. If you look at love that way and you get it wrong, you'll never be satisfied and you may well either end up in a miserable marriage, hating the man you're lumbered with and forever hankering after the one that got away, or you'll simply see out your days as a solitary old lady. I can see her ending up as one or the other. And as for the master...'

'Well, he didn't rush into a relationship after the late mistress died, did he? And that was even before both of us joined the household. We only ever knew her as a dead presence, watching over him from that portrait Miss Verity painted. I always thought he'd be bound by loyalty to her memory; it certainly seemed that way. No ladies or even strumpets were brought back here before Miss Orchidea appeared. I felt he wouldn't have entered into a union with her unless he thought she'd be the one he'd be with for life.'

'He obviously did – and it looks like she's not that one. But the fact he waited five years or however long it was until Miss Orchidea came along proves he won't just jump on any woman. He clearly won't commit himself unless he's convinced he's found the right one. And if this one isn't the right one, all that commitment has in the end counted for nothing. He might well not have it in him to commit again – and who could blame him? Why waste your breath and all that emotional investment that really takes it out of you? When I lost my Eddie – God rest his soul – I never once considered he could be replaced; that's why I went into domestic service. I wasn't interested, and I still ain't.'

Mr Wooldridge and Mrs Maggs shared a resigned sigh and then both snapped back into their respective duties. Neither had received confirmation that Orchidea wouldn't be returning to their home, but then again, neither had their master. For now, it was all about grinning and bearing the uncertainty. That uncertainty dragged on and on, draping the interior of the household in a dense cobweb of pessimistic pallor that virtually petrified all within it.

Beyond those doors, time's ambivalence to the life of Jeremiah Meadowbrook forcefully pushed events forward so that they gathered pace with such breathless haste that a day passed in an hour, a week passed in a day, a month passed in a week, and a year passed in a month. Before anyone under that roof realised it, Orchidea's paranoid prediction had been fittingly realised and history had repeated itself, for Great Britain was again at war with Germany.

Witch's Brew

The witches sat Orchidea down and then joined her on either side of the chez-longue; in theory, she was free to leave at any moment; but their attitude upon ushering her into their shared abode was one of welcoming bonhomie. It would have seemed unduly rude to spurn such hospitality. The conventions of niceties counted for a lot. She was seduced by the facile social rituals of the sisterhood, just as many had been before her and would continue to be after her.

After so many prolonged periods locked away with Biba, Orchidea now actively cultivated friendship, and the eager, outgoing Orchidea wanted to experience new things. Two women sharing a house in the neighbourhood rather than rotting away alone in one of each had extended the hand of friendship and Orchidea had grabbed it with gusto. Their arrangement seemed a sensible alternative to isolation, and Orchidea knew enough about that to sympathise with novel solutions to the problem. So what if they dressed rather oddly in matching tweed ensembles and also smoked pipes? Orchidea herself had attracted plenty of negative opinions for her own unconventional domestic arrangements and was not therefore likely to judge the lifestyles of others just because they challenged convention. Besides, the two women were so nice. She wasn't to know.

There was already a cup of poison steaming and begging to be consumed waiting for Orchidea on the table when she took her seat. Under any other circumstances, she would have relented from placing the cup to her lips when its contents had not been specified; but so convinced was she by the honest intentions of her hostesses that she sank into the cushions and sipped.

The poison began to take effect with remarkable rapidity, shooting through Orchidea's bloodstream quicker than the seconds it took to do so could have been counted. The line of communication between her brain and the words she spoke was broken so that they came out different from the initial signal that telegraphed them to her tongue – slower than she'd intended and worryingly incoherent. Orchidea was inwardly concerned by this unexpected development, but the suddenly wayward nature of the lexicon she'd mined with increasing ease since infancy was something she hadn't been prepared for and was powerless to arrest.

The witches smiled in unison at the speed of the effects as they showed on Orchidea's confused countenance; the formidable strength of character Orchidea depended upon for survival was instantly weakened by the abrupt invasion of a foreign body infecting every fibre of that rock. The steely structure of her persona had congealed into flexible material able to be manipulated against her will, and she could do nothing about it.

Orchidea could sense elongated worms wriggling and sliding in and out of her brain and then wrapping their slimy, sinewy bodies around every cell of the organ. Initially terrified by this unsettling experience, she wanted to scream but found her vocal chords had been paralysed; she was possessed by an urgent, desperate desire to get up and run away, but couldn't move. And then, amidst the panic, the fear was suddenly subsumed by an unexpected change in her response to what was happening. Her instinctive resistance to events began to lose its grip. The witches had tried before and failed, but now she was ready.

Orchidea's thoughts were the last to resist this detachment from her core personality, holding out the longest until the suggestions of her companions – suggestions enhanced by the overpowering colours of the dazzling new ideas swirling around her vision – started to sound like common sense. The instinct to fight off the worrying virus flowing unchecked into every nook and cranny of her head and to see it as an enemy was sedated by its overwhelming force and undeniably attractive qualities. It was her friend. It was her confidant. She could share her secrets with it and feel safe and secure that any advice it would dispense in response would be dispensed with the best of intentions. She could trust it. She could believe in it. She surrendered to its enveloping embrace because it cared. And the verbal foreplay it engaged in via the mouths of the witches was truth. She could see that now.

Yes, she said to herself; the witches are right. I must rid myself of Jeremiah Meadowbrook. For starters, he is a long way from home, too distanced from me to feel the loss of. He is an unstable and unreliable aberration, an imaginary soulmate I have allowed to dupe me into committing to a future that is unrealisable. I have been a fool sleepwalking my way through a fantasy simply because he set my flesh alight. I forsook the mundane for the magical and that is unforgivable. I must return to the comfort zone of the ordinary and unremarkable, for that is where I belong.

It is time to consign the unrestrained lost girl Jeremiah released from confinement to the locker I buried her in once before, back when I succumbed to the martyrdom of the system I momentarily rejected. This was her Indian summer, her last sight of daylight. She will not resurface again.

The witches winked as they watched the spell weave its wonders on their guest. Their green eyes still sparkled with indignant jealousy, but that would soon fade along with Orchidea's adoration of the desirable object that had prompted the witches into action. They knew there was only one way to put this ridiculous infatuation out of its misery, and Orchidea's reaction to the poison was precisely what they'd planned. Having enjoyed one final belated bath in the fountain of youth, Orchidea was now cleansing herself in the sober shower of old age, with each deadening droplet hitting the flesh that Jeremiah Meadowbrook had ignited serving to dampen her fire for good. It was a toxic detox for the soul. By the time the witches bade her goodnight, Orchidea would be as elderly as they were.

Her gnarled hostesses continued to infect Orchidea's head for hours, long enough for the right words to begin tumbling out of their guest's mouth with the ease of a native language. Before their eyes she was regenerating into the sensible provincial who would baulk at the prospect of giving herself over to passion ever again. The next contender would be cast from a more acceptable mould; she would consider his material value and coldly offer her body in exchange for the kind of security Jeremiah Meadowbrook could never provide.

That would be an eminently respectable business arrangement and not one that could excite the giddy gossips of the sisterhood because it would return her to their fold. Once again, she would be just like them – rich in goods, but an emotional peasant.

The witches converted Orchidea to their mindset throughout her duration in their company; it was only a matter of hours according to the clock, but to Orchidea herself it spanned months. These were months in which the witches dripped their words of wisdom into Orchidea's ears, persuading her that any embryonic doubts about her love were justified and she would be better off without him. For the witches, Orchidea's tales of erotic ecstasy in the company of Jeremiah Meadowbrook had been agonising. Their own personal erotic ecstasies were so distant that the passing of centuries had dimmed their appreciation of the sensation, and whenever they heard its resurrection in relation to others they exhibited envy that demanded its immediate extinction. Therefore, they set to work on poor unsuspecting Orchidea.

History was revised as the poison settled and took root in Orchidea's being. All expressions and declarations of unprecedented feeling with regards to Jeremiah Meadowbrook were either belittled or utterly erased. And any lingering memory of the impact he had had upon her, memory so vivid that even the witches couldn't entirely eradicate it, was reduced to a deviant diversion along the wholesome path Orchidea had foolishly veered from.

These embarrassing interludes would be locked away and never spoken of again, so contradictory were they to the life story she would henceforth tell. Jeremiah Meadowbrook would become just another conveniently obscured chapter in her lengthy autobiography, no more significant than a long-forgotten crime she'd committed in juvenile ignorance when she'd known no better. To remember him would not only be to evoke everything she now refused to acknowledge had ever happened, but would also jeopardise her application to rejoin the passionless masses. So she killed him.

Overjoyed that the seed they'd planted had inspired the murder they'd wanted, the witches waved Orchidea farewell after one evening that their guest imagined was merely one of many. The innocent recipient of their home-brew departed their abode believing she had dependable friends whose actions were motivated by caring concern for her wellbeing. They had rerouted her uncertain direction so that her destination was now a familiar and predictable one bereft of dangerous surprises.

Thanks to the guiding hand of such selfless sisters, Orchidea was back where she believed she belonged. Yes, there may now have been a strangely indefinable vacuum at the heart of the old place, one she had never previously noticed; but she turned a blind eye to it and proceeded regardless, oblivious to the motivations and machinations of those she regarded as sisters-in-arms.

That man she'd called 'Marianne' for the benefit of Meadowbrook was served-up as a far more sensible option for the future. With Biba now happily ensconced in his outdoor enclosure, the home Orchidea had intended to recreate in her own image can barely bask in the brilliant glow of her personality before she once more allows that personality to be suppressed as an interior imprint. Soon enough, all traces of that woman will be buried beneath the tasteful blandness of the consensus. She will yearn to fit in and sacrifices will have to be made. The bohemian spirit Meadowbrook freed will be returned to her dungeon and 'Marianne' will have his eminently respectable wife with the one solitary unique eccentricity that is permissible under the circumstances. All the rest must be cast by the wayside, abandoned as the flotsam of the swiftly forgotten.

****

The divide between country life and town living has rarely been underlined by such a vast chasm as the one separating them at this moment. Pleas fall on deaf ears when the servants huddle in the cellar and the master refuses to join them as the foundations are rocked by the shock; but ears are deafened by the nightly pounding the town is taking. Jeremiah Meadowbrook cares not if he becomes a Blitz fatality, for he is approaching the brink of surrender to forces within him even more malevolent than those dispatching swarms of bombs to rain down on the defiantly obstinate bulldog. Therefore, the malignant scarlet which the sky has adopted as its sole nocturnal spectrum is the ideal mirror through which he can observe his turmoil, and he looks long and hard into it every evening.

Even Devlin is unsettled by the shaking of the house and the plaster snowing on his feathers with every blast both near and far, but his father remains indifferent to the external onslaught; it is nothing compared to the fires raging within. He glances at the raven with a wry smile, as if to say – 'Isn't this what you've worked for all these years? Why not enjoy the inferno?'

He has felt her grip slip from his hand in agonising slow-motion for months, though every other day he manages to pause the process and regain a semblance of that connection she herself confessed to be unprecedented. He doesn't want to stare into the abyss awaiting him until/if she nudges him over the edge. It will be bad enough should that happen, so he will delay it as long as possible by simply pretending it isn't there. Blind eyes, deaf ears, denial, pretending – there's a lot of it about.

A long way from the urban warzone, a place where the flames are a faint flicker in the distance and the explosions are far-off thunder, a beautiful woman excuses herself from another night beside her 'fellow widow' and makes plans for a telephone call whilst the lines are still working. Orchidea applies her ruthless logic one more time. She can no longer see him, therefore he is not real; he is just a figment of her imagination, a voice in her head. She couldn't have done this face-to-face because she knows she would wilt if confronted by the reality of his presence; so she views her love as a glorified trick of the light that can be easily extinguished.

That relationship with Jeremiah Meadowbrook – it never happened. It never happened. *It never happened.*

Walking in a Winter Wasteland

I've no real idea how long I've been here now, but I haven't really been in synch with time since my youth; we went our separate ways a long time ago, keeping a respectful distance from one another, living our own lives and doing our best not to get in each other's way. A result of this approach was that the unfolding of time took place somewhere on the far distance of my peripheral vision, somewhere else altogether; many of the events it oversaw were no clearer to me than the blur of a passing dragonfly, for we inhabited different zones where the hands on our respective clocks moved at a different speed.

I'd become so accustomed to this arrangement that the abrupt shattering of the barrier between us was devastating. It first turned my hair white and then caused it to fall out altogether; my bones suddenly creaked and buckled under the weight of the air flooding through the cracks that let time seep in; and there I was, reborn as an ailing elderly survivor of another era, damaged, dazed and confused, staggering across a dusty winter wasteland that has no beginning and no end. It is merely *there* – as am I. The womb of timelessness I took for granted has been pierced and finally I have been contaminated by the same pollutants as all those who lived and died by time's laws throughout the century I avoided them.

I am not entirely alone, of course. He is here, that bloody bird.

Sometimes he sits on my shoulder when I am too tired to swat him away; at other times he flies on ahead and pecks at the bare branches of the occasional dead tree that enlivens the otherwise empty landscape. I suppose he feels hunger now in a way he never used to; he had always eaten from the negative energy he generated in me, but now there is little left. I am too drained and exhausted to care. I don't even know where I'm headed; I just keep walking. I know if I rest for too long I'll crumble away into nothingness, my every cell dissolving and blending with the surface at my feet so that I never existed other than as billion year-old carbon. And though that often seems wholly desirable, there's some annoying force inside that keeps driving me on in what looks like an utterly joyless journey, the purpose of which completely eludes me.

I must look like a poor man's Ghandi, a fragile stick-insect with ill-fitting rags hanging from him, supporting my brittle bones with a broken branch as I ceaselessly plod onwards towards nowhere; but a mirror probably wouldn't even be able to identify my phantom frame now any more than it would the image of Count Dracula. Every now and again I hold up my hand and it looks almost transparent; if I stare hard enough I can see my surroundings through it. I think I'm fading from the physical realm on a daily basis, if there are such things as days here. I don't even leave footsteps in this dust; I look over my shoulder and I can't see where I've come from; I look up ahead and I can't see where I'm going. It's neither dark nor bright here – just somewhere in-between; and you can always see the moon in the fuzzy, sickly sky – never the sun, only the moon; a curiously dim spotlight on my aimless progress.

Confirmation of my worst fears brought me here and those worst fears have kept me here; I don't know what the sentence of this exile is supposed to be, but not knowing what might await me on the other side is hardly a great incentive to bring about the sentence's end. Why abide by rules and regulations with rehabilitation in mind merely to have a few months shaved off for good behaviour when you've no idea what you're going to step out into once you've been released?

Having begun life all over again when Orchidea strolled into it from nowhere, the prospect of having to go back to the beginning one more time (and without her in it) doesn't appeal at all. It's too much of an upheaval too soon since the last one.

At least here there's the institutionalised certainty of the void; it is what it is, nothing at all – just as I myself am nothing at all now. Just keep walking through its unchanging landscape, not knowing if you're going round in circles or if you're closer to the end now than you were at the beginning. The repetitive motion of the journey is as easy as breathing or blinking, something you can enter into it without thought; you can let your body get on with it while you sleep. In this blank vista there's nothing and no one to bump into, anyway. It is an endless expanse of a world where all the scenery that had made it worthwhile has been removed.

In the end, we are all reduced to mere characters in oral stories recounted from one generation to the next; we are all eventually relegated to a past within no one's living memory. And it would seem Orchidea had attempted to banish what we had together to that very past in record time. It wasn't supposed to end like this. It wasn't supposed to *end*.

****

'I can't put this off any longer.'

Orchidea grabbed a broom and swept-up the lingering vestiges of stardust that were leftovers from a collaborative creation, not a solo album. She did so as though they were little more than the crumbs of a cake long since scoffed and shat away. She did so as though she owned exclusive copyright on them. She did so with a hardness of heart that chilled the blood, completing her gradual metamorphosis into this woman I didn't know or like, a woman I'd never held or kissed or loved. Someone else's woman. And, of course, that was the intention.

She'd been building up to it for long enough in her correspondence, but it hadn't worked then because the traces of *my* Orchidea were still in evidence, and I would always love *her*. So, that version had to be completely engulfed by the version she devised to alienate me. She erected a towering funeral pyre of all we had built together and made sure I was powerless to prevent it, with me being bound and gagged into inaction via fear of the inevitable; the part I had played was erased as sole responsibility for its fate fell to her.

I never anticipated that, of all the women I have known, she could do this to me – *her?* There are so many more deserving candidates that could have been thrust forward without any surprise to do this dastardly deed, but not *her* – not my Orchidea, the woman who won my trust as well as my heart, and then broke them both by abandoning me.

Backtracking, bullshitting and contradicting, she lit the flame behind my back and showed no emotion as she watched the lot go up in smoke, everything – every declaration, every gesture, every gift, every magical moment, every precious second together. None of it meant anything anymore to her. If she could reject all that and treat it so dismissively, as though it were no more than just another throwaway dalliance in which heavyweight words were casually recited with lightweight and cavalier conviction, then she didn't deserve to be loved and had never deserved it. I say so with the heaviest of hearts, but one indignant with anger.

It hadn't been the abstract holiday romance with an imaginary boyfriend that her revisionist rewrite depicted. And she bloody well knew it. There were genuine, flesh-and-blood casualties here.

'I'm moving on.'

The voice was stripped of all affectionate melody; it had acquired the unsexy, bland indifference of the government spokesman delivering an announcement on balances of payments during a quiet day in the Commons. Wondrous whispers of love had passed through those very lips, yet now listen to what was tumbling from them. Factors that had been in place from the beginning were recycled as reasons and justifications, though they were no more than excuses in disguise. None of it convinced. She was telling the story

281

she had scripted to fit the task, opting for fiction when facts had to be hidden.

Only when pressed did the small confession of another male presence confirm a long-held suspicion, but even then I knew there was probably a lot more being kept from me. She had learned to lie, so why would she abandon the practice when it had served her so well for so long?

What those who lie tend to forget when they become too reliant on their arrogant confidence is that they often let slip the actual truth as opposed to the version of the truth they choose to tell; that slippage will always register with the suspicious if it slips out too often, planting seeds of doubt in the ears of the recipient that cannot be ignored for long.

Orchidea clearly imagined she could keep doing it even at the very end, making it all so neat and tidy and painless, with no mess to clear up whatsoever. Then she could walk away with a fair-play English handshake and begin yet again without the chance of a glance over her shoulder prompting the unwelcome appearance of a conscience. Why spoil the washing of hands with something as distasteful as tears?

'We were never going to be married and live together. That was never going to happen.'

The contradictions of all that was once said or suggested continued throughout the dismissal. The absolute absence of the Orchidea I knew and loved was quite shocking. She addressed me as if we were just two strangers who'd had a passing acquaintance of no great substance and therefore any familiarity was unwarranted; there was nothing in her tone to imply there had ever been affection, intimacy or love.

She imagined her cold indifference in unnecessarily ending something that had at one time meant as much to her as it still did to me would somehow be mirrored in my own reaction to her decision, as though there would be no impact of any depth upon me at all. She appeared to have convinced herself this would be the case because that's how it was for her, ironically expecting our symbiosis to stretch to an amicable ending. The wilful delusion was remarkable.

It's a strange sensation, being suddenly deported from your homeland. Exiled overnight from Eden, it felt unreal to think my lips would never again make their mark on those shoulders or that back or those legs or any other cherished feature of a frame I had come to know as well as my own. Her body was barred to me forever now. I would be no more welcome there than the body of a stranger would welcome me. I thought I owned that body, but it seems I'd merely loaned it for a limited period, like a library book.

She had handed over the keys to a new tenant even before she had evicted me from the premises. Whoever he may be, I should imagine she slips into lingerie for him, and buys him presents, and cooks his meals, and tells him she loves him as she shares his sofa and sucks his cock. A woman's work is never done.

'And what about you?'

What about *me?* Yes, *what* about me? So nice of you to ask with all the passion of a shopkeeper attending to the next customer in the queue; well, let me see. I guess I'll just shrug my shoulders and go and pick another woman off the woman tree in the garden because I'm such a shallow male archetype that I can't cope without some cunt to poke. Yes, I'll pretend you meant nothing more than that and act as if we never happened. Would that make you feel better? I wouldn't want you to be as upset as me, so it's just as well you're not.

Of course, it would make your decision so much easier for you were I to declare that you're utterly replaceable – just like *I* am, eh? Never mind that I could never trust or believe the word of a woman who told me she loved me ever again. Therefore, I shall make what remains of my life's mission to ensure no woman ever will as my libido is encased in a mental chastity belt. It'll be easy. You were an aberration. You cured a yearning and you killed it. There will be no more women because I don't want them – and they won't want *me,* thank God. I'd rather be a monk or a man of the cloth or an autistic academic than a romantic; I *was* a romantic, but I've seen the futility of it now. The experience has made me a born-again widower.

Your farewell kiss is frozen on my lips like an immovable tattoo; these lips do not welcome the kiss of another, just as this flesh does not wish to be touched, caressed or undressed by another. All was reserved for you.

You weren't just 'another woman' – you were *my Orchidea,* for Christ's sake! You were the reward waiting for me at the summit of a mountain it had taken

284

many lean, long hard years to climb; and then when I was poised to plant the flag on the peak, I was cruelly and inexplicably pushed all the way back down. I picture that mountain now and the desire to ascend it again has gone. That particular ambition is dead.

Why don't you want to climb Everest, Mr Meadowbrook? *Because it's not there, Mr Mallory!*

****

If ever a place complemented a person, I have it here in this lifeless vacuum. But I am in harmony with the place. If it were a beautiful, blooming, green and living, breathing example of nature at its most breathtaking, it would make me feel worse. I wouldn't be able to relate to it at all and it would just frustrate and depress me; I'd be looking at nature having a great time and I'd be the emaciated urchin with his nose pressed against the sweetshop window. The bringer of joy is absent within, so I can't expect her to be present without.

No, this winter wasteland makes sense to me as it is. I am at home here because I am at one with the deadness of my surroundings, with the dry, barren soil where nothing grows and where there is the odd rotting tree decomposing in the dust. The air is vaguely acrid, as though a fire has recently fizzled out, and that too is perfect, to have my body passing through a place that my head already inhabited.

The location I once called home – that Georgian townhouse on the terrace that was reduced to rubble by the biggest air-raid of all – used to fulfil a similar function. Orchidea had gained instant access to the decor of my head and she seamlessly transplanted its contents to the rooms of that house with every object and ornament she festooned them with. When we were basking in our spring and summer, each of those rooms was a lovely looking-glass reflecting my happiness back at me.

Every eagerly-awaited unwrapping and unveiling of Orchidea's ingenious gifts was like being presented with little segments of her heart in weekly instalments, and I loved repaying the compliment in kind. It was a delightful experience for me, and I adored every minute of it. The novelty of being able to lavish a female recipient in love as embodied by exclusive presents with a motivation that was never in doubt or disputed or viewed as distasteful – and not having to concern myself with platonic dividing lines for once – was something I enjoyed.

How tragic that the gift I poured the most of my heart into, a collection of love poems that was ironically composed at a writing desk purchased for me by Orchidea, was then rejected by her. She received it like the unwanted product of an anonymous admirer's infatuation rather than the latest in a long line of missives from her beloved; and nothing was ever the same again thereafter.

I wonder where those gifts from me to her reside now. Has she destroyed them all because they're such an inconvenient contradiction of the path she chose to follow when she decided to dump me, despite the dedicated days devoted to their procurement purely out of love? Indeed, what *does* become of love's trinkets when their recipient rejects the sentiments behind them if they no longer complement the current narrative? Received with such touching gratitude upon receipt, they are worn or exhibited with pride, and then what?

I didn't display any ambivalence with hers; they remain amongst my most precious possessions, saved in storage and preserved in emotional amber. Some suggest their presence perhaps provokes pain, but what am I supposed to do – bin them or burn them? For me, doing so would be like binning or burning the precious expressions of love they embody. Why would I want to do that? It is hardly a commonplace expression expressed towards me. I need to commemorate the (rare) occasions as if to prove they actually happened.

I don't have the examples here, but I know they are in a safe place while I wander and see her in every speck of dust that brushes my lashes. As I see her, I wonder if Orchidea devotes any thoughts to me at all, for all my own thoughts are exclusively haunted by her as I drift through the desert she deposited me in.

I suppose this could well be a pattern with her, one that sees her dispense with lovers when her childlike attention span becomes bored with them and her passion quickly burns itself out; maybe most of her victims move on to other women when she employs her elbow, and therefore she naturally imagined I would do the same. This criminal ignorance of my character speaks volumes as to her blind eye. She could give herself to me yet think nothing of giving herself to somebody else, whereas I could never give myself to anyone again. To me, that contract was sacred and I could never break it. I could never desecrate consecrated ground. I am a bird who mates for life.

I used to try and inhale Orchidea on the clothes she left behind – all to no avail; yet, there are many times throughout this trek when I catch a whiff of her; I can fleetingly taste her flesh on the air again – or at least the deliciously delicate material she wore next to it. Often, the sensations merge together so it is difficult to distinguish the smouldering odour of her skin from that of her lingerie, the synthetic smell of which is enhanced and intensified from absorbing the natural scents released through arousal, though why I should catch the aroma I have no idea.

Maybe it's one of the imagination's wicked tricks, like conjuring a nonexistent oasis for the thirsty traveller. If only my eyes could summon her up as easy as my other senses can; but I can't make her materialise when the air is so thin; I can't turn back stuck clocks.

It's funny how the unreality of memory can become the norm so that our time together takes on the mythology of legend, so removed from the pattern I'd known up to that point that I find it hard to believe I lived it at all. *I* fucked up, though. I took her for granted with remarkable ease, probably because with Orchidea I'd been spared the desperate pursuit that had been the drawn-out prologue to my marriage with Alice. Did I merely dream Orchidea?

It's almost incomprehensible to me that any of it happened now. For a woman to appear out of nowhere – a woman in possession of all the qualities I had always admired in the fairer sex – and to stroll into the heart of my life with arms outstretched is so fantastical it's barely believable. How many other lives did she gate-crash before mine? How many did she shake-up and then bail out of, having taken what she wanted from them? I could have merely been one in a very long line and I'll never know because she convinced me our connection was special. I can see her crisscrossing the centuries, navigating broken hearts and accepting no responsibility for any of them. Yet, still I believe in her and I cannot dispute the goodness of her impact or my role in its curtailment.

I should have been on my knees every day, praising the Gods with gratitude for their gift instead of arrogantly assuming this was the way things are and will always be. How foolishly quickly we forget the way things were before; that neglect fails to prepare us for the swift resurrection of former arrangements.

Who was she, this woman who used to share my bed and shower me in tokens of affection and words of love? Where did she come from and where did she go? The suddenness of her appearance was only matched by the abruptness of her departure. The whole reality of the affair is a surreal blur to me now, even though every element that made it so memorable has left an almighty black hole in its wake. And I don't just miss my girlfriend; I miss my *friend.* I miss our friendship. But that couldn't have survived my dismissal as her beloved; it couldn't have continued along platonic lines whilst she resided in the arms of another. She couldn't have her cake and eat it while I starved. That wouldn't have been fair.

Feeling out of synch with the world and the way things are going in the culture surrounding you is a sensation familiar to me. Orchidea and I shared it, though our dissatisfaction gradually came to be expressed via wildly diverging routes that widened the longer our temporary separation stretched. Perhaps it was her own novel method of subconsciously preparing herself for a permanent severance, so that the day would soon come whereby *my* Orchidea would be so obscured by her less loveable successor that I'd feel there was nothing remaining to hold onto. It didn't work. She couldn't force my hand. I was already smitten by nostalgia for our beginning before she brought about our end.

When the head distracts the body from the monotony of pointlessly plodding on, I often pontificate upon what is left of *my* Orchidea now I can no longer see her. Despite events, I bet she still sometimes betrays her hidden past with a look in the eye or the raise of an eyebrow or the formation of a smile in the corner of her mouth. In that split second, when my successor is either not paying attention or is ignorant of the gesture's significance, it's probably possible to glimpse the woman I fell in love with. She can't eradicate her completely, no matter how hard she tries.

****

I have had to fight for everything. I have been bruised and battered by battle, but formed and moulded in conflict. I belong on the battlefield and I have no place in my heart for sentiment; my scars will always assert themselves when my defences are under threat. I am a realist, not a fantasist. Whenever my head drifts in the direction of the clouds and my feet leave the surface of the earth, I act swiftly. I will not allow myself to be rendered vulnerable by love or weakened by affection. I know it isn't fair. Life isn't fair. It is a hard, tough, cynical slog and we have to be hard, tough and cynical to last the course.

I was swept-up and softened. I let myself be put in a dangerous position, and I was foolishly irresponsible. I cannot capitulate to something as unreliably fragile as love. I have to survive and be ready for the next battle – for me and for Biba. Love has no feasible function; frustratingly, it is just love. Love is airy-fairy, impractical and illogical. It gets in the way. It disrupts everything, throwing the best-laid plans of mice, men and women into disarray and infecting your head with insane, unrealisable ideas. It is a devastatingly powerful force that cannot be controlled; it can only be curtailed – and curtailed by walking away from it. Doing so is the sole way to survive and to ensure one will never be so susceptible to it again.

I should never have allowed myself to fall under the insecurity of its spell, for I cannot submit to its crazed logic when I walk through eternity with Biba. There is no place for passengers afflicted by that sickness here. I move from one man to the next once a man has served his purpose – this is the way it has always been. I just pass through people's lives. I'm not a permanent fixture. This is the way I have survived. I must not break the cycle just for love. Otherwise, I shall perish.

I feel horrible for hurting him so badly; he is a lovely man; but it was unavoidable. I have to live amongst the earthbound, not float amongst the angels. This is the formula that has served me well so far, but this is the first time my actions have had consequences. I cannot look him in the eye or speak to him after this. I have to vanish from the realm he inhabits. We cannot share the same world now. I cannot risk encountering him again; it would jeopardise my decision to lock that girl back in her dungeon, and my composure would collapse – composure I fought tooth and claw to attain. I must keep it together and grit my teeth, not surrender to feelings that are ultimately destructive and may wreck everything I have battled for.

I can't let myself miss him, even though there are many times when I do. He healed me when I needed healing, but now I am healed I no longer need his healing hands, nor do I want to be reminded I ever did. It would be an admission of weakness. I have cried all my tears for Jeremiah...and for me.

And yet...if I can just send one last message to prove I am human, perhaps it might help ease my guilt and placate his anger. It would be an isolated missive, just so he will not judge me too harshly. It will be anonymous, but he will recognise the author of the sentiment. I love him, but I cannot be with him. I have to block him from my mind or else I shall succumb to forces only my weak heart, and not my hard head, can relate to.

I must disappear from his view, because if I linger he will suffer. It is an act of kindness he will perceive as a gesture of cruelty. The same puff of smoke from which I emerged will swallow me up for good as far as he's concerned. It has to be this way or we are both done for.

****

あなたがいなくて寂しいです

'I Miss You' – that's what it said. I don't know how I translated the alien language, but I did. Perhaps the strange impact of stumbling upon this unexpected message in the unlikeliest of locations spelt it out to me. I knew it was intended for me and I knew in whose hand it had been penned. It was written into a rock, carved so recently that the words hadn't had time to acquire the ancient, aged look that the logographic characters would ordinarily suggest when appearing on something other than bog-standard paper. It was the first pointer as to what part of the world my current home was situated in, as well as being the first sign that Orchidea was feeling the loss of our relationship, and that maybe *my* Orchidea still lingered a little, despite her best efforts to rewrite history.

I ran my fingers along the indentations made by those curious characters, almost as though expecting I could touch Orchidea's fingers deep in them, making contact with the author in the most intimate, personal manner. Doing so had the same effect on me that holding objects once held by long-gone figures historians admire has on them. She'd been here and she'd left her mark – for me. What was I to make of this?

There had been no communication between us since she walked away, and yet here was a message sent direct to me in a place I assumed nobody knew I now inhabited. But how was I supposed to respond to it? Perhaps it didn't require a response. Perhaps it was her simply saying she was sorry, and this was as much as I could hope for. Yet, her telling me she missed me, echoing my own sentiments at last, begged the question why we were not together as we should have been.

As if anticipating the inexplicable incursion of such a surprise into the landscape, the place had been slightly modified and altered to accommodate the sole indication I wasn't alone, the sole indication that the journey had so far suggested. After not much more than the odd dead tree to illuminate the route, I was beginning to make out other shapes in the mist, manmade ones. But none of them implied life any more than the bare branches before them had.

All I could see were the remnants and ruins of buildings that could have been rotting relics of ancient civilisations had their design not been too contemporary. Again, it was fitting that the first constructions I'd come across that hadn't sprouted from the earth looked as cadaverous as everything else here. I had been dispatched to a bombsite, albeit one unlike any bombsite in history let alone this current conflict. Maybe that had been Orchidea, now a fully qualified pilot, flying away in her Enola Gay and leaving me to walk the earth she scorched so successfully. Maybe.

I concluded I had a choice now – to remain here and eventually give up the ghost by lying down and allowing my aged frame to merge into the dust, or to plough on into the second half of a century I felt little affinity with. While I'd not been paying attention via my preoccupation with Orchidea, mankind had been devising evermore elaborate means of murdering its offspring in ever-greater numbers, and I had to ask

294

myself if such a world was one I wanted to live in. After all, I was already a man out of time, a man who had found a woman out of time and had then lost her. I used to be depraved, but now I'm just deprived.

I sat on the rock to ponder my future, if such a thing existed for me now. Devlin swooped down from the ledge of a recent ruin and settled on my shoulder; I didn't care if he was there; I had finally accepted our unhealthy union was for life. After a while, the fog swallowed up our surroundings anew and I again couldn't see further ahead than a few feet. These conditions play tricks on your vision, however.

After perhaps an hour or so of my eyes unable to see anything other than clouds of dust, I swore I could discern two hazy silhouettes somewhere in there. One looked like a female figure, not walking in a way that implied euphoria or being at ease with the world; the sluggish steps suggested sadness and surrender. The other figure was that of a large, heavy beast on four legs that followed the woman like a lumbering shadow she couldn't shake off; it appeared they were linked by a chain that joined them at the ankles like fellow slaves, and their journey seemed as pointless and laborious as my own. And then they were gone. Could it have been them?

Oh, Orchidea – my irresistible, incomparable Orchidea, love of my life and bride of my bereavement. Why? I will never really know the reasons behind the sad fact I have to face the remains of the day without your hand in mine. But on I go, alone and into the unknown – Orpheus on his fruitless quest for Eurydice, the siren who yanked his heartstrings from their moorings and cast them asunder when she fled to the embrace of Hades. Perhaps I shouldn't have strained my eyes to see you through this atomic smog; perhaps that was the shade of Eurydice shadowing me out of the Underworld, the shade that can now never materialise as my Orchidea again because you will never make it back into any light my eyes are capable of seeing. I should never have looked back.

One who has never known the cleansing, consuming glory of love cannot comprehend the magnitude of its loss and the almighty vacuum it leaves where the heart used to reside. It is grief at its most inconsolable and incurable.

God, I miss you.

Printed in Great Britain
by Amazon